THE SCROLLS OF PROVENCE

"Mary, my work here is finished. The Father calls me home. Before, it was too soon. Now, the Church is growing. You will follow, but not now. You must live. The Father has a purpose for you here—to record it all, to leave a testimony of how faith survives, and how hope and love take shape—or are betrayed—in the hands of those who claim to follow me. And to tell our story to the world when the time is right."

— The Diary of Mary Magdalene

ISBN 979-8-9999817-0-7

Library of Congress Control Number [Pending]

Silentii Press   New York, NY

Printed in the United States of America

Book Cover and Typesetting by HMDPublishing.com

THE SCROLLS OF PROVENCE

The Lost History of Christianity --- and
the Secret Order Sworn to Erase It

J. KIMBALL

Silentii Press

.

New York

AUTHOR'S NOTE

The Scrolls of Provence weaves historical truth with imagined discovery.

Many of the places, texts, and figures are real; others are speculative—reshaped to explore how much of history survives only in fragments and to provoke reflection on what lies between the lines of the recorded past.

This story invites readers to ask not only what was remembered, but what was deliberately erased by the powerful—and why they hoped it would remain forgotten.

The Ordo Silentii and the scrolls themselves are inventions, yet they echo real patterns of secrecy, suppression, and selective preservation within religious and political institutions.

Contents

History Is Written By The Powerful 8

Chapter One 9
Chapter Two 11
Chapter Three 15
Chapter Four 24
Chapter Five 36
Chapter Six 39
Chapter Seven 43
Chapter Eight 48
Chapter Nine 53
Chapter Ten 59
Chapter Eleven 63
Chapter Twelve 69
Chapter Thirteen 71
Chapter Fourteen 73
Chapter Fifteen 77
Chapter Sixteen 80
Chapter Seventeen 84
Chapter Eighteen 87
Chapter Nineteen 94
Chapter Twenty 98
Chapter Twenty-One 102
Chapter Twenty-Two 105
Chapter Twenty-Three 107
Chapter Twenty-Four 111
Chapter Twenty-Five 115
Chapter Twenty-Six 120
Chapter Twenty-Seven 123
Chapter Twenty-Eight 127
Chapter Twenty-Nine 131
Chapter Thirty 138
Chapter Thirty-One 140
Chapter Thirty-Two 147

Chapter Thirty-Three 153
Chapter Thirty-Four 158
Chapter Thirty-Five 166
Chapter Thirty-Six 172
Chapter Thirty-Seven 176
Chapter Thirty-Eight 181
Chapter Thirty-Nine 184
Chapter Forty 194
Chapter Forty-One 199
Chapter Forty-Two 204
Chapter Forty-Three 210
Chapter Forty-Four 215
Chapter Forty-Five 221
Chapter Forty-Six 225
Chapter Forty-Seven 229
Chapter Forty-Eight 235
Chapter Forty-Nine 240
Chapter Fifty 242
Chapter Fifty-One 246
Chapter Fifty-Two 252
Chapter Fifty-Three 256
Chapter Fifty-Four 260
Chapter Fifty-Five 263
Chapter Fifty-Six 269
Chapter Fifty-Seven 274
Chapter Fifty-Eight 277

Epilogue **281**

About the Author **283**

HISTORY IS
WRITTEN BY THE POWERFUL

THE TRUTH HIDES IN WHAT THEY ERASED

For nearly two thousand years, whispers have drifted through archives, monasteries, and ruins—rumors of lost gospels, letters struck from memory, testimonies ground into earth and ash.

Some say they were destroyed to guard the faithful. Others say they were erased to guard the powerful.

But what if—despite everything—one voice refused to be silenced.

The Scrolls of Provence imagines that collision of two worlds: the fragile dawn of Christianity and the shadowed forces bent on shaping it for their own ends.

Across centuries, a secret order has moved unseen, its oath unbroken, its purpose unwavering…to erase whatever threatens the power of the Church.

In the hills of Provence.

A forgotten voice.

A deadly hunt.

CHAPTER ONE

St Cyr, South of France – May 2060

It was unusually warm for late spring, even under the centuries-old cypress tree that shaded the stone plaza and village fountain at the center of St Cyr. A small restaurant, run by a local family for an unremembered number of decades, was tucked into a corner of the plaza. Its tables overlooked a field of olive trees in the valley below—some older than memory.

Alice Hale sat quietly at a table near the fountain, waiting for the words to come. Sophie sat across from her and waited too. Since meeting as sorority sisters thirty-six years ago at college in California, they have remained friends through the years, their relationship growing closer as they shared most of life's chapters. Alice was about to share another of those chapters, but this one was more important than all the others combined.

"I'm sorry I've been out of touch," Alice said softly, her eyes lowered to the edge of her wine glass. "Yesterday," she paused for a long moment to steady her voice, "… my mother passed away."

Over the years, Sophie had met Alice's mother, Susan Hale, many times. She reached out to touch Alice's hand.

"As you know, Mom been ill for some time, but the end came faster than we expected. Still, she knew it was close. And in these last two weeks, she asked me to come to be with her—just the two of us. She said there was a story I needed to hear. One she'd never told anyone. Not fully. Not even me."

Alice's voice was steadier now, but her expression carried not just sadness —something more ominous.

"Mom told me about something that happened almost thirty-five years ago. It all happened quickly, over just six months—but it changed everything. Her life, my life…maybe even things far beyond that. She said I'd always had questions."

The server approached, and they ordered a light lunch—the kind that filled more time than appetite.

Alice continued. "Mom told me it was a complicated story that spans two thousand years. That it could undermine everything we believe. 'It's still unfinished,' she said over and over. And then—before she could finish telling me the last part—she was gone."

She fell silent, her breath unsteady. Then, looking past the plaza, Alice spoke again, softer now. "I think I know why she kept it hidden for so long. And why some pieces may never be complete."

Sophie leaned forward, eyes intent, waiting for what would come next.

Alice touched the rim of her glass, then raised her eyes. "The only way to tell you the story is just as she shared it with me. From the beginning."

She paused. "…and Sophie, once you hear it, everything changes. Are you sure you want me to go on?"

And as the midday bells echoed from the Church below the plaza, Sophie nodded, and Alice began telling the story…the unfinished story…just as her mother, Susan Hale, had during the past two weeks.

CHAPTER TWO

*The Ancient Burial Ground Beneath The Vatican
Easter Sunday 2026*

On this cold, rain-soaked night, they waited.

It was Easter Sunday—the day chosen for their induction.

The day they would be born again into a new life.

Of the hundreds who began the journey as children, only seven stood here tonight. They had been chosen for the rarest of traits—those of natural-born predators. Capable of violence, deception, and sacrifice. Unflinching and without remorse. Each had been stripped of personal identity long ago. No family. No past. No future beyond their mission.

They would become alpha guardians of orthodox Church history—future *Silentii*, trained to be invisible shadows, weapons honed to perfection.

They stood cloaked in simple woolen robes, barefoot upon an ancient stone floor, eyes forward, waiting. The chamber where they stood reeked of iron, old blood, and damp earth. Shadows from candlelight flicker across its stone walls, polished by time, and carved more than seventeen hundred years ago. They were deep within an ancient burial ground beneath Saint Peter's Cathedral. On tourist maps, it's called the Vatican Necropolis.

This chamber, hidden in the oldest wing of the Necropolis—forgotten by time and unmarked on any map—had been sealed nearly two millennia ago behind a false tomb door. Accessible only through a secret tunnel known to the initiated, it was called the *Chamber of the*

Seventh Seal. Seven sacred candles flickered along its walls, symbols of God's plan unveiled in the Bible's Book of Revelation: the seven hills of Rome, the seven seals that bound heaven's secrets, the seven plagues of judgment, and the seven angels who would sound the end of days. For the *Ordo Silentii*, the cipher **OS**7777 is a symbol of their commitment to orthodox Church history, etched with their blood… the seven hills, the seven seals, the seven plagues, and the seven angels.

Tonight, in this sacred chamber, these seven new members would be baptized into the Order's shadowed lineage.

The rite was swift. Brutal.
No pageantry. No waste.

Words came from a darkened corner of the chamber:
"You have no name. No past. No identity beyond what the Church commands. You are the silence between breath and blade. The eyes that do not blink. The hand that leaves no trace."

Then, without warning, a red-hot branding iron was pulled from the coals—a cross entwined with protective vines—and one by one, it seared into their shoulders. No screams. Only smoke.

From the shadows, a single man emerged.

His presence was absolute.
Tall, straight-backed, with a precision that bordered on cruel.
His voice was low. Calm.

Cardinal Vallente.
Supreme Prelate of the Ordo Silentii.
To the initiated, he was Il Giudice Nero.
The Black Judge.

Tonight, these seven new members would meet him for the first time.

The air thickened as he stepped forward.

"I once stood where you kneel," he said. "You are not clergy—you are now the Church's shield."

The induction was complete.
Only one step remained.

A black-robed aide entered, carrying a sleek metal case. Each new *Silentii* was handed a sealed folder containing their first assignment.

Leadership considered these tasks minor: a fragment recovered in Crete, a suspect dig in the Balkans, and a papyrus theft in Cairo. But they were tests—watched closely. First rites of passage. Final trials.

The seventh initiate was the last to open his folder.

He was by far the most dangerous.
Brutal in exercises. Powerfully built. Utterly without empathy. His white-cropped hair and scarred cheek made him impossible to forget. Even among killers, he stood apart.

The others gave him space. He demanded none.

He had already forgotten his birth name.
He was known only as:
Corvus.

He opened his folder. No expression. Then bowed.

The lead came from an informant in southern France, flagged by a mid-level Mafia courier in Nice. A shipment of ancient material had passed through customs uninspected, bound for New York under a private museum registry. The point of origin was unlogged. The courier had mentioned only one name:

Dr. Susan Hale, Metropolitan Museum of Art, New York.

That was all.
Corvus moved like an animal—calm, dangerous, sure. The corners of his mouth twitched in something like a grin.

"Susan Hale," he thought. "My first prey."

His sole objective in life was to become the next Supreme Prelate of the Ordo Silentii.
And he would let nothing stop him.

He passed through the ancient tunnel, damp and echoing, emerging into the rain-slicked cobblestones of the Vatican's northern court.

He paused to open his encrypted phone.
Code: OS7777.
Then called the operations center.

"Prepare the Gulfstream," he said. "New York. Tomorrow evening."

Tomorrow is Easter Monday, he thought. *Perfect.*

As St. Peter's bells rang out across the Roman night—echoing and sonorous—Corvus began to walk, whispering to himself:

"It's called Monday of the Angel. A good day to start the hunt."

CHAPTER THREE

New York City, Easter Sunday 2026

The city stirred under a brilliant, cloudless April morning—the kind that tricked New Yorkers into thinking winter had truly given up its fight and spring had finally won. Sunlight streamed through the east-facing windows of the apartment, casting golden streaks across the hardwood floor.

It was Easter Sunday.

Susan Hale stood barefoot in the kitchen, black coffee in hand, wrapped in a robe. She and her husband, Bob, had just returned from ten sorely needed vacation days at their peaceful stone house in a small town perched in the hills above ancient olive groves in Provence, southern France. Now, back again in their comfortable New York apartment, she felt a quiet calmness overtake her.

She had no way of knowing that she had just become the prey in a deadly hunt. Nothing would ever be the same again. The tremor that shook those ancient hills during one evening in Provence two weeks ago would change her life—and perhaps the world itself.

For now, however, Susan felt all was well in the Hale household, as her eyes fixed on the trees of Central Park, just beginning to soften with pale green. Her ceramic mug, purchased in Jerusalem nearly two decades ago, felt warm against her palm.

"Today is Easter," she said quietly.

Behind her, Bob lay half-asleep on the couch, the Times open across his chest. He stirred but didn't look up, folding the paper lazily.

"Yes, and…?"

"And we need to get ready for church," Susan said, turning slightly toward him.

Bob raised a brow. "We just got back yesterday. It was a great trip, but the jet lag has worn me out. Can't we take off just one year?"

"No, we can't. I haven't missed Mass on Easter since I was sick with the flu when I was a kid in Boston." Her voice carried a soft defiance, touched with a smile.

He smirked and returned to his coffee. "Twenty years together, and your dedication still surprises me."

Susan kept her gaze on the trees. A couple jogged past on the lower path, side by side. Her thoughts drifted—back to South Boston, to Easter Sunday at the triple-decker on Dorchester Avenue where she and her brother Thomas had grown up. Religion had not only anchored their childhood—it had shaped their futures. Susan pursued early Christianity through college and graduate school. Thomas became a Jesuit, eventually serving as the head of a university in Korea.

Easter morning at the Doyle household had its own sacred rhythm. The scent of Maureen's corned beef from the night before still hung in the air. Dishes clattered in the kitchen. Their father, Patrick, rustled his newspaper while waiting for everyone to get dressed. The bells of St. Augustine's rang through the open window, and Maureen, already half into her coat, would call down the hall, "We're not going to keep the Lord waiting!"

Susan could still see the shafts of colored light filtering through stained glass, hear the chant-like rise of Latin responses, feel her mother's steady hand on her shoulder as they knelt in the pew. Even as she grew more questioning with time, the order and reverence of those mornings had never left her.

"We're going," she said to Bob. "We've been at St. Pat's for Easter since before Alice. Get dressed."

With a mock sigh, he sat up. "Then I guess I'm going."

Susan glanced at the photo on the bookshelf—two college students grinning after a late-night lecture on first-century Christianity. That night was still vivid: the darkened hall, the spirited debate. Bob had waited just outside with a question about the Dead Sea Scrolls— though the question wasn't really about the scrolls.

They'd gone for coffee. Talked for four hours. And never stopped.

They'd made it through his business degree at Columbia and her doctoral work at NYU's Institute for the Study of the Ancient World. Now she was a respected curator of religious antiquities at the Met. He was a successful commercial real estate broker whose client list included Fortune 500 companies. They'd raised a daughter who got into the Ivy League and stayed married through careers, deadlines, and doubt—with effort, with faith, and, Susan believed at least until now, with love.

"This afternoon after church, we need to unpack from France," she said, tugging open the French doors to the patio.

Bob groaned. "That too…give me a break!"

Susan picked up a small carry-on duffel from their trip that he had left by the door when they arrived home the night before. She dropped it at his feet."You can start with that."

With a smile, he replied, "Fine. But now I don't have time because I need to get dressed for Church."

She kissed his cheek, "Thank you for being a model of Easter virtue," she deadpanned.

By the time they reached St. Patrick's, the bells were already pealing across Fifth Avenue—deep, resonant tones that sent pigeons scattering from the eaves and signaled the beginning of the 12 o'clock Mass.

The morning sun lit the grand stone façade with almost heavenly precision, gilding the Gothic spires in gold.

Inside, the sanctuary was full. Every pew packed. A reverent hush hung in the vaulted air, broken only by the rustle of worship aids and the occasional cough muffled by a sleeve.

They slipped into their usual spot—midway down the right aisle, beneath a great stained-glass window alive with light. The ceiling arched high above them like the ribs of a ship turned skyward. The scent of incense still lingered from the procession, mingling with the sweetness of lilies arrayed around the high altar. The crucifix—massive and golden—rose behind the candles and Easter vestments, glinting beneath the chandeliers.

Then the organ surged to life, and a choir of sixty voices lifted as one. As the voices of the congregation joined softly, Susan remembered a past Easter morning, she couldn't recall precisely, when Alice had clutched her hand and swung her pudgy legs under the pew, humming off-key.

Alice had attended St. Pat's Nursery School and, as she got older, Sunday school at St. Pat's. At Easter Mass that year, she sat with them in her spring dress and black Mary Janes. How quickly it all goes by.

That was over a dozen Easters ago. And this was already Alice's second spring break away at college. It wasn't he same without her. They went alone to JFK ten days ago for the evening Delta flight to Nice in Southeastern France, a region that the world calls Provence. The name is ancient, dating back before early Christian times, 2,000 years ago, when the Romans first arrived. They called it *Provincia Romana*—literally 'the Roman province'—because it was their first conquest outside of Italy. As the language evolved, the name was shortened to *"Provincia"*, which eventually became *"Provence"* in the local French dialect.

Provence is beautiful in the springtime, but Susan now recalled that she had an uncomfortable felling in the pit of her stomach, somewhere just beneath the excitement, that this trip would be different. It wasn't that Alice wouldn't be there with them. It was more than that.

A sense that something was already there, in Provence…ancient, and waiting for them. Something that would change everything.

As the choir's voices faded, her mind wandered. Just last year, they had purchased their home in the hills of St Cyr—an ancient village in Provence, 25 miles from Nice, overlooking a Roman olive valley once vital to the Empire's trade routes through Gaul. It was near the port town of Fréjus, located along the Via Domitia, the ancient Roman trade route that once connected Italy to Spain.

However, the region's history paled in comparison to the stories of the town's early inhabitants. St. Cyr was once a fiercely defended village called Seillans, which had earned its reputation from residents pouring great cauldrons of boiling oil on invaders who tried to breach the town's medieval ramparts. There was much more to what happened here in those ancient times, but Susan and Bob had no way of knowing that…yet.

Bob and Susan had fallen in love with the house instantly—a three-bedroom stone structure built two centuries ago atop the foundations of a Roman-era olive farmer's home. The builders had preserved its original terrace overlooking the olive groves, connecting it to a summer kitchen shaded by jasmine vines and fig trees.

It was just two weeks ago that they were there, so she could still remember the warm and still evening air on that terrace in St Cyr. Two-foot-thick stone walls framed the patio on two sides. One open edge overlooked the pool deck, about a hundred feet out in the garden; the other looked out across fifty ancient olive trees, their silvered leaves flickering in the last light of day. Adjacent to a deep wine cellar and accessible through a thick stone doorway from the summer kitchen, the terrace was both charming and practical.

Oddly enough, this part of the home had been added by the previous owners—the Johnsons, also a couple from New York. Susan and Bob had smiled at that coincidence when the real estate agent showed them the place last fall. They bought it on the spot.

They had only owned the house for nine months, but after just two short vacation stays, the terrace patio had already become their favorite spot at the close of the day. They had sat in easy silence, watching the sun dip behind the hills—just as countless couples must have done on this same slope over thousands of years.

The hymns continued to resonate through the Church, as Susan remembered that night vividly…the fading evening light shimmered on the pool's surface, casting a warm glow on the olive grove below. It was, she recalled, all anyone could ever ask for.

It was unusually warm for early April, almost 72 degrees. Perfect, she recalled, slowly swirled a glass of chilled rosé they'd bought that morning at a local Fayence vineyard in the next town. She leaned back in her chair and glanced at the old support column at the patio's edge.

"That column was probably built from the rubble of a Roman ruin—maybe by the olive farmers who lived on this very spot thousands of years ago. We should give it a name," she said, raising her glass in mock ceremony.

Bob smiled. He knew this game. Over the years, Susan had bestowed grand historical names on nearly every corner of every place they had lived. Here in St. Cyr, she had named the poolside dining nook where they could see the village of Fayence light up every evening in the setting sun's rays: *Vue de Fayence*. The old stone face with a carved mouth in the garden wall, once meant to channel water? *The Fountain of the Lost*. As Bob often reminded her, no water had ever flowed through it.

And where they sat, the terrace patio, their favorite evening spot, "*Column du Roma*," Bob added that the name has "a nice tourist guide ring to it."

They laughed together, the easy laugh that only comes after decades of shared shorthand. The day had been long but peaceful—baguettes in the morning, a slow lunch, and a visit to the chapel at the foot of the road that led to their house. Susan thought the chapel had predated Christianity in the region, perhaps built over something still older. She couldn't know it then, but a secret was buried deep below that chapel's altar—trying to break free and speak to her after 2000 years of silence under the stone.

It was in that quiet moment, as dusk settled and the light dimmed to a deep purple, that the ancient land around them began to speak in a voice from two millennia past.

It started softly, as a low rumble rolling up the valley, like a truck struggling uphill. Then, the terrace itself shivered. Glasses rattled. A wood dove flapped off the roof tiles in alarm.

The tremor lasted no more than ten seconds—but it was enough.

A dull, crumbling sound came from the edge of the patio, followed by the dry crunch of stone against stone.

"Uh oh," Bob muttered, rising. "*Column du Roma* has a problem."

Three stones had dislodged at the base of the column, falling into a shallow cavity beneath the terrace. Dust curled into the air like incense.

"Strange," Bob said. "I thought this whole terrace was on solid rock. No cavity underneath."

The rest of the house seemed untouched. Old stone construction is resilient. No cracks, no fallen frames. Just a broken patch beneath the oldest part of the structure. All seemed well. Nothing seemed urgent—just a tremor.

So they decided to look more closely in the morning and call it a night.

All was well. Or so they thought.

Susan rose early the next morning to inspect the damage. Bob was inside making coffee. Kneeling at the base of the collapse, she brushed away loose stone and dirt.

Then she saw it—a curved ridge of something terracotta, half-buried behind a rock.

She reached in carefully. It wasn't part of the construction. Not a pipe. It was warm to the touch, smooth and ancient, shaped like a storage jar, and sealed at the top with a hardened resin.

"Bob!"

He came out with two mugs of coffee and stopped cold at the sight of what she held.

The jar was heavy and weathered, mottled by centuries of soil. Faint inscriptions were etched near the neck. Susan turned it slowly in her hands.

"This could be Roman," she said. "Or older."

Inside, nestled in crumbling straw and wrapped in ancient linen, was a scroll. A single, tightly wound roll of darkened papyrus—fragile, but intact.

She laid it gently on a cloth napkin and unrolled just enough to see the writing.

"I think this is Aramaic," she whispered.

Bob raised an eyebrow. "You're sure?"

"I'm not fluent," she said, "but I've handled scrolls like this at the Met. The script, the brush strokes—it's definitely Aramaic. First century, maybe older."

Bob gave a low whistle. "So what are we talking about here?"

"Too soon to say. It could be anything. A tax record. A merchant's account. Maybe an olive harvest report. Probably someone local—someone who lived and died here."

"So not the Gospel According to St. Cyr? The guy who built that chapel down the road?"

Susan smiled faintly but didn't laugh. Her brow furrowed as she stared at the scroll.

"We should protect it. Take it back with us. I'll ask someone from the Aramaic working group to take a look."

She carefully wrapped the scroll again and slipped it back into the jar. They packed it into a canvas tote and tucked it deep in their bedroom closet—behind a stack of books, extra linens, and a pair of hiking boots.

"For now," she said, "let's just enjoy our week."

Later that night, as they readied for bed, Bob spoke casually.

"You know… if that thing turns out to be the next Dead Sea Scroll, I will want royalties. It could be worth a fortune."

Susan chuckled. "It's probably just a farmer griping about olive yields."

She remembered that the night was still, and cicadas hummed in the trees, while Bob's comment lingered with her — it left an uncomfortable feeling. As she pulled up the covers and closed her eyes, a phrase surfaced from years ago—something she'd once heard in a lecture. She let the thought drift through her as sleep pulled her under. The future, it turned out, would prove it prophetic.

When real wealth or power is involved, you can trust no one

The Mass was ending, and she was drawn back from her memories of Provence. Around her, a thousand people, misty-eyed, whispered the words together,

He is risen. The Christ.

Across that grand cathedral, person by person, they were anchoring themselves to something older and larger than any of them.

She understood the power of belief. But what struck her now was how deeply they believed. Neither of them could have guessed that what they found under their terrace two weeks ago would challenge that deeply felt shared belief, so vivid this Easter morning. And it changed their lives. Completely.

CHAPTER FOUR

Their vacation was over, and all the excitement of the Easter weekend was fading into just a memory. It was Easter Monday, but Susan preferred the way the church referred to it: Monday of the Angel.

Susan and Bob stood shoulder to shoulder on the subway platform at 72nd Street and Broadway, their coffees in hand, already half-lost in their own thoughts. The train doors slid open, and they kissed briefly before parting—heading uptown to the Met, Bob downtown to his office in the nineteenth-century Gothic Revival skyscraper that housed Dalton, Kessler & Keene Properties in the Financial District.

As she walked from the subway exit on 81st Street across to the east side of Central Park, the scroll jar, which housed an ancient voice that could change the world, was absent-mindedly tucked into her backpack. She hadn't forgotten about it—but so much else was on her plate, and it had seemed, at best, an intriguing artifact from an old olive farm. Interesting but not very exciting.

After their lovely week in St Cyr—alone together for the first time in what felt like years—she thought she would tuck it away for safekeeping in her climate-controlled locker in the Met's research basement. She planned to carefully wrap and label it with a temporary identification code and file it under "Potential Gaul Farming Curio." Curators often left items like this waiting for further study or budget approval.

As she stepped through the staff entrance of the Metropolitan Museum. Susan felt the familiar hush settle over her.

She'd worked here for nearly two decades. She loved the quiet before the public arrived—these early hours—before the marble floors echoed with schoolchildren's footsteps or the murmur of tourists—were her favorite. The building breathed differently in that quiet, as if it remembered what it was meant to be.

She often reflected on how improbable it all was. The Met hadn't begun with grandeur. It started as an idea over dinner in Paris in 1866, when John Jay and a few others discussed the need for an American museum to rival Europe's finest. New York had no public collection at the time, just borrowed halls and private salons. The ambition was almost laughable. But it took hold.

The early years were improvised—exhibits in a former dance academy on Fifth Avenue, canvases arriving in wooden crates from Europe, volunteers scrambling to decide what went where. Then came Cesnola, the Italian-born Civil War veteran who seemed to have excavated most of Cyprus and then shipped most of the country back in barrels. It wasn't subtle, nor was it always ethical, but the treasure got the museum started. It gave the collection's weight, volume, and presence. The antiquities department Susan now led could trace its roots directly to his chaotic enthusiasm.

She walked the corridor slowly, glancing at the darkened galleries. The museum now stretched more than a quarter mile end to end—over two million square feet, more than twenty times the size of its original 1880 footprint. And yet, despite its monumentality, it still bore signs of its incomplete past.

Most visitors never notice the uncut blocks crowning the four massive columns at the Fifth Avenue entrance. They were meant to be sculpted into allegorical figures representing the great epochs of art: Ancient, Classical, Renaissance, and Modern. But the work was never finished. Funding dried up. The architect Richard Morris Hunt passed away. And no one could agree on what "modern art" should even look like. The stones remained untouched—silent, jagged, unresolved.

Susan passed beneath them every morning, and she thought the same thing each time: they were perfect that way. The Met wasn't a finished monument. It was a question still being asked. She liked it that way. Unfinished. Honest.

To most people, it was just a museum. To Susan, it was something more—a layered argument for why history mattered—a place where belief and facts quietly wrestled beneath the surface of every display.

She opened her locker and gently laid the scroll jar inside. On her first day back, it wasn't top of mind. Instead, she would work on a grant proposal and a Byzantine exhibit. There was also Alice's third call from California regarding her thesis on women in early Christian liturgy.

An ordinary first day back…or so she thought, until she looked at the Met's internal calendar of visiting scholars. An associate and old friend unexpectedly turned up. A wide smile spread on her face as she spotted his name.

Dr. Alister Duran was scheduled to speak at a closed-door symposium on "Gospels: Visions of Jesus Before the Church Took Control." They were old friends. Alister was brilliant but still an oddball. After completing his studies at Oxford, he had returned to New York to pursue his doctorate at NYU, where the two of them first met, deep in the world of early Christian studies. While she had moved more into the public eye, focused on developing exhibits at the Met, Alister had grown more reclusive, immersing himself in arcane linguistic mysteries and theologies that made other scholars shift uncomfortably in their chairs.

Over the past ten years, Susan had noticed that he had taken on the look of a professor straight from Central Casting at a movie studio, one who slept in his office with uncombed hair, a rumpled linen jacket, mismatched socks, and a shoulder bag stuffed with research journals.

But as she waved him down as he entered the west corridor, he grinned as if no time had passed at all.

"Lunch, she asked, giving him a big hug… it will be just like the old days at school; we can talk about some interesting stuff that's been happening to me."

"Sure," Alister said with a wide smile, "I'll meet you right here after my presentation?"

Just before noon, two hours later, they descended the west stairway, which had windows overlooking Central Park. With Susan's fingerprint passkey, they entered the climate-regulated receiving room adjacent to the Egyptian galleries. There, with dusted crates and cabinets of unexhibited artifacts surrounding them, they sat down at one of the examination tables. It felt like the old days at school again, with sandwiches from the café and two cans of Perrier.

"I want to show you something weird," Susan said, half-laughing. It came from the wall of a house where we were on vacation earlier this month. There was a very small earthquake tremor one evening. It knocked a section of a stone column loose, and I found this wedged in the rubble."

She opened her locker and gently lifted out the scroll jar, still unlabeled, but carefully wrapped in the Museum's standard cotton cloth, which she had used to ship it here using the museum's private shipping vendor to avoid customs complications.

As she carefully removed the scroll from the jar, still wrapped in its ancient linen covering, she said, "It's probably just a personal journal or agricultural log," she added. "There are some strange markings on the jar that I don't recognize—but no symbols of significance. Still, it feels early. First-century, maybe?"

Alister, eyes widening as he noticed the writing on the papyrus scroll, had already stopped chewing.

As he unrolled the scroll, his eyes slowly scanned the first few lines. Then, several more. Then, the first full section. His hand trembled a bit.

And then he froze.

His breath caught. His body stiffened. Color drained from his face.

"Alister...?" she whispered.

No response.

She leaned closer. "What is it?"

Finally, he slowly exhaled. He hadn't even realized that he was holding his breath. Then, he carefully rolled the scroll closed, like handling an explosive.

"We… we can't talk about this here," he whispered.

She blinked. "What are you talking about?"

He glanced toward the security camera in the corner of the ceiling and lowered his voice to a whisper. "Not here. Put it away. Wrap it. No labels. In your locker. Now."

Susan, suddenly alert, followed his instructions. They walked briskly through the service corridor and out the glass double-door back exit, into the corner of Central Park that backs up against the museum's west side.

They walked for several minutes without saying a word. Alister was thinking, and Susan was growing increasingly concerned and nervous. They circled the Great Lawn until they found a shady, unoccupied bench.

It was a picture-perfect spring day—light breeze, children laughing, joggers weaving between strollers, lovers lying tangled in sun and shade—the serene, simple, unknowing world.

Alister sat still, his sweating palms pressed flat against his thighs, leaving damp marks on the trousers.

Finally, he spoke.

"What I'm about to tell you… can't leave this bench."

Susan nodded. Now, even more concerned.

He spoke very slowly. "To understand what you've found and how dangerous it is, I need to tell you a story. You know the beginning, but you won't know the end.

"In the early fourth century, the Roman Emperor Constantine authorized Christianity for the empire, not out of belief, but because he needed a unifying ideology. But he soon realized dozens—maybe hundreds—of different Christian texts were in circulation. Gospels. Letters. Oral accounts. Some authentic, many altered, and most anonymous. The Church had become fractured, and so were the teachings of Christianity. Constantine saw this as a threat to his unification plan."

She nodded, following him easily—he was right; this was familiar territory.

" So, he had the Church collect all the texts they could find. Filtering, excluding, and pulling together the ones that presented a consistent doctrine. Over the next century, they agreed on a canon. Twenty-seven books. That became the New Testament. A consistent Christian doctrine. Everything else became heresy."

He paused. "Now, here is the part you don't know."

"There have always been rumors," he said, "persistent ones, among very small groups of research scholars, some of whom are my closest colleagues. It's said that one Gospel they collected was so dangerous, they concluded, that it could bring down the Church itself—the Gospel of Magdalene. The rumors are that Mary Magdalene was more than a disciple. That she knew something no one else did. Something about Jesus. About what really happened to him. Something that would undo everything that Rome hoped to accomplish by authorizing and empowering Christianity to unify the empire."

Susan leaned forward. "What was in the Gospel…what was so dangerous?"

"The rumors don't tell us. No one seems to know. That's been a very carefully guarded secret. But whatever it is, they believed it would destroy everything. The beliefs of the Church. The divinity. Crushing the souls of billions of followers and destabilizing Western culture."

Susan almost whispered, "What did they do with the Gospel?"

Alister continued. "So the story goes. They didn't just suppress it. They destroyed the existing copies and rewrote it. Created a forgery in its place. That's the text we have now."

She stared at him, stunned.

"But there was a problem," he said. "They weren't sure they got all the copies. And even more concerning, they needed to find the original, if it still existed."

Alister paused, thinking. And then quietly added, "To make matters even worse, some years later, rumors surfaced claiming that Mary also kept a diary, which she used to remind herself of details as she wrote her gospel years later. If true, it would be even more dangerous because it was recorded at the time the events occurred, not written by an old woman years later."

"That must have terrified them." Susan said, "What did they do?"

"They built a secret arm to hunt the rest down and destroy them."

Alister paused momentarily, then continued, "But that's not where the story ends. It wasn't long before paranoia reared its ugly head. If Mary had known this damaging truth, others might have known it as well. So their focus slowly grew beyond just copies of Mary Magdalene's Gospel. It expanded to include any documents, copies, or originals discovered in the future that might contain this damaging truth." He paused for a long moment, looked her dead in the eyes, and then continued slowly, "*AND* to eliminate anyone who had learned the truth that Mary wrote in her gospel."

"That was almost 2000 years ago; they called it The *Order of Silence—Ordo Silentii* in their native Latin. Over the centuries, they became simply *The Silentii*. Last year, one of my colleagues, who often talks too much about these rumors, told me he heard their motto was *"Silence Becomes Eternal for the Erased."*

Suddenly, Susan felt very cold despite the warm spring day around her.

"And they've existed ever since. Passed through generations. As Christianity took root as the foundation of modern civilization, emperors and kings began supporting the Silentii. Quietly. Ruthlessly. They couldn't risk destabilizing the morals and laws that gave them power. And today they operate globally with the support of modern governments and their intelligence agencies..

"You're saying they still exist," she whispered, "…and that I, or we, may have what they search for."

A shiver went up her spine.

"They're more powerful than ever," Alister said. "Encrypted funding. Private satellites. Facial recognition. AI analysis. If someone uploads a fragment with certain phrases—anomalous Aramaic syntax, for example—it's flagged. Instantly."

Susan's breath was shallow now.

"There are rumors about what they are capable of… the Kennedy brothers learned the secret and threatened to expose it—even Lincoln, the rumors say, they thought he was becoming a problem. And that MLK accidentally learned too much."

"People whisper about these rumors. But no one talks aloud. Not in writing. Not online. Because they monitor everything, one rumor is that the Silentii has partnered with the Mafia since their inception in early 1800s Sicily, when they were just a loosely organized group offering protection in rural areas where the official government was corrupt and weak. *The Silentii* engaged them to keep a lookout in local churches, universities, museums, archaeological dig sites, and even in bars for any loose talk about early Christian documents. Today, their partnership is worldwide…and their involvement has grown stronger. The Dead Sea Scrolls give you an example of their extraordinary reach. I understand that the Mafia was immediately alerted to the scroll's discovery in the late 1940s near Khirbet Qumran. They informed Silentii before anyone else knew. Have you ever wondered why the Scrolls are completely silent regarding Jesus, despite being written during the same time period as his life and the early stages of his ministry? Before anyone else got to see the scrolls. *Silentii* had already silenced them of any reference to Jesus. My colleague thinks that the Mafia's incorrect use of the term

Omerta, to mean Silence, signals their close connection with *Silentii.* Just consider that the definition of the word Omerta says nothing about Silence; it is actually the root of Manhood.

Susan sat quietly, trying to digest the story. A teenage boy passed by with headphones. A golden retriever barked.

Alister turned back toward her. "I am not fluent in Aramaic, the language of Judea in the time of Jesus, but I can read enough to get the general ideas. That scroll you have—I can make out the basic names, phrasing, the handwriting, and the references—I think Jesus himself may have written it along with Mary Magdalene. I'm not sure, but I think it mentions them traveling to Gaul, living together, and having a family. What puzzles me is that it would appear that it is after the crucifixion."

The sentence hung in the air like a storm. The implications were devastating. Dangerous.

Alister added, "The scroll has much more, but I'm not skilled enough to have read it so quickly before we put it away."

"But what's so important is that no original manuscripts from that time still exist," he added. "Not even one. No original gospels. Just copies. Copies of copies. Thousands of them, centuries removed." The scroll you found appears to be an original, not a copy, and it looks to me like Jesus himself was one of the writers. If *Silentii* believes the Magdalene Gospel was dangerous, can you imagine how they will feel if they learn about what you've found?

"And if they do find out?"

"They will do anything to stop it. Stop you. And stop anyone else who has seen it. To the Church, it's much more dangerous than the Magdalene Gospel, containing the same damning information, but written by Jesus himself."

Deep in their own separate thoughts, they walked slowly back to the museum, passing an oblivious world: children playing, lovers kissing, and scholars discussing minor exhibits.

At the staff entrance, Alister stopped.

"Earlier, when we were inside, I only had time to look at the scroll's first few paragraphs. As I mentioned, I possess only rudimentary skills in reading ancient Aramaic, particularly in a Galilean dialect, so I could only grasp the gist of what it said. But that was enough. I need some more time to read and study the scrolls and then think about what to do next. With all the security cameras inside the museum, it would be better for me to take it home, study it there," he said. "Could you go back in and grab it from your locker. Boring bag—paper or gym. Meet me outside in front."

Susan tried to remain calm as she retrieved the scroll and brought it to Alister, who waited on the front steps of the museum on Fifth Avenue. "Smart," he said, "a brown paper shopping bag, perfect."

As he began to leave, he said, "Let me call you tomorrow or the next day. In the meantime, don't contact me, don't email, and don't text."

He looked around cautiously. "Don't tell anyone. Not your team. Not Bob. Not the museum director. Not your daughter. *The Silentii* monitors everything."

Susan felt her legs weak beneath her as he started to walk away.

Then Alister paused. "One thing," he said over his shoulder. "Where did you say you found the scroll?"

Susan hesitated.

"I didn't."

He nodded once, turned, and became just one of the crowd as he crossed Fifth Avenue and headed for his apartment on Morton Street in the far West Village. It was just 1:30 in New York—a sunny and warm midday afternoon.

The stress of the day was almost too much. Susan stood in the museum's west corridor long after Alister had disappeared on the street, the weight of the encounter pressing against her chest. She couldn't go back to work. Not now. She needed time to think. To breathe.

Bob would be home today. He often worked from their apartment on Mondays, buried in proposals and financing deals. His analytical mind—rational, a relentlessly practical dealmaker—had always helped steady her in moments of uncertainty. Even when they disagreed, his clarity helped her find her own.

Alister had warned her not to tell anyone. Not yet. Not even Bob. But they had built a life together on honesty, right? And wasn't just about a piece of ancient papyrus—it was something bigger, something terrifying.

She made her decision. She would go home and tell him…but not everything.

She would tell Bob that she thinks the scroll might contain original writings of Jesus himself. She would leave out the rest. The Silentii. The danger. The chilling warning Alister had whispered in the park. There was no need to frighten him. Not yet.

As she gathered her things, she tried to convince herself that this was the right choice—just a fragment of the truth.

Her memory of that evening just before bed last month in St Cyr had faded, that fleeting recollection just before sleep.

When real power and wealth are involved, you can trust no one.

It would have been wise to remember it, but she didn't.

At that exact moment, separated by 4300 miles and six hours on the clock, that same sun was setting through chilly, rain-soaked evening clouds at Rome Ciampino Airport, 10 miles from the Vatican.

The Silentii Gulfstream G800 jet was fully fueled and cleared for departure on Ciampino's 7,000-foot runway 33 for its trip to New York.

The black fuselage glowed under the Ciampino night lights.

"Ciampino Clearance, Gulfstream OS7777, requesting IFR clearance to Teterboro, New Jersey."

After a brief pause at the holding point,

"Gulfstream OS7777, Ciampino Tower. Wind two seven zero at five knots. Runway Three Three, cleared for takeoff."

Almost imperceptibly, a smile touched the corners of Corvus's mouth as thirty-seven thousand pounds of thrust from the twin Rolls-Royce Pearl 700 engines pressed him back into the seat. In less than 30 seconds, the wheels lifted from the runway, and the cabin fell into near silence as the G800 accelerated through its 130 knot rotation speed and arced upward into the dark North Atlantic sky.

His first hunt had begun.

He would be in New York tomorrow morning. He would find Dr. Susan Hale. He would find out what was in that shipment from Nice to the Metropolitan Museum in New York.

As he thought, an image of the Silentii chamber walls emerged from his subconscious. It bore the seal of the Ordo Silentii and its motto, carved centuries earlier: *"Silence Becomes Eternal for the Erased."*

CHAPTER FIVE

Alister Duran stepped into his Morton Street apartment, the door quietly locking behind him. The afternoon sun reflected off the Hudson River. Bands of rippling light moved across the high-ceilinged walls, decorated with modern art and understated elegance.

He stood for a long moment in the silence, taking it in.

Safe, he thought. For now.

The apartment was a sprawling prewar coop—clean lines, cool colors, and a massive terrace that overlooked the Hudson and the path of pedestrians and cyclists down below. Across the river, the Jersey shoreline hummed with harbor traffic. The place never failed to surprise the few visitors he allowed inside. It didn't match the image of a rumpled professor that his colleagues knew. But Alister never explained.

He liked it that way.

Even Susan Hale, who knew him best in their earlier days, had no idea who he was. To her, he was just a fellow doctoral student from NYU, a scholar with deep knowledge and quirky habits.

She didn't know about Harrison Duran—Alister's late father—self-made, quietly powerful, and once one of the most connected men on Wall Street. He had built a global mining empire and forged friendships with Nobel laureates, world leaders, and financiers whose names never appeared in public headlines.

From childhood, Alister had traveled beside him—dining with statesmen, absorbing the way true power operated behind closed doors. And yet, when the time came, he'd chosen a different life. Languages, theology, history. The quiet pursuit of meaning over influence.

His father had respected that decision, even if he hadn't entirely understood it.

Alister shrugged off his jacket and walked into the kitchen, still feeling the adrenaline of the past day rattling through his chest. He poured a bourbon—his father's favorite—and took a long, quiet sip in his father's worn leather chair. It was a Ralph Lauren Writer's chair, and its traditional style didn't match the rest of the apartment's modernist feel. But it stayed. It always stayed—a small rebellion against the cool anonymity of the rest of the place.

The bourbon worked quickly, softening the hard edges in his mind.

He ordered a meal from a small Italian place on Carmine Street—grilled vegetables, pasta, and olive oil cake. While he waited for delivery, his thoughts drifted to another life—one summer long ago, when he had stayed with *Luca Severin* on Italy's Amalfi Coast.

Luca had been his father's friend—fifteen years younger, endlessly brilliant, and intensely private. He held multiple doctorates in ancient languages, Near Eastern religions, and biblical studies. First, a consultant to powerful governments and institutions, then the chair of a major department at Harvard, Luca had retired years ago to a villa perched above the Mediterranean.

That summer—his last before finishing his PhD—Alister had spent a month there. Days were filled with quiet research. Evenings were spent on the terrace, overlooking the cobalt Tyrrhenian sea, discussing ancient texts, hidden histories, and questions of faith over glasses of Brunello and platters of grilled fish. Luca had shaped his thinking more than any professor ever had.

He hadn't spoken to him in years.

But that would soon change.

The buzzer jolted him from his reverie. It was Frank, the doorman, sending up the food. Alister thanked him absently and settled in to eat, but his exhaustion finally caught up. Half the food went untouched.

He drifted into an uneasy sleep in the same chair, bourbon on the side.

As he slept, a sleek black shape had already cleared air traffic control at Ciampino in Rome and was cruising at 690 miles at an altitude of 51,000 feet, high above commercial traffic. It would be at Teterboro in 7 hours and 10 minutes. Then it would be just a 30-minute drive to the Metropolitan Museum of Art in Manhattan.

CHAPTER SIX

Corvus reclined in the rear seat of the Gulfstream, its tail number—OS7777—broadcasting nothing unusual to air traffic control but speaking volumes within the Ordo Silentii. The sevens were their number. Their shield. Their creed.

He unfolded his black titanium laptop on the polished walnut desk beside him and activated the secure satellite link to the Silentii Surveillance Operations Network. Within seconds, a comprehensive schematic of the Metropolitan Museum of Art's security system appeared on the screen, including video archives, staff credentials, keycode logs, and thermal mapping overlays.

The Vatican had learned early how to wield its influence. When its priceless art collections toured the world, part of the agreement for lending artifacts always included "technical enhancements" to ensure protection. The receiving museums never knew that these enhancements gave Silentii permanent access—ghost software inserted deep within their systems, impossible to trace or remove.

Corvus moved with quiet precision, pulling up staff credentials. Dr. Susan Hale, curator of religious antiquities. He studied her profile photograph, scanned her recent keycard activity, and ran a facial recognition scan across the museum's internal surveillance footage from the last month.

There she was—routine days of work, unremarkable entries and exits until yesterday.

She had entered the sub-basement storage wing at 1:23 p.m. with a second individual: a male with glasses, a tweed jacket, and unkempt hair—another academic, clearly. The footage showed them seated at a long metal table, facing each other. Susan carefully unwrapped a bundled object.

A terracotta jar.

Then—briefly—a scroll.

They spoke for several minutes. Alister Duran. That name came back flagged. Corvus studied the man's posture, the reaction as he leaned forward, his frozen expression. Then they packed it away. Too quickly, Corvus thought. Far too quickly for something of real value.

His initial read was that the item wasn't important. If it were significant, they'd have lingered.

Later footage showed Susan returning alone. She removed something from her locker, placing it in a brown paper bag before walking out through the service doors. It could've been groceries. Gym clothes. Nothing about her behavior suggested anything unusual.

Still, Corvus had learned never to assume.

Before the plane touched down at Teterboro, he accessed the museum's admin panel, pulling Susan's locker number and overriding access codes. Then, with a single keystroke, he temporarily disabled the motion sensors in that section of the sub-basement for a two-minute window. He encrypted a copy of the backup footage and deleted the override logs.

The jet touched down in light crosswinds. A black Mercedes waited on the tarmac, its license plate—also OS7777—gleaming under the afternoon sun. Corvus stepped in, silent as always.

By 2:45 p.m., he was inside the Met.

Security passed him without a second glance. His forged ID, drawn from a Vatican-linked academic partnership, identified him as Dr. Marco Silvani, a restoration consultant assigned to the Byzantine wing. No one questioned him.

He descended the basement stairs without hesitation. The corridor smelled faintly of cleaning solvent and dust. Locker 1128. Susan Hale.

He opened it.

Empty.

No jar. No scroll. Nothing but a faint trace of paper dust and museum-standard cotton wrap.

He turned to leave—but a voice stopped him.

"Excuse me, sir. That locker's not assigned to you."

Corvus turned slowly. A museum archivist—young, earnest, wearing a name badge—stood near the end of the corridor.

"Security audit," Corvus said."Random checks. Two minutes." Corvus said smoothly. His voice carried the perfect inflection of official confidence. "We've had a small breach reported. Random spot checks."

The archivist hesitated. "I haven't heard about that."

"Then I suggest you speak with your department head. I'll finish my check and be gone."

Corvus walked away before the young man could respond. He was out of the building in under four minutes.

In the car, his phone vibrated—a direct encrypted call from the Silentii Intelligence Operations Center.

He answered with a single word. "Yes?"

A voice crackled on the other end. "We've received a report from our Roman affiliates. Dr. Susan Hale's husband—Robert Hale, a commercial real estate broker working with global corporate clients working with religious antiquities—made contact yesterday with a known laundering intermediary."

"For artifacts?" Corvus asked sharply.

"Yes. The intermediary flagged the term *scroll written by Jesus*. No physical description. But we've confirmed this intermediary has ties to the old syndicate network. He reported the conversation to his handler. The handler reported to us."

Corvus's eyes narrowed. "Jesus himself?"

"That's what he said."

The call ended.

Corvus logged back into the museum's system. He ran a secondary scan on the video logs, searching for Alister Duran. The AI flagged the footage. Outside the museum service entrance, timestamped 3:12 p.m. the day before, Susan handed a brown paper bag to Alister. No doubt. That was the scroll.

It wasn't groceries. It wasn't gym clothes.

It was gone.

He cross-referenced Duran's residential files—pulled from Vatican-backdoored academic databases. A condo in the West Village. Morton Street. Sixth-floor corner unit.

"Take me there," Corvus said to the driver.

The Mercedes turned south. Traffic was thick, but the car moved steadily through the maze of downtown Manhattan.

It was just after 4:00 p.m. when they reached Morton Street. Corvus's fingers tapped slowly on the armrest, a flicker of excitement in his otherwise unreadable face.

This was no longer an ordinary retrieval.

This could be his defining opportunity—the defining moment of his career.

He stepped from the car.
The hunt had begun.
Again.

CHAPTER SEVEN

unlight filtered through the linen curtains, casting a warm glow across the room. Alister stirred awake in his father's worn leather chair, the scent of bourbon lingering in the air. The half-eaten meal from the night before sat untouched on the table.

He rose slowly, stretching to shake off the remnants of sleep. Had he known to look, in the distance, he could have seen the Silentii G800 on its final approach to Teterboro. It would be later today before any of that would matter.

For now, after a quick shower and a strong cup of coffee, he returned to the scroll, laying it carefully on the polished desk beneath a soft white lamp. The ancient papyrus crackled faintly as he unrolled it, its ink fading but legible under the right light.

He began working.

Though not an Aramaic specialist, years of linguistic training had made him just skilled enough to grasp the text's contours. He took his time now, unlike the rush he had yesterday at the Met with Susan. A few words caught his eye. Again, he saw the same names and places.

Mary Magdala... the first-century name for Mary Magdalene.
Maryam bat Joachim... Jesus's mother.

Golgatha...the crucifixion hill.
Gaul...A village of olive trees.

His eyes narrowed on the sentence that mentioned children.

His pulse quickened. He leaned back, his eyes wide. The few words he could recognise were painting a confusing and fragmented picture.

The crucifixion. Jesus with Mary Magdalene and his mother in Gaul. A family. It couldn't be right…could it? He needed to find someone fluent in Aramaic who could read this for him.

A sharp buzz from the intercom broke his focus.

"Yeah?" he answered, voice still rough.

"Mr. Duran? It's Frank. A courier just dropped something off. Says it's urgent. And, uh… he's been asked to wait for a reply."

Alister froze.

"From whom?"

"Susan Hale, sir."

Susan!

He swore under his breath, already moving. This wasn't good. They had agreed—no contact. Not yet. Not unless absolutely necessary. And even if she had used the Met's private courier, it still risked exposing his connection to her.

Until now, he'd assumed the Silentii hadn't yet flagged him. Just another academic on the fringes. But a delivery here? Today? It might've just painted a target on his back.

He took the elevator down to the lobby and retrieved the envelope. Sat in the corner chair and opened it.

Her handwriting was as familiar as her voice:

Alister—
I used the Met's confidential courier service, so technically I haven't broken our agreement. But we need to meet. There's been a break-in at the Met. My locker was targeted.
Call me. —S.

His stomach dropped.

So soon.

The Silentii were moving faster than he'd feared.

On the back of her note, he quickly scribbled the address of a quiet café he knew well in Tribeca that would be far from prying eyes. After he wrote at "4:30 this afternoon," he added, "Bring your passport. I will explain." He handed the envelope back to the courier.

"Take this to her. Now."

Back upstairs, pacing, Alister ran his hands through his hair, heart racing. He had to move—fast.

He pulled out his phone and scrolled to a number he hadn't dialed in nearly a decade. Lena Bartelli, his father's personal buyer at Bloomingdale's from years ago, was a second-generation Italian from Queens who'd built her career with the same street smarts and tenacity his father had admired. During his teenage years, she'd outfitted both Duran men, as his father liked to say, and despite not hearing from him since Harrison died, he had a hunch she'd still be there.

The line clicked.

"Bloomingdale's, personal shopping, Lena speaking."

"Lena," Alister said, surprised by the familiarity he felt in her voice. "It's Alister Duran."

A pause—and then, delighted: "Alister! Look who's calling out of the blue! Ten years, at least? I still have you in my phone, you know. How are you, honey?"

He smiled despite everything. "I'm better now that you're still there. I need a big favor—fast."

"Anything," she said, all business now. "Tell me."

He gave her a quick rundown: a woman, mid-40s, slim, about 5'6", stylish but understated. A professor type. He needed a casual travel wardrobe for her—layers, flats, essentials, everything for several days. Remove the labels. All packed in a simple carry-on bag. And he'd pick it up in three to four hours.

There was the briefest pause. Then: "Done. Don't worry. Discretion's my middle name." Alister could only imagine what she was thinking.

"Thank you, Lena. I owe you."

"You already owe me ten years' worth of catch-ups," she quipped. "See you soon."

He hung up, exhaling hard. Then quickly dialed his Amex Black Card personal travel agent.

"Get me two business-class tickets tonight, JFK to London. Anything you can find."

A pause while she searched.

"We've got the last two seats on Lufthansa, midnight departure."

"Book them. And after that, Eurostar to Paris, TGV to Aix-en-Provence. Plus a rental car in Marseille."

"Understood. Anything else, Mr Duran?"

"No. That's it."

He ended the call, staring at the New Jersey skyline as the sun sank lower. His mind flashed to Luca—Luca Severin, the man who had shaped his path as much as his father: biblical scholar, linguist, historian, multiple doctorates, friends with Nobel laureates. There was no one alive better suited to decipher the depths of these scrolls. Luca would help them. He had to...otherwise?

Alister sent a brief text using an encryption app he had used only for confidential university business:

Luca, I'm coming. I'll be there the day after tomorrow. I need to see you. It's urgent. I will explain everything.

He packed quickly and efficiently, throwing essentials into his bag: a jacket, layers, ID, and a backup drive.

And as he zipped up the carry-on, the weight of what was happening suddenly hit him.

This might be the last time he ever sets foot in this apartment.

The hunt had begun—and now, they were running to stay alive, and caution would need to be part of every next move.

Alister Duran stepped quickly into the late afternoon sunlight from his apartment lobby. He hailed a yellow cab—not his usual Uber, which would have provided a digital footprint that the Silentii could track.

As the cab turned the corner from Morton Street and merged onto the West Side Highway, a polished black Mercedes with the license plate OS7777 caught his eye. Turning to look over his shoulder, Alister noted it was pulling up in front of his Morton Street apartment. He didn't recognize the car, nor the man with the cropped white hair that stepped quickly onto the sidewalk. It wasn't a usual ride-share car ride. And he didn't know of any neighbors who owned a car like that.

He shook off the unease and leaned back in the seat, unaware of the danger that had just arrived at his doorstep.

CHAPTER EIGHT

Alister arrived in Tribeca just before four. He walked a few blocks to a quiet corner of Harrison Street and stepped inside a tucked-away café called *Le Faubourg*. The dining area was narrow and long, with tables spaced discreetly apart. The kind of place where you could talk, and no one was seated close enough to overhear.

On the way there, he'd stopped at a local telecom shop just a few doors down and bought two burner phones, each loaded with prepaid international calling plans. When he told the clerk he needed coverage across Europe, the man didn't blink—good, he thought, that it wasn't an uncommon request, and the clerk wouldn't remember if someone would come around later asking questions.

The café was nearly empty. He chose a rear table near the kitchen. Quiet, and out of view. As he waited, old memories stirred. He'd come here often, years ago, with someone he had loved. Maybe he still did. It was a whirlwind courtship, and they married after dating only eight months. The relationship lasted only two years and hadn't ended with drama, only the slow, aching drift of two people heading in different directions. With time, he began to see the marriage as the path not taken, and perhaps he should have put more effort into it. A noise from the kitchen brought him back to the present—and Susan. And everything that had happened over the last forty-eight hours.

He found himself wondering why he'd chosen this place to meet. There were other, safer options. Closer. Less conspicuous. Perhaps, he thought, some part of him wanted a second chance to rewrite something. To work harder the next time.

Susan arrived moments later. She slipped into the seat across from him, breathless and visibly rattled, her eyes scanning the café as if expecting someone to follow her.

"You okay?" he asked.

"No. Not really."

He studied her. Since her time at NYU, her looks had remained striking. Her signature poise was still there—but now it was edged with something unfamiliar. Vulnerability. He had never seen that in her before. It softened her. And it made her, somehow, more approachable and, what was the feeling, attractive.

They ordered cappuccinos.

Alister leaned in, keeping his voice low. "Susan, what I've been able to translate from the scroll…it's enough to be dangerous. I can only read fragments, but what I've seen—it's serious. We need help. There's someone I trust. Luca Severin. A former professor, linguist, biblical scholar—he was my mentor. Brilliant. He lives in seclusion now, in a villa on the Amalfi Coast. We need to go. Stay with him. Let him read the scroll. He'll know what to do."

She lifted her cup with a trembling hand. "That seems… extreme. Are you sure they're tracking me?"

Alister nodded, careful not to alarm her further. "If what you described in your note is what I think it is… then yes. Silentii doesn't make casual visits."

She leaned forward. "You mean the break-in?"

"Yes. Tell me what happened."

She explained that a young archivist had noticed someone near her locker. Security had been alerted. They asked her to review the security footage.

"He wasn't anyone I knew," she said. "Early to mid-thirties, maybe younger. Medium height. Powerfully built. He moved like…like an animal. White hair, cropped short. Scar on his cheek."

Alister tensed. He recalled the figure stepping out of the black Mercedes that had pulled up outside his apartment.

He pulled one of the burner phones from his bag and dialed his building.

"I need to check something," he murmured.

The voice that answered wasn't Frank, his doorman.

"This is Alister Duran. Who is this?"

"I'm Marcus, the night guy. Came early to drop off my uniform. I… I'm sorry to tell you, sir—Frank's dead."

Alister froze. "What happened?"

"Security footage shows a man walking in, asking for you. Frank tried to stop him. The guy snapped his neck like it was nothing. Pulled him behind the desk. Powerfully built. White hair. Scar down his face."

"My apartment?"

"He went straight up—only your unit. The place is trashed—closets, drawers, everything turned upside down. Nothing else touched. I called building security. NYPD's there now."

Alister hung up. His face had gone pale.

"Susan, it's the same man. He was at my building. The doorman is dead."

Her breath caught. She took the burner from Alister and called Bob, who was working from home again.

He answered, his voice tight, panicked. "Susan? Where the hell are you? Some guy came—said he was a courier from the Met. Claimed he had documents. I thought you'd sent him. I let him come up. When I opened the door, he asked for the jar. I hesitated, and he pushed past me. Tore the place apart."

Susan's voice went cold. "How would he know about the scroll? Did you tell someone?"

"I… I called a client last night—someone I trust. I'm sorry. It was just to ask—hypothetically—what something like that might be worth. Susan, the guy knew. He knew I made that call. He told me if I went to the cops, I'd be dead before morning."

"Bob, what have you done?"

"Me! He knew about the jar, Susan. Said if I call the cops, I'm dead."

Controlling her growing anger, Susan took a deep breath and said slowly and calmly, " Bob, pack a bag and stay with friends, or go to a hotel. Just stay away from the apartment until I get back. I'm going out of town. I'll call you when I know more. It might be a few days, maybe even a week or more."

She hung up.

"It's him," she said to Alister. "Same man. Scar. White hair. Bob called one of his clients and told him about the jar. Wanted to know how much it could be worth. Alister, he already knew about the call."

Alister's voice dropped to a whisper. "Then we have no time. We leave. Now."

Susan's hesitation vanished. Her expression sharpened. Her voice turned calm and steady.

"Ok, let's go."

As soon as they were in the cab, Alister gave her the rest. He told her about Lena—his father's longtime personal shopper—who had already packed a travel bag for Susan with everything she'd need for the next several days. Their first stop would be at Bloomingdale's to pick it up.

Then he opened his notebook.

"We leave on the midnight flight to London. From there, Eurostar to Paris. Then the TGV to Aix-en-Provence. Rental car in Marseille. We'll drive the rest of the way to Luca's. It's not the route they'll expect."

"They'll be watching for departures to Nice," she said, already thinking several steps ahead.

"Exactly. They'll assume you've gone back to where the scroll originated. And if they're scanning airline manifests, it'll take them time to spot us heading to London."

She studied him now, as he had studied her earlier. And just as he'd noticed her vulnerability, she saw something she hadn't before—quiet resolve, a sense of control, the sharp clarity of someone who had lived close to power but never flaunted it.

It was…comforting. And unexpectedly attractive.

She smiled faintly and said quietly. "You've changed, Alister."

"So have you," he replied

And for a moment, the danger she felt receded—just a little—and the cab sped on into the falling night.

CHAPTER NINE

The Business Class cabin slowly returned to life after a smooth flight through the transatlantic night. As the cabin lights came back on, Alister awoke to the rustle of refastening seatbelts, quiet yawns, and the sound of window shades rising. The cabin lit up from a brilliant sun already high in the late morning sky. They were an hour from Heathrow, scheduled for a noon arrival.

While it was bright above the clouds, a thick gray cover below signaled the usual fog and rain of a typical London day. They were traveling by rail to Paris this afternoon, Alister thought, so the rain would not be a problem.

Next to him, Susan stirred. Despite the last-minute booking, they'd managed to get seats together. A small miracle.

The night before now felt like a blur—tense, adrenaline-charged, unreal.

After leaving Bloomingdale's with the travel bag Lena had prepared, they took separate cabs to JFK, being careful not to be seen together. Check-in had gone smoothly. Too smoothly. There was a brief moment when Alister thought he saw someone watching them near the security area. A man, nondescript but oddly still. But he turned and boarded a different flight.

It was nothing, he thought.

That judgment had been right—yesterday at JFK. But it wouldn't be today at Heathrow.

Back in New York, Corvus had waited for three long hours in the shadows of Central Park across from Susan's apartment. He had watched patiently, carefully. She never came home. He knew then—she was gone. And if she was gone, so was Alister.

He didn't know where they were—maybe still in New York, maybe hiding in another borough, maybe halfway across the country. Or perhaps they had taken the scroll and fled overseas.

Corvus didn't hesitate. He couldn't risk failure on his first assignment. This was too important for his future with Silentii. He unlocked his encrypted device and tapped in a code he knew would carry weight: OS7777.

A silent channel opened to Silentii Intelligence Operations. He uploaded dossiers on Susan Hale and Alister Duran in seconds and activated the organization's global surveillance system.

At airports across Europe, silent alerts were issued. British Intelligence, Vatican attachés, and embedded agents within airport security staff—all were quietly mobilized.

But Alister's strategy had bought them time: the indirect route, the late booking, the circuitous flight path. The data didn't surface in time. By the time Silentii learned they were on the Lufthansa flight to London, the wheels had already lifted.

Now, Susan and Alister were on board, and the tension was ebbing, if only slightly. Susan sipped her bourbon, a habit Alister hadn't remembered from their NYU days.

"Always been your drink?" he asked with a faint smile.

She gave a small laugh. "You think because I'm a curator, I should prefer white wine and delicate cheeses?"

She paused, then added more softly, "It started with my dad. I grew up in a triple-decker in South Boston. He was a captain in the Boston Fire Department. A quiet man, not overtly religious like my mom, but wise in ways that mattered. He saw things clearly, without pretense. When I was sixteen, I got into a bad situation at school—dumb choices that most teenagers make without thinking of the consequences. While I excelled at my studies and got excellent grades, I wasn't the most outgoing or popular kid. I secretly wanted to be part of that 'in crowd'. So, I just did it when one of them asked me to stand in the hallway and drop a book to make noise if I saw the teacher coming. I thought that if I helped them, it would prove I was cool, and they would ask me to be part of their group.

Boy, was I wrong. I didn't know they were looking through the teacher's desk to find the exam. The whole thing blew up in my face, and I would be suspended even though I told them I didn't know what they were doing. I was terrified. But my dad wasn't angry, didn't scold me. He came to get me from the principal's office, laid out a plan to make it right, take responsibility, and helped me fix it, with no excuses. When it was over, we sat on the back porch…we called it our 'piazzas'…as the sun went down. He poured two bourbons—his drink of choice. Told me if I was old enough to get myself into trouble, I was old enough to share his bourbon. It's been my drink ever since. Reminds me of being able to depend on someone strong—that I don't have to shoulder everything myself."

Alister raised his glass. "To a strong shoulder to lean on."

They clinked gently as Susan replied, "And to getting out of a tough spot."

She leaned back, letting the warmth settle her. "I keep thinking about Bob. Not just what happened last night. But who he has become lately. Treasure does that to people. The idea of it. But I worry that perhaps he was always that way, and I never saw it before."

"You think he'll be okay?" Alister asked.

She was quiet for a long moment. "I don't know. But if that guy from Silentii came to the apartment—if he got to Bob—he knows… enough about what we have to make it… very dangerous."

Alister took a breath, glancing around the cabin, then leaned in closer. "There's something I didn't tell you yesterday. I think there might be another scroll. Maybe even more than one. Like I said, my Aramaic is far from perfect, but I think there was something about... disappoint-ment. Jesus was hearing rumors from back in Galilee and Jerusalem. The apostles, something about them abandoning their promises. He was very disappointed about it."

Susan's eyes locked onto his.

"Does it say he did anything about it?"

"I think the scroll mentions a journey. Remember, my Aramaic is far from perfect. If my reading is even close to correct, I think it says he may have returned to Jerusalem…not as Jesus, but as Paul."

Her voice dropped to a whisper. "As Paul?"

Alister nodded. "It sounds like Jesus returned, using the identity of Saul of Tarsus. It would make sense, because he couldn't return as Jesus; the Romans would arrest him immediately."

Susan sat back slowly, her face pale. "Could that possibly be true ?"

Alister exhaled slowly. "If it is, then the entire Bible story about Paul and his transformation on the road to Damascus was entirely fabricat-ed. And all the stories about his missions…there never was a Paul, just Jesus building the Church using his name."

Susan stared at him, then said quietly, "My brother Thomas used to say the Church was built on miracles and marble dust. Beautiful, fragile, but full of cracks and always in need of repair."

Alister turned. "Your brother, the Jesuit?"

She nodded. "Was a Jesuit. He left the order about seven years ago. He'd been promoted—oversaw a Jesuit university in Seoul. But some-thing happened. A faculty member uncovered records—buried disci-plinary files from the '90s, implicating a senior official in… well, let's say it wasn't just financial abuse."

Alister's brow tightened.

"The official died before anything came out, and the order pushed for silence. Not justice. Just containment. Thomas fought them. Thought transparency mattered. They told him loyalty mattered more."

Alister said nothing for a moment.

"He left," Susan added. "Came back to the States. Worked for UNESCO for a few years, leading preservation efforts at archaeological sites across southeastern Turkey, Jordan, and northern Syria.

"He is currently in New York, working with an international non-profit organization called Covenant Partners International (CPI), which focuses on securing archaeological sites from illegal trafficking in those same areas. It still believes in God. Still prays. But he doesn't trust institutions anymore."

She looked over. "If he knew what we've found—what this scroll suggests—if we need it, I think he'd help. He's already lost his illusions about the honesty of Church history."

They fell into silence, their eyes heavy from the day's excitement. The bourbon was working its magic as the engines hummed beneath them, finally lulling them into a relaxed sleep.

Four hours later, as the cabin returned to life, the flight attendants moved through with coffee and breakfast trays.

Landing was smooth. Passport control was uneventful. They exchanged no words until they reached the Lufthansa lounge. Behind frosted glass and soft music, they reserved two shower rooms, changed into clean clothes, and regrouped.

They had four hours until the Eurostar to Paris—they could relax and take their time.

But that feeling changed when they stepped out of the lounge and headed toward the exit to catch a taxi to St. Pancras.

Security staff glanced at them. Twice.

This time, they weren't imagining it.

A man near the escalator touched his ear. Another by the doors adjusted his position as they passed.

No alarms. No overt actions.

But it was clear—Silentii was closing in.

Alister caught it—a small communication gesture. Not police. Not customs. Something else.

He grabbed Susan's hand.

"We're going now. Fast."

They ducked out through a side exit and into a queue of black cabs. The moment they were inside, Alister gave an address just south of the station. Not the Eurostar entrance. A street nearby.

As the cab pulled away, Susan looked back.

Two men stepped outside the terminal. One pointed. Then the cab turned the corner, and they were gone.

Again, they thought, we are still one step ahead.

Back in New York, Corvus was already on the move. He stood in the private hangar at Teterboro, staring at the sleek black Gulfstream marked only with its tail number: OS7777.

He turned to the pilot. "France. Marseille. Now."

Silentii Global International had already informed him of Alister and Susan's next destination after Paris—a rental car facility near the port. He would not be one step behind this time.

He would be waiting when they arrived.

The engines began to roar, and the sleek black Gulfstream climbed sharply, disappearing into the dark North Atlantic night.

CHAPTER TEN

The cab merged into late morning traffic, a typical London knot of buses, delivery vans, and honking black taxis. Alister sat back, scroll tucked safely in his backpack, watching the blur of rooftops and double-deckers pass by. Their complicated itinerary should have bought them more time, kept them at least one step ahead of Silentii. But what just happened at Heathrow said otherwise.

They had arrived only three hours ago. And Silentii already knew.

Still, they'd moved quickly, been careful, and now, for a fleeting moment, it felt like they might be ahead again.

Susan still held his hand. Not in panic—something steadier. The silence between them lasted several blocks. Then she spoke.

"If they knew where we were this morning," she said, now more slowly, "they already know where we're going."

Alister met her eyes. "The Eurostar. Then the TGV to Marseille. They'll be waiting. If we show up for that rental car, they'll follow us right to Luca."

Susan nodded. "They're not guessing anymore. They know."

The weight of her words sank in. Alister straightened and tapped on the plexiglass.

"Change of plans," he said to the driver. "Take us to Gatwick Airport."

The man blinked. "Gatwick? That's out of the way, that is."

Alister nodded. "So's a good tip."

Alister opened the map app on his burner phone as the cab rerouted south.

"We can book a flight to Naples from Gatwick. Luca's place is only two hours from there—just outside Positano."

Susan raised an eyebrow. "Why not go back to Heathrow? It's much closer."

 "They'll still have eyes there," Alister said, "…we were just at Heathrow this morning. Too risky."

Susan nodded, thinking it through. "And they'll assume we're on the Eurostar by now—headed toward Paris and Marseille."

"And let's keep it that way." Alister confirmed

Alister signaled the driver to stop when he spotted a sports shop off Kensington High Street. A few minutes later, he emerged with two wide-brimmed baseball caps—navy for him, grey for her.

"Keep your face angled down," he said, handing her the cap. "CCTV's everywhere. Silentii probably has a real-time AI feed running off the UK's camera network. Facial recognition, movement tracking. These help us vanish."

Susan tucked her hair into a low ponytail under the cap.

Their next stop was a bank. Alister withdrew a large stack of euros and pounds from two separate accounts—small amounts, no flags, no trace. His father had taught him that. Keep some parts of your life off the grid.

Ninety minutes later, they arrived at Gatwick. They blended in with the terminal buzz of casual chaos of holiday travelers—families, backpackers, businessmen. Perfect camouflage.

They found the nearest easyJet kiosk and paid in cash for two last-minute tickets to Naples. No ID required. Just boarding passes printed with gate numbers and departure in forty-five minutes.

In the security line, Susan kept her head down, face in shadow, moving with the rhythm of the crowd. No delays. No attention. Their false trail in London was growing cold.

Three hours later, as the wheels touched down in Naples, Alister powered up the burner phone and sent a short, encrypted message.

We're coming. Two hours. Looking forward to seeing you again.

Luca's reply came quickly. *Can't wait. Safe travels. Curious already.*

They exited the airport into the warm early evening of southern Italy. No ride shares. No digital footprint. Just a cab and a driver named Sergio—silent, grizzled, and competent. He knew where Positano was without being asked twice.

Meanwhile, Corvus stood across the street from the port's car rental center in Marseille. He had been watching for hours. No Alister. No Susan.

The final ferry from Corsica had docked. A family loaded a red Peugeot. Staff began closing up. No sign of the reservation.

Corvus didn't speak. He paced once, in tight circles. Then he climbed back into his car, jaw set. Something had gone wrong.

Back in the cab, Susan stared out at the winding coastline. The tension of the last 72 hours had dulled just enough for her mind to start processing what she'd missed before.

Alister was not who she thought he was.

He wasn't just a rumpled academic with dusty books and quiet offices. He was...something else. Her natural penchant for observation and stubborn curiosity finally took over. She couldn't ignore it any longer.

She turned to him. "I need to ask you something. Who are you?"

Alister looked over, taken aback by her urgent curiosity. For a long moment, he waited.

"I mean, really," she quickly added, her voice low, softening. "You're calm under pressure. You see what no one else sees. This life, this escape, it's not something you just stumble into."

He exhaled slowly, eyes now on the road ahead.

"You're right, Susan, underneath it all, I'm not really what I appear to be. When we get to Luca's," he said, "when we've stopped running... I'll tell you everything."

She watched him without speaking, then slowly nodded.

"Luca shaped a lot of who I became," he said quietly. "And my father... well, you never met him. But he prepared me for the world. Luca helped me decide what I wanted to do in it."

The cab rounded a bend, revealing the rugged terrain of the Amalfi Coast below, with the sea painted orange, yellow, and pink from a fiery setting sun. Susan leaned back, silent, taking it all in.

They were almost there. Safe. For now.

CHAPTER ELEVEN

As they approached Positano, the road began to climb, winding high above the glittering Mediterranean coast. Alister leaned forward in the seat, his eyes scanning the familiar landscape. It had been over a decade since he was here last, but nothing had changed—at least not the things that mattered.

He recognized the turnoff before the driver even slowed. There was no street sign, no markers—easy to miss by anyone unfamiliar with its location. Just a narrow gravel path, almost hidden behind a stand of olive trees, descending gently toward the cliffs below through the dense shade of carob trees.

"This is it," Alister said, tapping the driver's shoulder. "Turn here."

Susan glanced at him. "You've been here before?"

He nodded. "The last summer before I finished my doctorate. I spent three months here—studying, thinking, talking late into the night with Luca about everything from Babylonian seals to Christian Apocrypha." A pause. "It was the best summer of my life."

The cab's tires crunched over the gravel, the lane winding downward. The dense canopy gave way to a view that took Susan's breath away. Luca's villa clung to the cliffside above the Mediterranean like something carved from myth—its white stone walls rising in levels among terraced gardens and cascading wisteria. The sea stretched out beyond, a vast canvas of silver and blue.

They pulled into a small, sunlit courtyard just as the villa's two weathered wooden front doors creaked open. Crafted of solid cypress silvered with age, they had withstood decades of salt-laden winds and had silently witnessed uncounted arrivals.

Luca Severin stood framed in the pale limestone arch, barefoot in white linen, his silver hair swept back by the breeze. He looked older than Alister remembered—thinner, maybe—but the intensity behind his eyes was unchanged.

"Alister!" he called out, his voice echoing in the courtyard.

Alister stepped from the cab just in time to be enveloped in a strong, familiar hug.

"You look terrible," Luca said, smiling wide. "Which means you must be doing something important."

Alister laughed. "This is Dr. Susan Hale," he said, turning toward her. "Luca Severin. My mentor."

Luca extended both hands warmly. "I've been expecting you, in a manner of speaking. In his text, Alister mentioned a friend. And any friend of Alister's is family here."

Susan smiled, exhausted but grateful. "Thank you for having us."

"Come," Luca said. "Let me show you what I've done with the place since you were last here."

They followed him inside, through a sun-drenched foyer that opened onto the main hall. The renovation had added modern touches but preserved the villa's ancient bones. Arched doorways opened into rooms filled with hand-carved furniture, shelves of old books, and windows with views of large sailing yachts on the open sea that made Susan pause more than once just to stare.

The tour wound upward—past the guest suites, through the upper galleries, and into the skylight-filled attic level, which housed Luca's eclectic collections of sculptures, manuscripts, and relics from around the world.

"Up here," he said with a mischievous grin, "is where I pretend I'm still needed by academia." "Alister, we can reminisce about those days later over dinner."

Back on the main floor, Luca led them outside through another pair of carved wooden doors onto a terrace overlooking the sea. A trellis covered with flowering vines shaded a tray of olives and cheeses, a white wine carafe, a large serving bowl of salad, and a loaf of freshly baked bread on a long stone table. A breeze stirred the trees as they sat for a light dinner. Luca proudly mentioned that he walks to a nearby town called Agerola every morning to purchase Pane di Agerola bread, one of the most famous breads from the area.

The feeling was enchanting, with olive trees and lemon trees stretching out beyond the terrace to the glittering pool framed by pale stone.

Susan turned slowly, taking it all in. "This place is… it's unreal."

"It's real," Luca said quietly. "It just took me a lifetime to find my way here."

They ate slowly, letting the ocean air and fading light begin to wash away the stress of the last three days. The villa felt like an escape to another world—safe and untroubled.

But the reason they were here remained close behind, so as the sun dipped closer to the Mediterranean, Alister reached into his backpack and pulled out the scroll jar. Luca's expression changed as he leaned forward, hands on the table, the air around them tightening.

"Now that we've unwound, it's time to tell me everything," he said.

For the next hour, as the sun seemed to disappear into the sea, Alister and Susan took turns recounting the story from the beginning—the house in St Cyr, the earth tremor that unearthed the scroll, their unplanned meeting at the Met, the break-in, the man with the scar, their hasty flight across Europe, and how they ended up here, at his door.

Luca listened without interrupting, nodding slowly, asking only some clarifying questions. It was clear that he was beginning to understand.

When Alister mentioned the name Silentii, Luca's brow furrowed. "I've heard the name in certain circles," he said slowly. "Rarely, and always in connection with things the Church prefers to keep well away from public debate. They were formed, as I understand it, to protect the faith from heresy—evaluating disputed writings, separating truth from distortion. In their early days, they were seen as methodical, even principled."

"But something shifted?" Susan asked.

Luca gave a small, reluctant nod. "Power can be addictive. Over centuries, it can blur a mission. Guarding the truth sometimes becomes… shaping it. And once you start deciding which truths are safe and which are dangerous, you're no longer just a guardian—you're an editor. And what they fear most isn't violence or scandal—it's contradiction."

He leaned forward, lowering his voice.
"Here's what's always struck me. We have papyrus documents dating back to long before Jesus—Egyptian tax rolls, Greek tragedies, fragments of Homer, and even early Hebrew scripture. But not a single original Christian text from the first century. Not one. Everything we know comes from copies, and copies of copies, often made centuries later."

Susan studied him. "You think that's deliberate?"

"There are old accounts," Luca said, eyes narrowing slightly, "that when Christianity became the state religion, the Silentii were given extraordinary authority. They gathered any documents that didn't align with the emerging canon. Then they 'Cleansed' them before allowing a copy to circulate. And over time, as they silenced the voices of those heretical documents, what they came to fear most was unexpected discoveries that contradicted what remained."

Alister looked at him sharply. "You're saying that the original Christian writings have been altered or destroyed, and surviving copies were planted?"

Luca seemed to wince at that comment, and then replied, now thoughtfully and very slowly, "You may be holding not just a surviving original scroll from the first century—but one written by Mary Magdalene and Jesus themselves, then the danger is far greater than you realize.

He leaned back slowly.

Susan shivered. The late Mediterranean breeze had cooled, but that wasn't what raised the chill in her spine.

Luca rested his hands on the table. "You're right to have come here," he said. "This must be handled carefully. And quietly."

He stood, gently lifting the scroll jar from the table. "Let me keep this tonight. You both need rest. I'll get up early and read it before you wake. I want to study it thoroughly before we talk again in the morning."

Susan hesitated, then nodded.

Alister agreed. "There's no one else I would trust with it."

Luca walked to the far end of the room and opened a concealed panel on the stone wall. Behind it, set into the villa's ancient stone foundation, was a secure vault. He placed the scroll inside, spun the combination dial on the door, and turned back to them.

"It will be safe here. And by morning, I'll have some answers."

At that very moment, Corvus stared out on the same waning sunset aboard a sleek black shape sweeping silently in over the Mediterranean coast on its final approach to Rome. Though Corvus didn't know it, he was only 120 miles north of his targets.

He was frustrated and angry, but showed no emotion.

He had lost them—his first assignment—and with them, a potentially dangerous artifact. They could be anywhere. Unless corrected and fast, this could be the premature end of his career…or his life.

He had considered his options. While Silentii's surveillance systems remained on high alert, he had ordered AI-powered recognition sweeps of CCTV footage across Europe. Nothing yet. But one additional lead remained.

Last month, Susan Hale had personally dropped off the scroll for shipping at a location in Nice. That meant the scroll must have been found nearby. He needed to find out where. He regretted not using painful force with her husband, Robert Hale, to fully extract what he knew. That had been a mistake. He would correct that if he got the chance.

Corvus had ordered deep searches into local property records—recent purchases, rentals, leases. So far, nothing. But he knew France's archaic bureaucratic system ran months behind in updating its national database. Silentii's bots would continue scanning hourly for new entries.

 Until then…he would wait. Reluctantly, but not idly. Waiting was dangerous. Waiting could invite scrutiny from Silentii leadership.

New entries should be swept daily. It was only a matter of time.

He didn't know that the sweep would pay dividends in five days. The Hales' purchase of a house in St Cyr six months ago would be updated to the national database providing him with its location

…and the hunt would start again.

CHAPTER TWELVE

The southern Italian sun rose into a warm, clear blue morning on the Amalfi coast. Despite Susan's bedroom facing east, she slept late, the brilliant light streaming through the window finally waking her. On the western side of the villa, Alister's room remained shaded, allowing him a few extra hours of rest.

Her hair still damp from showering, Susan stepped barefoot onto the terrace, blinking into the sunlight. Luca was already in the garden, seated at the stone table beneath the flowering trellis. The scroll lay open before him on a linen cloth, the azure blue Mediterranean Sea stretching wide behind him. A cup of espresso steamed beside a half-eaten piece of bread, untouched since sunrise.

Susan carried her coffee to a shaded bench beneath the olive trees and gazed out northward toward the coastal Gulf of Salerno. Alister followed about a half hour later, pulling on a fresh shirt, his hair still wet from the shower.

Luca finally looked up. For a long moment, he said nothing. Then:

"This scroll is remarkably well preserved."

Alister yawned. "It's written in the Galilean dialect of Aramaic. We were hoping you'd be able to read enough of it to tell us something," he replied, still easing into the morning.

Luca nodded, eyes scanning the ancient papyrus. "I am fluent enough… well, actually more than enough. It was a requirement for much of the first century research work I did when I was at Harvard."

They joined him at the table as he gently re-rolled part of the scroll, gently tapping his finger on it.

"Over the years, I've seen many very sophisticated forgeries," he said, "…but this scroll is not like any of them; I'm sure it's real." Then he added, slowly, "And dangerous."

Susan leaned forward. "Dangerous?"

He met her eyes. "Because the content is not only explosive to church orthodoxy—it's all very plausible and hard to refute."

He paused momentarily, thinking, then resumed, "Let me tell you what I mean. The Papyrus scroll itself is authentic to the period. We could carbon date it to be sure, but I'm certain it is. The handwriting is primitive but marked by early regional Aramaic forms. The phrasing, the Galilean dialect—it's raw. Unfiltered. It doesn't read like theology; it reads like lived experience."

Luca added. "It was written by someone who was theologically naïveté and with a linguistic style and vocabulary clearly dated in the early first century. Simulating this is the most difficult challenge for later forgers.

"Considering all the markers we use to evaluate ancient documents… this one, it feels true."

Alister gestured toward the scroll. "What does it actually say?"

And with that…Luca told the ancient story that began on this first scroll of Provence.

CHAPTER THIRTEEN

Golgatha, Friday, April 3, 33 CE

I t was already past three in the afternoon, and still he remained patient. Watching. If anyone had noticed, they would only have seen a dark figure standing in the shadows of a limestone wall. He watched, still anticipating something and becoming more confused as darkness came over Jerusalem.

He had trusted that divine intervention would come when the final hour arrived. The skies would crack open, the armies of heaven would descend, the faithful would be delivered, and the wicked would be punished.

Like so many others in this troubled time, he had been certain that the end of the world was near, very near. No one yet called it 'apocalypticism'; that description would come centuries later. But countless men and women across Judea believed it: that history itself was about to be torn open, that God would come down and judge the living and the dead. Most Jewish groups and countless desert mystics and street preachers in Jerusalem live by that same breathless expectation.

And so did he.

"Why?" he now mumbled to himself. It had not happened. The world had not ended. There was no divine rescue—only stillness.

He stood alone now. The executioners and the restless, curious crowds were gone, along with the soldiers. Only the crucified bodies remained, nailed on their crosses. In days to come, they would be defiled by birds of prey, adding a final insult and punishment, even after death. All the crucified bodies remained except for the one body he had been watching. He saw that his close friend and supporter, Joseph of Arimathea, had been permitted to take that body to his new tomb in an adjacent olive garden. This was unusual, but he suspected that the authorities allowed it to *avoid protests and possibly riots from supporters of that crucified man during the Passover weekend.*

Now alone at the day's end, he watched as the moon rose over the dusty and hot crucifixion hilltop that locals called Golgotha, the 'Place of the Skull'.

And with a shiver throughout his body, he saw the rising moon appear blood red, and the long shadows it cast over the walls seemed to echo the cries of the crucifixions.

And with that, he felt a sudden urgency to leave before anyone saw him standing alone. So, under the pale light of the blood-tinted moon, he moved quickly. He could let no one see him…because his face was a mirror likeness of the crucified Jesus.

Except he was Jesus, not just his likeness
And the man on the cross was his twin brother.

He had to think, collect his thoughts, and decide what to do next. A short distance down from the hilltop, he slipped quietly into the gardens and burial grounds surrounding Golgotha. He was surprised when he saw a Roman guard posted at the tomb, but after some thought, he realized they were afraid his followers would steal the body. So he retreated quietly to the garden's edge and lay on the soft earth beneath an ancient olive tree. Since the Sabbath had already begun at sundown, he could sleep, comfortable knowing that the guard would soon leave and no one else would be at the gravesite. Exhausted, he slept through most of the next day, and in the twilight, just before awakening the following evening, he dreamed what he needed to do.

CHAPTER FOURTEEN

Since the next day began at sundown, when Jesus awoke, the Sabbath had already passed, and he could follow the plan revealed in his dream. He needed to work quickly; there was little time. Save for the scraping of stone and shoveled earth, and finally the sound of a body falling into the soft ground, he labored until after midnight. And now, breathless Jesus stood in the moonlit shadows of the olive trees, his back aching, his robe caked with dirt and torn at the hem. Beneath the tree roots in the far corner of the garden, a fresh grave was hidden—soon to be his brother's true resting place.

He pushed away the heavy stones that sealed the tomb entrance and removed his brother's body under the cover of night. The tomb had been too exposed, too danger-ous. The women, preparing the body for burial, would have noticed the differences between him and his brother, slight but obvious after more than three decades of living. He couldn't take that chance.

And so, while the city slept and the moon still hung heavy in the sky, he had buried his brother deep in the soil and covered the grave with stones and olive branches.

Now, at last, he could breathe. But only after one last chore.

He returned to the tomb at first light—quietly, cautiously—just to be certain. Had he left anything behind? A scrap of fabric? A sandal? His deception, uncovered by an overlooked mistake, was a risk he could not afford to take.

He pushed aside the last brush of branches and stepped into the open tomb.

Empty.

Good.

The air inside was cool and damp, still clinging to the memory of the body it once held. He stood a moment longer, steadying himself, heart still thudding with exhaustion and dread.

Then—a sound.

Footsteps on gravel.

He froze.

Three figures approached from the far side of the tomb entrance—small, solitary shapes, wrapped in the soft grays of the early dawn. Each moved like someone in mourning, slow and unsure. Jesus stepped deeper into the shadows.

But they had already seen the tomb—open, gaping. Two turned and ran. But one remained. Now she moved quickly toward the open tomb, her breath catching.

"Mary," he whispered to himself, not meaning to, just beneath his breath.

She did not hear.

Instead, she dropped to her knees at the entrance. Her hands trembled against the stone. "They've taken him," she whispered into the morning. "Oh God, they've taken him."

Jesus's mind raced.

Being seen so soon, He hadn't prepared for this. He was angry with himself for his carelessness. Not yet, I'm not ready, he thought as he stepped back into the gloom, trying to retreat, trying to think—but his foot brushed a stone, and the sound of a faint scuff was enough.

Mary turned, now looking directly at him.

But what she saw was not Jesus. Just a cloaked, disheveled man. A dust-streaked face. Tattered clothes.

Startled, she squinted, frightened and unsure—paused and then cautiously took a step forward. "Sir," she called, her voice nervous, echoing in the open tomb. "If you have taken him away, please… tell me where you have laid him. I—I will take him…not you."

Jesus said nothing.

She stared harder into the half-light, her breath catching again. Something in the posture. The Silence. The eyes.

Then he said quietly, "Mary."

She froze. The familiar sound of his voice reached through the haze of grief like lightning through fog.

"Rabboni...?" she breathed, the word for 'teacher' in Aramaic, their native tongue.

Jesus didn't move. He felt lightheaded, suspended in the silence between her question and the realization that his world had changed completely and forever.

She believes.
Not just that I live—but that I have risen.
From death.

His mind raced like a storm.

She believes that I was crucified...and returned.

His breath caught. He could hardly breathe. The pain of the past five years, the failure, the wall of resistance he had faced as a teacher, a prophet, a voice crying in the wilderness—all of it had changed in this one moment. This...the resurrection...could become the proof. The sign. The divine confirmation of who I am... truly the Christ.

And if Mary believed—others would too.

He stepped forward—but not too close.

"No," he said gently. "Do not touch me."

Mary's eyes widened.

He steadied his voice. "Tell no one."

But after a pause, he added, "Except my brothers. Not yet. Please. I will come to them soon."

She blinked, confused. 'Brothers' was a new way of referring to his close followers. Before this moment, they were disciples, apostles, or even servants. But her face— radiant—nodded slowly.

She would obey.
She would hold these commands in her heart like fire.

And Jesus, cloaked in Silence and dirt, turned once more into the olive trees, his thoughts racing toward a new beginning.
Not as the twin who survived.

But as the Messiah, the anointed one, who rose from the dead. The Christ.

CHAPTER FIFTEEN

Jerusalem, Monday , April 6 33 CE , Early Morning

The sun was climbing now—slow, deliberate, stretching its golden limbs over the ridges of Jerusalem. Shadows retreated into alleyways and under trees. Birds stirred among the cypresses.

Jesus moved quietly along the garden's edge, ducking beneath twisted olive branches still wet with dew. His robe was stiff with dust and sweat. Earth clung to his fingers. His feet ached, his legs trembled from the night's work, but his thoughts ran faster than his body could move.

He had not expected Mary or anyone else to be at the tomb so early.

And when she recognized his voice, his mind searched for a way to explain.

But she provided an answer — a resurrection. He didn't expect that—but it opened a path. One he had not seen clearly until the moment her voice trembled with joy and called him Rabboni.

And yet, he would still have problems to deal with.

His pace slowed as he reached the low stone wall that marked the edge of the olive grove. Below, the city still slept in the blush of morning. Smoke began to rise from early fires. The Temple Mount loomed in the distance, its gold encasement catching the first light.

He looked away as he thought. Problems. His followers. The night of his arrest. That final meal. The warnings.

And his arrest when they had all left him.

Peter, swearing boldness one moment, denying him three times before sunrise.
Thomas, silent and unreadable.
James and John, sons of thunder, reduced to shadows, slipping away into the dark.
And Judas… Judas, with the kiss.

Jesus clenched his jaw. Angry.

Only a handful had remained near the crucifixion—the women, mostly. His mother. Mary Magdalene. Salome. And John, perhaps, standing in the distance. But the rest—those who called him teacher, swore allegiance and said they would follow to the end—had vanished.

Had he died in his brother's place, and not one of them would have tried to stop it.

Was it cowardice? Or had they simply stopped believing?

But now. Now everything had changed.

Mary believed. And if Mary did, others might. And if others believed he had risen—then he could speak again. Preach again. Not as a failed prophet. Not as a fugitive teacher.
But as Christ, the one who had conquered death.

That idea pulsed in his chest as he moved through the city's outskirts. The streets were still mostly empty—traders not yet stirring, children not yet chasing goats through alleys. He kept his head down, slipping past shuttered doors and low stone homes. He crossed the dried streambed near the potter's quarter and avoided the watchful eyes of Roman sentries stationed near the city gates.

By the time he reached the lower town's eastern edge, the sun had fully risen. The city yawned and stretched to life.

Jesus ducked into a narrow path between crumbling walls, then behind a half-burned stable. At last, he reached the small structure he had remembered from years before when visiting Jerusalem as a child—a storage shed abandoned and used only seasonally by migrant workers who came during the olive harvest.

He pushed the creaking door open and stepped inside. The air was musty, filled with the scent of dust and old straw. Light pierced through gaps in the roof, tracing bright stripes across the floor.

He sank to the ground, back against the cool wall, and let his body go slack. The fatigue was total. Every part of him ached—not just from toil, but from the enormity of what now lay ahead.

He closed his eyes. Visions flickered behind them—Mary's stunned face, the shadowed garden, the broken tomb.

They will believe, he thought, because they want to believe.

Sleep came quickly as morning bells began to ring in the city above, and a new day began—one that, centuries in the future, would be called Easter Monday, or what Susan liked to call it, Monday of the Angel.

CHAPTER SIXTEEN

Jesus sat alone on the hillside above Bethany, watching the sun sink over the stone rooftops and olive groves. The wind picked up slightly, brushing his robe and carrying the scent of wild thyme.

So much had changed since the frantic uncertainty of those early days after the resurrection—when he wandered the city's edges, unsure of what would come next. He felt calm now, like the quiet golden land stretching across the plains below. The plan to spread his teachings was underway. His apostles would carry it out. In the dust of these hills, the future of his church was being written. He was sure of it.

But the future would prove him wrong.

Forty days had passed since Mary had mistaken him for a gardener and wept beside the empty tomb. He had sent her to the apostles first to keep them from despair. But it didn't take long for him to realize words alone would not be enough. Their faith was too fragile—flickering in the shadows of fear, guilt, and confusion.

So he had appeared to them. Sometimes briefly, sometimes for hours. Always teaching and always preparing them for their mission to take his message to all nations, and the ends of the earth.

He reminded them again and again that the Kingdom of God was near, that the end of time was coming, and that he would soon return as the Messiah — the Anointed One. Each of the Twelve, he said, would sit on thrones, judging the twelve tribes of Israel. He told them that this was not a metaphor—but a prophecy.

He had appeared to them all, but especially to Thomas, whose doubt had pierced like a knife, and to Peter, whose shame still hung heavy around his neck. He visited others, too: the women who waited with broken hearts, the travelers on the road to Emmaus, and the frightened men who still hid in the upper room.

He spoke to them all. Of urgency. Of promise. The end was near. The reckoning would come. They must be ready.

But now, he thought, he had accomplished what he set out to do. His work here was finished.

He could see it in Peter's renewed boldness. In the steadiness in John's eyes. They would carry the message. They would build the church communities. They would spread the word. They would be ready for God's kingdom and his return as the Messiah.

He no longer needed to remain. They were ready. Or so he thought. It was still half a decade before he would learn the disappointing truth that they would all abandon their promises... except for one.

But for now, he couldn't know. So he decided to leave; he needed distance—a place beyond reach, beyond rumor. Somewhere, where no one knew him, and he knew no one.

He needed a place to wait—for the final trumpet, for the heavens to open, for the armies of God to descend. When that moment came, he would return in glory—not hidden, not disguised, but fully revealed—the Messiah.

Yet history would take a different turn. The crucifixion would become the very heart of his church, a sign that the final trumpet had already sounded. His return in glory would be through resurrection, not conquest—no longer hidden, no longer disguised. But for now, as he began to plan, he could not see the changes that lay ahead.

He had considered many destinations, but none felt right—until a memory returned to him one morning in the pale light of dawn. Years earlier, he had spoken with a spice merchant who described a cousin's olive farm in Gaul, tucked within a hidden valley of remarkable beauty. Thick groves, stone terraces, and ancient shelters clung to the hills like secrets. The locals called it Olea Vallis—the Valley of Olives. It lay in the Roman province of Gallia Narbonensis, on the southern slopes of a mountain range a day's walk above Frejus and two days west of Nice. Travel to either port was possible, the merchant had said—both were naval bases and thriving commercial hubs along the Mediterranean coast. His ships docked there weekly.

It was perfect. Quiet. Remote. A Roman olive farm. Far from the turmoil of Judea. But not too far from the extensive Roman roads and sea networks that could take us there.

It was a place people forgot. A place where no one would know his ministry. Nor of the crucifixion. Where no one would know his name. This was perfect…he wanted to be forgotten.

His departure would be simple to explain. He had already told his followers that he would soon ascend to heaven. When he disappeared, they would believe it. The appearances would end. The story would settle. And the myth would take root. Or so he thought.

Only two people knew the truth.

Mary Magdalene, who had given more than he ever asked. So much more. And his mother, who had always suspected the truth. Mothers always know.

He told them everything—not just because he needed shelter and food during these past forty days, but because he needed them for the long struggle ahead. In the village where they would settle, they would help create the illusion of a small, stable household—a wife and a mother, tending to a quiet man who kept mostly to himself.

He didn't know how long they would stay in Gaul. Years perhaps. But hopefully less.

They would go with him. They had already agreed.

As twilight deepened, he stood, brushing dust from his robe. Tomorrow, they would begin their long overland journey—north through Antioch and Tarsus, past mountains and rivers, toward the far valleys of Gaul.

They would live quietly there, tucked into the rhythms of a simpler life, while he waited—for the right moment, for the end of days, for the world to be ready. When the time came, Jesus would reveal himself as the Messiah. Until then, he and Mary would write—chronicling their past forty days that had changed everything.

The story captured in their first scroll would be enough one day to rattle the foundations of a world not yet born. But it wouldn't end there. Three more scrolls would follow, each peeling back another layer of the history the Church thought it had sealed. Each growing more dangerous to Church Orthodoxy and power.

The second would be hidden just steps from the first, beneath the same weathered stone terrace of the ancient hut where they had lived, and raised their children.

The third—buried hastily in the Near East, during a desperate flight from Roman arrest.

And the fourth—interred beneath the stone altar of a remote chapel, where olive farmers once gathered to hear the voice of Christ.

CHAPTER SEVENTEEN

The fragrances from the garden in the soft afternoon breeze filled the air as they sat quietly, almost speechless, on the terrace of Luca's villa, as Luca paused the story to take a much-needed break. The afternoon sun was beginning to move closer to the Terranian Sea. Susan, realizing that just over two weeks ago, their paths had been separated only by time and place, as their paths were destined to cross. Bob and Susan Hale packed for their trip to St Cyr just as Jesus, Mary, and his mother began packing for their journey to Gaul.

She said, almost to herself, "Our worlds would soon collide." Two families were preparing to leave for the same destination—separated only by time.

Luca's voice cut through her thoughts, "Many early church groups believed that Jesus had an identical twin. For example, the Gnostic Gospel of Thomas refers to a 'twin.' Other stories mention Judas Thomas, the twin brother of Jesus, and some have tales of his identical twin traveling to work in India.

He paused, thinking, then continued, "There were probably hundreds of copies of those Gospels and documents, not to mention all the oral stories in circulation. Silentii couldn't erase the actual documents, so they erased their credibility. They succeeded, and none of them made it into the accepted canon of the New Testament…and, even today, the stories of a twin are considered creative fiction."

"But the story on this scroll is dangerous. It tells us that Mary bore two children, Jesus and a twin brother. The scroll only calls him 'the other one.' When Herod ordered the massacre of male infants, Joseph and Mary fled to Egypt. However, managing two infants on such a journey would be both dangerous and impossible. So they left one child—'the other one'—with a trusted Galilean family. The plan was to reunite later, but in those troubled times, they lost contact. Years passed."

"And the twin comes back?" Alister asked.

"Just after Jesus' ministry begins and only a short time before Judas betrays Jesus, the twin hears rumors, sees him preaching, realizes the resemblance, and reunites just days before the last supper. They reconnect. Only a few others learn of him…that would explain why there are no contemporary writings, only later rumors. Then—on the night of Jesus' arrest—Jesus asks his twin to take his place. Unseen, Jesus wants to observe his disciples, to test their loyalty and readiness to be apostles."

Susan raised an eyebrow. "But why would the twin agree to something so dangerous? He would have known that Pontius Pilate, local Governor, could order punishment at the trial the next morning."

"Because he believed the world's end was near, so it didn't matter," Luca said. "Apocalypticism had gripped Judea. Many believed that God's judgment was imminent and that He would punish the evil… mainly the Roman oppressors. Jesus and his twin believed nothing bad would happen to them—they thought God would intervene."

He paused.

"According to the scroll, that's why the twin went silently to trial. Why didn't he protest or resist his death sentence? He believed divine protection would spare him."

Susan sat back, stunned. "And Jesus thought they would both survive…not just him alone?"

"And then?"

"After appearing and ministering to his apostles and others, he leaves with Mary Magdalene and his mother. They sail west to Gaul. A Roman outpost. A land of olive groves and friendly enclaves of farmers. No questions. No one would know him there. No one would care where he came from. And a place where the memory of Jerusalem won't follow."

"St Cyr, of course," Susan whispered, almost to herself

Luca nodded.

"And the scroll is co-written, apparently," Luca said. "A joint testimony recording their life in Gaul. A record for the future in case the apocalypse didn't come soon."

A long silence followed.

Then Luca added, "And you must be asking an important question."

He looked at both Alister and Susan. "You should be wondering how Jesus, an illiterate carpenter, could write. The scroll answers that."

Alister raised an eyebrow. "How? Where?"

"In India. When Jesus was about twelve, a wealthy Indian merchant traveling through Jerusalem happened to see him arguing Jewish law with leaders in the Synagogue. He was so impressed that, after talking with Joseph and Mary, he brought Jesus to his home in India, where tutors taught him to read and write Aramaic, Greek, Sanskrit, and basic Latin. It answers questions about what he was doing when he disappeared from biblical writings during his 'lost years' from 12 to 25. When he returned to Galilee around age thirty, he was educated, literate, and ready to teach, argue, and—perhaps—rewrite history."

Susan whispered, "OK, let's continue with the story."

CHAPTER EIGHTEEN

The early spring sun dipped behind the hills above their hamlet of Olea Vallis. It cast a golden shadow that crept eastward across the olive trees lining the valley below on its way to the neighboring hamlet of Fayence. A warm breeze stirred the branches—a welcome change after the coldest, wettest winter in years. On a stone patio halfway up the hillside, where the olive trees thinned and gave way to scrub and stone, Jesus and Mary Magdalene sat on a weathered terrace bench, sharing a woolen cloak. Behind them was the modest stone house they settled into after arriving in Gaul five years ago. Like most evenings, it was quiet, save for the faint sounds of laughter and soft footsteps—his mother tending to the children and preparing the evening meal.

Mary turned her face to the last light of the day. "I never thought I'd love a place as much as this."

Jesus didn't answer right away. There was stillness in him—but it was not contentment.

As his eyes traced the shadows lengthening through the valley, he said, "Do you remember the first time I preached under those olive trees?"

She smiled, knowing this path of thought. "Seven people. A few farmers, one merchant, and a boy who fell asleep halfway through."

He gave a soft chuckle. "And now they come from three villages. Some walk half a day just to hear the message."

"They come for you."

"They come for hope," he said. "For the promise that death doesn't win."

She turned toward him. "You never preached that in Galilee, before we came here."

"I didn't know it then," he said quietly. "But after what I've learned here… preaching the resurrection—not just mine, but the very idea of it—it has become everything."

She reached down and took his hand. "I remember the tomb. When I thought you were the gardener."

He nodded. "You believed I had risen. And in that moment, your belief gave birth to something bigger than either of us. That moment shaped my message. The resurrection gave our followers a second life—a second chance—if only they believe."

Something about those words—a second life…a second chance—stirred a memory deep in her.

"You gave that to me also," she whispered to herself. And then her old life, before Jesus, replayed in her mind's eye.

She had been twenty-one when she left Magdala. Almost a decade ago, yet it still lived in her memory as vividly as if it were yesterday.

Nestled on the lake's western shore, Magdala was little more than a fishing outpost—but her family's house stood apart. A tall stone villa at the village's northern edge, with its own courtyard and a cistern-fed bath, surrounded by olive trees and shaded awnings. Her father was among the wealthiest men in the region, a strict Pharisee and ruthless in business. He owned boats. Nets. Workers. He owned the men who caught the fish and the merchants who sold them.

But he did not, however, own her.

She had always been different in that house—tenderhearted, too quick to cry, too easily overwhelmed by the severity that ruled their lives. Her older brothers obeyed, strong and silent. Her sisters married young, dressed plainly, and spoke only when spoken to. Mary would disappear for hours, wandering the shore, sketching driftwood in the sand, or listening to stories from the boatmen's wives.

She had no patience for the long scrolls of law her father demanded she study. When she questioned them, his voice thundered down the halls. Once, he struck her for defying a rabbi.

Her mother said nothing. Never did. But one evening, after Mary fled the dinner table in tears, her mother slipped into her room and placed a carved box beneath her sleeping mat.

"Your dowry," she whispered. "Use it only when you must."

Over the years, her mother quietly took from the household accounts and added to the box until it could hold no more. It would be Mary's lifeline.

At eighteen, home became unbearable. She slipped away often to meet young men from the lower docks—sunburned, rough-handed, soft-eyed. When word got out, her father seethed. At nineteen, she became pregnant. The child did not survive. Her family responded with silence and shame. Her father said she was cursed.

And she believed it.

By twenty-one, she could barely breathe in that house.

So one morning before dawn, she rose, packed a satchel, and walked the stone path to the road that led south to Jerusalem. She didn't say goodbye. She carried the carved box and never looked back.

Jerusalem was chaos. She rented a small upper room behind a tanner's stall and wandered aimlessly. The noise, the dust, the smells—dung, cumin, sweat—blurred into confusion. She had no plan. No friends. No family. But for the first time in her life, she was free.

And then one morning, near the temple steps, she heard a voice.

Not loud. Not theatrical. Just… sure.

A man was speaking to a small crowd by the well. His tunic was plain, his hands work-worn. But his words—his words were everything she had been searching for.

"The kingdom of God will not come in clouds or thunder," he said, "but in the quiet turning of a heart."

She stopped walking.

He looked up, and their eyes met. He kept speaking, but something shifted. She listened, transfixed—mercy, brokenness, healing. Not ritual. Not punishment. Not fear.

Afterward, she approached him. Not yet as a follower. Just a soul desperate to be seen.

She asked if he was a rabbi. He said no.

She asked what he wanted. He said nothing—except that she listened.

And so she did. Every day. Every evening. At first, behind the others. Then, beside him. One night, under a sycamore, he touched her face.

"You have always been free," he said. "But now, you believe it."

She cried. And never wanted to leave his side again.

His voice returned her to the present.

"That place," he said, pointing toward the mound of stones under the olive trees at the base of the valley, "it's not a temple. Just olive branches and clay. But it's ours. It's where the weary come—and they leave with hope."

Mary rested her head on his shoulder. "It's where we married. Where the children were baptized. Where you finally preached your truth."

In recent months, the gatherings had grown. Word spread beyond Olea Vallis— beyond their quiet valley's olive terraces and stone paths and into the neighboring hamlets. One of those who came regularly was a Roman merchant named Lucius Barrius, a wealthy gentile from Antioch. He owned a sprawling seasonal villa in Callian, a prosperous hillside town a morning's ride away.

Lucius was a God-fearer—respectful of Jewish customs but not yet converted. He'd first heard of Jesus's preaching from village tradesmen and tenants near his olive oil estate, where he grew a rare, delicate varietal pressed for his personal use and select clients in the East. He owned Domus Lucullus et Filius, an enterprise that operated an extensive shipping network from Syria to the Italian coast. But Callian was his retreat—a place of rest and reflection, where his mind turned from commerce to the soul.

At first, Lucius had come to the chapel anonymously, lingering at the back of the gatherings. But over time, Jesus noticed his questions—curious, probing, educated. Their conversations deepened, often extending long after others had left. He was unlike most Roman elites: direct, but not arrogant. Wealthy, but not entitled.

One evening, after a sermon on mercy, Lucius stayed behind. "You speak as if words could change the empire itself," he said.

Jesus smiled. "Only by those willing to listen."

They began to meet privately, sometimes at Lucius's villa, sometimes beneath the fig trees near the chapel. Mary welcomed Lucius cautiously. But soon, she, too, saw the sincerity in his friendship.

It was Lucius who first offered safe travel for Jesus's eventual journey. "My ships run between Caesarea and Antioch almost monthly," he said one afternoon. "No questions asked. Use them if the time comes."

Now, as the breeze stirred the branches and dusk deepened the valley's color, Jesus exhaled and turned to Mary.

"Mary, I have to leave."

She sat up. "You want to leave this life? This peace?"

"I don't want to. But I must."

"Why?"

"My apostles' message is splintering. I've heard it from Lucius and from other traveling merchants. Too many voices. No clear doctrine. They cannot write. No two stories are the same. Unless this changes, the Church won't grow beyond Jerusalem."

She held his gaze. "So you'll go back. To fix it?"

"To preserve it," he said. "To give it form. I can write. I can teach through papyrus. Carry the truth to every village, not just in Jerusalem and Galilee, but across the empire."

"But they think you ascended," she said. "You're not who they expect."

"I know. That's why I must go as someone else."

He paused. "Saul—our friend—died yesterday. A sudden fever took him, swift and merciless. I laid him to rest beside the little chapel where we had so often gathered. I will miss him—his voice in the quiet evenings, our talks that lingered late into the night."

"I remember his arrival. He was worn thin by the endless disputes of the Pharisees—arguments over law and ritual purity, debates that never seemed to end. Though well-schooled in the traditions, he confessed that his heart ached at their harshness. 'Where is the mercy?' he once asked me. Beneath the weight of doctrine, he longed for something gentler. He crossed the sea from his home in Tarsus to these distant valleys, seeking a life the noise of Jerusalem could not give him. And when at last he reached Gaul, it was as if his lungs filled with air for the first time. He loved the quiet hills, the people who listened without judgment. Here he became less a Pharisee and more a brother—less a scholar and more a friend."

Tears glimmered in his eyes. "He was different. Learned. A Roman citizen. Like me, he could read and write Aramaic, Greek, Latin—and even Sanskrit. In his last days, I told him who I truly was, and we found our final bond on a common ground: the hope that the soul endures beyond death, and the promise that the righteous will be raised in the world to come. And in the hours before he passed, I shared with him God's call to carry the Church to the ends of the Empire."

His voice broke. "He believed me. And he asked me to bear his name."

He believed me. And he told me to take his name."

She froze. "You would go as Saul?"

He nodded. "Our ages are close. Our features, similar enough. I can avoid those who knew him. I will use his Roman name, Paul, instead of his Hebrew name, Saul. As Paul, a Roman, I can move more freely. Preach. Write."

Jesus paused for a moment, realizing Mary's real concern. Falsely claiming to be a Roman citizen was a capital offense, punishable by death. How could Jesus prove it?

Jesus said," Saul was a Roman citizen by birth. His grandfather served in the Roman military and was granted citizenship for himself and all his family. Saul gave me his citizen document just before he died. The Romans call this document a diptych. I will carry it with me, wear it around my neck on a string. "

Satisfied, Mary said quietly, "I'll come with you. As your sister, I will also be a citizen. And your companion. I'll write down every sermon, as I have done so far. Every vision. I'll help you record everything."

"You will. But not now. The children are still young. My mother is growing too frail. Stay here. Raise them. When I return, we'll go together to Cilicia, Galatia, Asia…"

They fell into silence. The light was nearly gone.

Mary asked, "And when it ends?"

"When I've built the Church," he said, "we'll return here. To this spot. And grow old watching the sun set over the valley. We'll build the chapel into a church."

He paused for a long while, watching the sun set over the neighboring village, "And the scroll that's about these last six years, what will you do with it?"

"I'll continue to write while I wait for you. Then I'll seal it in a jar and place it under the terrace—here, where we sit each night. It will wait for us."

They didn't know it yet, but only his writings would return to this enchanted hillside —and speak to the world from deep below his beloved chapel.

But that was still to come.

Susan whispered, "And if Silentii learns what we already have in this scroll and that there is more in a second scroll…"

"They'll stop at nothing," Luca said.

CHAPTER NINETEEN

A soft afternoon breeze curled through the stone plaza as the late spring sun reached its peak. Soon, the air would cool, but for now, it remained warm enough to linger. The gentle splash of the village fountain mingled with the clink of wine glasses and the hum of conversation from surrounding tables.

"Excuse me…" A polite voice interrupted Alice Hale's story.

She blinked, momentarily pulled from the weight of memory. A young waiter stood by their table, smiling as he nodded to their empty plates.

"Shall I clear these for you? Would you like the dessert menu?"

Alice's friend Sophie, who had been utterly absorbed in the tale, seemed startled. "Oh—yes, of course. Thank you."

The waiter gathered the dishes, clearing the table, except for the empty wine glasses. "Another glass of wine?"

"Rosé, please," Alice said. Sophie nodded, still watching her closely, still stunned by the story she was hearing.

As the waiter retreated, her friend leaned in. "You know, I never realized that none of our Christian beliefs today, and nothing in the New Testament, are based on primary, original writings from the time of Jesus…just copies."

"Right, it surprised me also. No first-century original Christian writings survive. Only later copies. But this scroll— a firsthand account—it's a new history, changing everything."

Sophie swallowed. "And the Silentii?"

"If they still exist," Alice said softly, "They wouldn't allow that truth to come out."

She took a breath, then continued.

"Luca told my mother and Alister that the scroll chronicled what happened after the crucifixion. How Jesus, Mary Magdalene, and his mother fled Judea and settled in a quiet Jewish farming village in Gaul. Lived quietly. Worked in the olive groves."

Sophie stared, entranced.

"They were welcomed by a young couple who offered them shelter in their stone house while they searched for a place of their own. The couple had three infants—two girls and a boy—whose laughter filled the small rooms. But Luca told them that soon after, and suddenly, a sickness killed them. Not a plague, but a poisoning from tainted grain. They had no way of knowing that their harvest that year carried a black fungus that weakened them and brought fevered dreams. We now know that it's called Ergotism, and we can detect it. But they didn't know then. Within weeks, both parents were gone."

"There was no family left to take in the children, no one to keep them alive. So Jesus and Mary opened their arms and raised them as their own. They baptized and brought them up in the way of Jesus."

"They stayed in that stone house, built their life around the olive groves, and lived as a family."

She leaned closer, her voice dropping.
"But Jesus couldn't remain quiet for long. He began preaching again—not the old apocalyptic message, but something new. A message rooted in believing the resurrection as the pathway to salvation and forgiveness. At the start, only the local olive farmers

listened. But word spread quickly, first to other villages, and then even the traveling merchants on trade routes began to listen."

She swirled her wine glass slowly.

"He started by building a small chapel at the bottom of the path leading to their house—just a simple place to pray and teach."

Sophie gasped softly. "Alice—could that be the Chapel of St Cyr? The one near your home?"

Alice looked across the plaza toward the distant hills. "That's what we've always called it. But the locals say it's older than the town itself. The story they've passed down through the years tells of a gifted olive farmer—though no one seems to realize he was Jesus—building a mound of stones where he preached to the workers in the valley. They only remember the name he gave it: *Chapel Olivarum Christi*—the Chapel of Christ's Olive Workers."

She paused, her voice lower. "But Mom said she always thought there was something more to that story. When she looked up old parish records and found that this town was originally named *Seillans*. Then, a century later, the name disappears—replaced with *St Cyr*. The same happened with the chapel. Both names erased and rewritten."

Sophie looked up sharply. "St. Cyr… the child-martyr from Tarsus?"

Alice nodded. "That's the official account. But it feels too convenient. Tarsus was Saul's home—Paul's home. Remember, Mary Magdalene came here to live out her days writing her Gospel. What if the name change wasn't about honoring a child saint at all, but about secretly marking something older—something only Mary knew, and passed down through the centuries to a select few others? Perhaps the name secretly remembers whose bones truly lie beneath this hill. Paul. The man Jesus became to carry his message across the empire."

Sophie was silent, thinking, and after a long pause said, "To me it feels more ominous…like the memory of *Chapel of Christ's Olive Workers* was scrubbed clean by Silentii until only a safer story remained."

They sat silently until the waiter returned with a fresh bottle of rosé, refilling their glasses with a quiet smile before disappearing again.

Alice took a sip. Then leaned in.

"Either way, if the story ended there, it would be damaging enough, confirming as truth what they had claimed was rumor, heresy, or myth. That would be powerful."

"The second scroll described what Jesus did next," she paused. "And what he did…continues to change the history we've all been taught."

She set her glass down and looked directly at Sophie.

"It's why my mother kept it secret for forty years. Why Silentii would do anything to find those scrolls. And it's why, forty years ago, Mom and Alister left Luca's villa so suddenly that afternoon, heading for the house in St Cyr. They found out that the second scroll was buried with the first scroll under the terrace at the house in St Cyr. And it was only a matter of time before Silentii would identify the location."

"They had to get there and find out what was in it before Silentii could find and destroy it."

Sophie's eyes narrowed. "And what was in it?"

Alice paused for a moment, thinking, and finally just said. "Let me tell you the rest of the story. It's really the only way to answer that question."

The bells from the church tower below began to toll. Alice leaned back in her chair, her voice quiet and final, as she continued a story from an ancient world, 2000 years past. The story of the second scroll.

CHAPTER TWENTY

In the fading light of the Mediterranean sunset, Provence's ancient mountains blurred in streaks of gray and green as Luca's battered Peugeot struggled to keep pace with the faster traffic on the A8. Soon, they would exit the motorway for the narrow, twisting roads that ribboned through cliffs and valleys toward St Cyr. Just an hour more. But it was no time to relax.

Alister gripped the wheel, knuckles white. Susan sat beside him, bone-tired from taking turns behind the wheel for the past eleven hours, yet too wired to rest. They had changed into soiled work clothes taken from Luca's garden shed—dusty caps pulled low—to avoid toll booth recognition. Every roadside camera, every sensor, might be watching.

They had left Positano in the late morning after a needed full night's sleep. It would be a long 12-hour drive to St Cyr. They pushed hard through Naples, skirting the edge of Rome, then northward into France, without stopping to sightsee or engage in conversation. Two brief stops—for fuel, sandwiches, and bathroom breaks—were their only concessions to necessity. To the world, they looked like tired garden workers heading home at day's end. But they felt like fugitives chasing a ghost buried under stone.

The sun had long set by the time they crossed into the Var region. Under a rising full moon, they passed the Aerodrome Fayence-Tourrettes, a small glider airport in the town before St Cyr, and began the final eight-mile climb to Susan's house.

Near midnight, they rolled through the St Cyr town center that was perched high on the ridge above the house. The streets were dark, shuttered, the kind of stillness where a single car could stir curiosity. Taking the familiar road to the front gate at such an hour risked drawing the eyes of nosy neighbors who lived along its rising curve. Instead, Susan suggested another way—an obscure back approach she had found on her last visit.

It was a forgotten gravel track that dropped steeply from the ridge behind town, choked with brush and rarely used. Alister cut the headlights and eased forward until the car disappeared beneath cypress trees, fifty feet short of the property. From there, they went on foot, carrying the borrowed pickaxe as they pushed through bramble. With care, they climbed down the five-foot retaining wall that bordered the back of the property and quietly crossed the pool deck, determined not to alert any sleeping neighbors or their dogs.

The house stood silent in the moonlight. No lights. No movement. The terrace, still cracked and uneven from the last tremor. Susan remembered that they had decided to wait until after their next visit to have it repaired. An unintended stroke of luck, Susan thought.

Meanwhile, eight miles away, the beating thrum of rotors broke the silence above the Aerodrome Fayence-Tourrettes they had passed just an hour before. A matte-black Sikorsky with no external markings and a tail number—OS7777—circled in for landing. Earlier that evening, in Rome, Corvus had received the information he'd been waiting for: a fresh update from the painfully slow French property registry. The St Cyr house had surfaced.

The Sikorsky S-76C swept low over the darkened valley, its four-blade rotor slicing the night with a muffled, mechanical rhythm. On 129.975 MHz, the pilot's voice came steady, clipped, self-announcing into the night: *"Fayence traffic, Helicopter Oscar Sierra seven seven seven seven, five miles north, inbound for landing, Fayence."* The call was routine, but in the stillness of Provence it carried a quiet menace. Below, a handful of late diners at Les Voilure, the airfield's small restaurant just off the runway, glanced up from their wine glasses as the heavy machine's navigation lights drifted overhead, astonished to see an unscheduled aircraft arriving at such an hour.

The pilot banked gently into the downwind leg, then base, his voice punctuating each turn: *"OS seven seven seven seven entering base… final, runway two-eight, Fayence."* The helicopter descended smoothly, nearly twelve thousand pounds of matte-black precision, settling onto the field with the grace of a predator alighting. The skids kissed the ground almost noiselessly, rotor wash sending napkins fluttering across half-cleared tables on the restaurant terrace.

Corvus sat motionless in the cabin's dim light as the turbines wound down. Outside, a waiting car idled at the edge of the tarmac, headlights dark, engine already warm, the GPS pre-set with Susan Hale's St Cyr address. Without a word, he stepped out onto the tarmac. He would be at her house in thirty minutes. If they were there, they wouldn't know he was coming…he would catch them unaware, sleeping perhaps. And retrieve the scroll. If not, he would search the house and the property.

Back in St Cyr, Susan held the flashlight low while Alister wedged the pickaxe into a seam between the heavy flagstones. With a grunt, he pried one loose. Dust spilled. Another stone shifted. They worked quickly, pausing often to listen—the rustle of leaves, the distant call of a nightbird, the stillness of breath.

Just after half past midnight, metal struck something hollow.

Alister dropped to his knees. "Here." He whispered.

Within moments, they had quietly and carefully pulled it free—a clay jar, tall as a wine bottle, sealed with wax and cloth and coated in ancient dust.

Susan knelt beside it, her breath catching. "This is it."

"Now, let's get out of here," Alister whispered.

But as they lifted it from the earth, the quiet around them exploded—an engine roared as it sped up the road to the house, tires skidded on gravel, and headlights slashed across the front gate. A car door slammed.

Susan's voice dropped to a whisper. "Let's go. Now."

They bolted, scrambling up the retaining wall, the scroll jar held tightly under her arm. Behind them, heavy boots hit stone. A flashlight swept across the pool.

Corvus.

His silhouette appeared at the terrace's edge, eyes locking onto the rubble—and the fleeing figures. He surged forward, pistol already drawn. One of them, he recognized as Susan Hale. And she was carrying something. A jar.

Too late.

He raised his Glock and fired. The shot cracked through the valley. Dogs barked in the distance. The round struck metal—rear fender. Sparks flew.

"Drive!" Susan shouted, diving into the car.

Alister didn't hesitate. He slammed the accelerator. The Peugeot skidded forward, gravel spraying as they tore up the winding track. Headlights off. Moonlight showing the way.

Corvus reached the wall too late. The car vanished into the trees above, back road too narrow, too disconnected. There was no way to intercept from the front. By the time he looped through the village, they would be long gone.

He stood still, breathing hard, Glock lowered. His eyes swept the broken terrace. A shovel. A pickaxe. The jagged mouth of freshly disturbed earth.

He knelt, gloved fingers tracing the loose soil.

They had been digging for something.

Another scroll. In the jar Susan Hale was carrying. He was sure.

And once again, he had failed.

CHAPTER TWENTY-ONE

The small Peugeot kicked up dust as it wound away from the retaining wall behind the Hale house, vanishing into the pines that cloaked the back roads above St Cyr. For the first time in hours, Alister dared to glance at Susan. Her hands trembled in her lap, still clutching the scroll jar. She removed her coat and bundled it protectively around the jar.

"We can't go back tonight," she said quietly.

"I know," he replied, his voice tight. "We're too tired. And he'll have the whole area under surveillance within the hour."

They pulled off the road into a shadowed grove, engine idling, and weighed their options. The near-empty roads would betray them long before the Italian border. Corvus was close—too close—and deeply connected. The Silentii didn't need to catch them in person. Cameras, drones, and automated checkpoints could do the job if they were careless.

"There's a hotel in town," Susan said finally. "Deux Rocs. Small. Discreet. Right in the center. He won't expect us to stay so close."

Alister nodded. "We'll check in as husband and wife. Say we got delayed on the road."

Ten minutes later, they parked on a remote side street and slipped into the old stone inn under the cover of darkness. The night clerk barely looked up when they signed in as Monsieur and Madame Duran. Just a pair of tired travelers, waylaid on winding mountain roads.

The room was modest but clean—two twin beds, a small shuttered window, and a heavy wooden door that locked with a solid click. They didn't speak as they washed up and changed. When Susan finally pulled down the covers, she looked across the room.

"We made it," she said—almost whispering to herself.

But when she turned out the light, she glanced over at Alister, holding the gaze for just a moment too long. She felt that something was changing. Not just the aftermath of danger. A shift. A tension. Within moments, they were asleep.

They had the front desk ring their phone just after sunrise. Too little sleep, but they needed to be on their way. The early light of late May washed over the rooftops of St Cyr and bathed the olive groves in a brilliant morning sun. Outside, on the terrace beneath an ancient cypress, they had breakfast in near silence —coffee, fresh croissants.

The sound of swallows overhead and the gentle splash of a stone fountain should have calmed them.

"I keep hearing that shot," Susan said at last, staring into the hills.

"I keep seeing his face," Alister replied. "He's not just angry. He's desperate."

"And the scroll?" she asked. "What could possibly be in it?"

Alister shook his head. "We'll know soon."

By 8 am, they had packed up and slipped back into the same worn gardener's clothes and caps they had worn the day before. It would be a long trip—thirteen hours if they were lucky. But they wouldn't take the coastal highway. Instead, they turned north toward Grenoble, then east through the Alps, avoiding toll roads and major junctions where surveillance would be heavy.

It was the right decision.

Corvus had worked through the night to secure the area around the Hale house. Local enforcers. Silentii assets. He had moved quickly. But even with his reach, the full net around St Cyr wasn't in place until mid-morning—two hours too late.

By then, the Peugeot was already climbing into the foothills of the Alps, well beyond reach.

At dusk, Corvus stood on the terrace behind the Hale house, staring at the disturbed earth where the scroll had been buried. Another had slipped through his fingers.

He kicked a broken stone across the yard, rage simmering, and growled into his communicator. "They're gone. Get me full border logs. Every toll cam. Every drone feed."

In Rome, silence answered him first. Then a voice. Flat. Deliberate.

"We'll call you."

Corvus's jaw tightened. He knew what that meant. Disappointment. Doubt. A shadow darkening from above.

CHAPTER TWENTY-TWO

They reached the villa just after midnight, the old Peugeot groaning up the final curve of the cliffside road. Below, the sea lay ink-black under a canopy of stars, and endless. Alister eased the car onto the narrow gravel path that wound down through a stand of carob trees. The tires crackled over stone—the only sound in the Mediterranean night.

As they rolled into the small courtyard, the villa's weathered doors opened before they could stop. Luca stood in the doorway, silhouetted by the soft light behind him.

He had been waiting.

They climbed out, road-weary and hollow-eyed. Dust clung to their clothes. The scroll jar was still wrapped tightly in Susan's coat.

Luca said nothing. He simply reached forward with trembling hands and took the jar. Then he nodded—once—turned, and walked silently down the hall toward his study.

Susan and Alister didn't speak. They barely made it to their rooms before sleep claimed them.

When they woke, it was already late morning. Sunlight poured through the windows, golden and warm, scented faintly by lemon blossoms drifting up from the terrace below. Susan splashed water on her face, pulled on clean clothes, and stepped outside to find Alister already on the terrace, coffee in hand, a half-eaten croissant beside him. His expression was still drawn tight from the night before.

Luca was in the study.

He had not slept.

The scroll jar sat open on his broad mahogany desk. A section of the papyrus—fifteen feet long, by Luca's estimate—had been gently un-rolled and pinned beneath velvet-lined glass panels. A magnifier and soft brushes lay nearby. The ancient ink still shimmered faintly in the light slanting through the arched windows. The papyrus was intact. Legible. Miraculous.

Luca looked up as they entered. His eyes were red-rimmed—not only from sleeplessness but from something deeper.

Awe.

"This one," he said softly, "is unlike anything I have ever read."

Alister stepped forward. "What does it say?"

Luca didn't answer right away. His hands hovered reverently above the papyrus, seemingly afraid to touch what it revealed.

"It picks up where the first left off. Jesus goes back to Jerusalem, but as Paul, the name of a close friend in Gaul who had recently died. He shaves his hairline, alters his voice, his posture—he becomes someone else. Someone unrecognizable."

Luca began to tell the story.

CHAPTER TWENTY-THREE

Spring, 41 CE

The first light of day crested over the hills of Narbonensis, the Roman Empire's province in southern Gaul. After walking since dawn the day before, with only a brief rest at a roadside guesthouse, Jesus finally reached the outskirts of Frejus.

He paused on a ridge above the harbor. He could hear and feel the energy radiating from below. In contrast to the rural countryside he had just traveled through, it was an awe-inspiring sight. With almost 400 military ships and countless commercial vessels docked in its natural harbor, it was the second most important naval base in the Empire. Located at the crossroads of two major Roman trading routes, it was also the hub of commercial activity in the Mediterranean basin.

Behind him, more than twenty-five miles away, the peaceful olive-lined valleys of Olea Vallis lay quiet in memory, still cloaked in morning fog. The wind tugged at his tunic. He was about to enter a different world, marked by the scent of salt and pine in the air, and the tang of tar and fish. Dockworkers called to each other in Latin and Greek over the creak of timber and the clatter of amphorae. In the distance, gulls circled above the sails of anchored merchant ships.

He imagined Mary gathering the children, perhaps standing on their terrace, watching the same horizon he had followed.

He pressed a hand to the pouch slung across his chest. Inside, wrapped in cloth and sealed in a terracotta sleeve, was a scroll—the second of many he and Mary hoped to write. And on a string next to his heart was the document with his Roman citizenship and a new name. With this, he would become Paul when he reached Jerusalem.

Down at the docks, the Pax Romana waited. A squat, sturdy cog with a weathered hull and a broad square sail already catching wind. Cargo was being loaded—oil, wine, grain, and rough-wrapped bundles of wool. Among the crew stood Lucius Barrius, Jesus's friend and supporter from Olea Vallis—the same man who had once stood silently in the chapel shadows. Now, his voice rang sharp and confident as he gave orders to the bosun.

When he saw Jesus, Lucius approached and clasped his forearm in the Roman style.

"Welcome, my friend. Right on time, as I knew you'd be. My ships are safe—and fast," he said, eyes glinting. "While the gods favor speed, Captain Vorenus will see you safely to Rome and the port at Ostia. Beyond that… the wind will decide."

Then more softly: "While you're in Jerusalem, I'll visit my estate and stop by Olea Vallis—to make sure Mary and the children have all they need in your absence."

Jesus nodded. "Thank you, my friend. For your trust—and your support."

Lucius met his eyes. "Speak carefully when you arrive. The world beyond our hills is less kind to miracles. Caesarea will be your last port before Jerusalem. When you return, find your way back there. Any of my captains will bring you home."

As the Pax Romana pulled away, Jesus stood at the stern, watching Gaul's coastline vanish into haze. Centuries later, the world would come to know it as the Côte d'Azur—a place of emperors and exiles. For now, it was a trade route. The waves rolled steady and mild.

He had made this voyage once before, five years earlier, arriving with Mary and his mother. Then, he had traveled not by sea, but over land, with hope and a belief that others would build his Church. Now, he traveled with purpose—and a weight heavier than when he left. At every port, he would ask the same questions. And with each answer, the same dismay: the apostles had scattered, the promises had faltered, and the message was splintering.

Unless he stepped forward, his Church—his truth—would fade into obscurity, forgotten among the ruins of forgotten prophets.

But amid the disappointments, something new took shape. His confidence grew— not in doctrine, but in the power of resurrection. He saw its reach in the eyes of ordinary people: sailors, widows, pagans, and dreamless men who listened when he spoke of hope and rising again.

He saw it first aboard the Pax Romana. Just two days out, storm clouds gathered off the Etruscan coast. Rain swept the deck sideways. The mast groaned. Passengers clung to the railings, crying out to their gods.

Jesus stood silently, drenched, calm. Then, to test the strength of the message even here, he knelt—hands clasped, not in panic but in prayer.

A young deckhand named Felix, barely sixteen, gaped at him. "Aren't you afraid?"

Jesus opened his eyes. "No man commands the sea. But faith anchors the soul."

The storm passed, as storms do. But the memory of his stillness lingered. He saw it in the eyes of the crew. The message had entered.

The next day, they docked at Ostia, Rome's churning port. He would return here years later, in a very different role. But for now, he couldn't know that so he stiffly through a city loud with commerce and incense. He stayed two nights near the Forum Holitorium, meeting quietly with Jews who shrugged at his questions. None had heard of a new faith. The promises of his brothers echoed hollow. He couldn't know it then, but he would return here in a decade, having successfully founded his church, which was rapidly expanding in the Empire.

But for now, he booked passage aboard the Invictus, a massive grain ship bound for Alexandria. On the third day, fierce storms diverted them south along the Tyrrhenian coast—within sight of cliffs that, two millennia later, would house Luca's villa and the scroll Jesus now carried.

Days blurred. Some with wind, others with none. Tempers flared during long calms; fights broke out and were silenced by the bellow of the first mate. Other days, storms slammed the ship broadside. Sails cracked like whips. The Invictus listed hard, barrels breaking loose. Jesus helped haul the wounded, lifted the fearful, and steadied men with words drawn from the mustard seed, the lost coin, and life beyond death.

One evening, Captain Valerius found him alone at the prow.

"You're either mad," he muttered, "or blessed. Either way…they listen to you."

When the lighthouse of Pharos appeared at last, Alexandria lay before them—its domes and temples rising from the shore like carved marble from the sea. Jesus stepped ashore in silence.

The markets roared. Philosophers bickered. He found a few Jewish merchants who had once heard the name of Jesus. But their news confirmed his worst fear: the apostles had drifted apart. Messages diverged. Doctrines split.

He stayed only briefly. The weight of their abandonment burned cold in his chest.

He moved on—eastward, to Caesarea. The journey was not over. Now, he carried not only a scroll, but a burden.

In early June, six weeks after departing Gaul, his ship arrived at Caesarea Maritima. Jesus stepped onto Judean soil—his beard salt-stiff, his robes worn, his eyes tired but burning with fire.

He joined a merchant caravan for the final leg. Through the dry hills of Samaria. Past olive groves and fig trees. Along dusty Roman roads lined with whispering pines.

On the seventh day, just before dusk, Jerusalem rose ahead—its towering Temple silhouetted in the sun, its gates heavy with history.

He passed Calvary Hill, the site of his brother's crucifixion, without looking, without stopping.

He did not flinch.

Jesus was gone.
Paul had arrived.

CHAPTER TWENTY-FOUR

The afternoon sun was moving west, shining too brightly through Luca's study windows that overlooked the villa's terrace and the Tyrrhenian Sea, where sailboats leaned into the afternoon wind. Luca rubbed his eyes, pausing for a rest, and drew the shades down to soften the glare. The story riveted Susan and Alister, but they had slept until almost midday, were well-rested, and eager to hear more. Yet they could see that Luca, who had worked late into the night, needed a break.

They went down to the kitchen together and assembled a simple but typical meal: fresh mozzarella Di Bufala with ripe tomatoes and basil from the terrace garden, drizzled with Luca's own olive oil; thin slices of prosciutto laid over wedges of melon; a basket of warm focaccia from the village bakery; and a carafe of crisp Falanghina white wine from Campania. For dessert, there were figs picked that morning from the tree just beyond the stone wall.

Carrying the platters outside, they settled at the long table on the terrace, shaded by the trellis of vines. The sea stretched away in a blaze of silver light as they ate slowly, savoring the food and the pause, before turning again to the words that had carried them across centuries.

In Luca's study, after the break he needed, Luca continued. " The scroll is quite long and detailed, and there is quite a bit to absorb, so before I read it to you, let me give you a quick summary."

"When Jesus arrives in Jerusalem, he is a nobody. He watches from the shadows, hoping to hear echoes of the message he once preached. But what he finds is disturbing. The apostles—those he once trusted—have done little. After witnessing what happened to Jesus, they remained clustered in Jerusalem, hiding and clinging to safety. They rarely preach. The movement is fragmented. Confused. Some followers have developed distorted versions of his teachings. No one is carrying the message into the empire."

Susan leaned in closer. "So he doesn't reveal himself?"

Luca shook his head. "He can't. To them, he has already ascended to heaven. If he returns as a mortal man… everything collapses. So he decides to lead his Church again—quietly, intentionally—this time preaching as Paul, a disciple of the risen Christ."

He glanced at them both, lowering his voice.

"This approach had worked in Gaul when he preached at his chapel. There, his followers were mainly pagan—open to new ideas. His message was that salvation didn't come through law or sacrifice, but through faith in the crucifixion and resurrection. It signaled that the Kingdom of God wasn't coming soon—it had already begun. Anyone—Jew or Gentile—could be made right with God simply by believing. The rituals, temple, and priesthood were no longer essential."

He paused.

"When he preached to poor gentile communities, this message gave hope to men with little else. Fishermen, tax collectors, tradesmen—suddenly, they had a destiny. A divine role."

"But in Jerusalem," Luca continued, "his audience was Jewish and steeped in tradition. There, the context was different. His message wasn't just radical—it was offensive."

Alister drew a breath. "More than offensive. For those traditional Jewish sects in Jerusalem, that message would have been heresy."

"Exactly," Luca said quietly. "And it led to him running for his life."

Susan stared at the scroll. "And none of this exists in the Gospels?"

"Not a word," Luca said.

"The Paul of the Bible—his letters, his backstory, his miraculous conversion on the road to Damascus—it's a carefully constructed myth. A fiction built to unify doctrine while hiding the truth."

Luca looked up.

"Jesus returned and continued to shape Christianity—but now as a ghost with a mask. Forever hidden beneath a lie."

Susan's breath caught. "You think the Silentii erased this, too?"

"They had to," Luca said. "If people discovered that Jesus and Paul were the same person, that most of the apostles abandoned their promise, and the Gospels were fabricated, the entire foundation of power they derived form Church history would fracture."

Alister turned to Susan. "Remember what I told you in Central Park? About the Gospel of Mary Magdalene—how it was so dangerous to the Church that the Silentii destroyed it…and then rewrote it? I think we are hearing the beginnings of that original story."

He touched the edge of the papyrus gently.

Susan stepped back, shaken. "And this scroll… is only the second? There must be more, but where?"

Luca nodded slowly, tapping the glass. "Yes. We need to find them before Silentii does. Together, they reveal the true history of the Church's origin—buried under two thousand years of silence. And the Silentii will stop at nothing to keep it that way…and then silence us."

Luca paused as an uncomfortable quiet fell over the room. He added slowly, "In the same way, Jesus found himself in the same situation two thousand years ago. The scroll tells us that when he returned to Jerusalem, the Jewish leaders would stop at nothing to suppress his new message and silence him."

Silence settled over the room.

Then Alister spoke, his voice clear.

"Amazing. Thank you. Now take us through it. Slowly. Tell us what he actually wrote."

Luca reached for the magnifier.

And the true history began to unfold.

CHAPTER TWENTY-FIVE

Jerusalem, 44 CE

The city had become familiar, yet foreign.

Two years had passed since his return from Gaul. Two years of narrow alleys and overcrowded markets, of whispers and glances, of sandals worn thin walking the old routes under a borrowed name. Jerusalem had not changed. But everything else had. The change he had expected to find wasn't there. And he now realized it never was.

He entered as Paul, an educated convert and minor merchant from Tarsus. He practiced his new identity until it was second nature—his Aramaic fluent, his Greek sharper than most, and his Latin tinged with just enough Gallic curl to pass as an outsider with local ties. He found lodging in the upper city, in a narrow stone house beside a spice merchant whose nephew owed him a favor from Gaul.

He began at once to search for the others—his apostles—the men who had sworn loyalty during those final days after the crucifixion. The ones who had promised to spread the message, build a church, and carry on what he had begun.

But they were gone.

Thomas had fled, some said, to Egypt or even farther east. Andrew was rumored to be fishing again in Bethsaida. Philip had vanished. Matthew was teaching quietly near the coast, careful not to speak openly. And Peter—Peter had left no trail at all. Some claimed he'd gone north. Others whispered of a journey west. But no one knew for sure. He had simply disappeared.

Only one Apostle remained: James, son of Zebedee. The brother of John. Once headstrong, now solemn, older. And the only one still preaching in public.

Paul did not reveal himself. Not yet. He wanted to observe—watch, and see the reaction of those who came to listen. So he blended into the crowd—sat quietly behind carts and cloaks, listened in alleyways and temple courtyards where James spoke to gatherings of tradesmen and day laborers. The message was familiar, but faint. A weakened echo of what had once ignited their movement. It lacked the power and drive of Jesus's delivery.

Even so, James drew listeners. His humility, his certainty, his endurance—they stirred something ancient in the crowd.

However, as Paul joined these groups, he began to notice that not everyone came to listen.

Over several weeks, he saw three men appear regularly at the edges of the gatherings: Simeon, who dressed as a linen merchant; Damaris, who claimed to be a stonemason; and Eliezar, who wore the plain tunic of a carpenter. They stood close together. Nodded at all the right moments. Smiled at the parables.

Paul had seen people like this before. They were watchers, not believers—gathering information for their leaders.

In secret histories of the Temple, they would later have another name: Enforcers. They were spies, agents of the Temple elite, trained to detect heresy, deviation, and disorder. Every religion had them—silencers.

But James didn't notice. And Paul couldn't say anything.

Then, one day, while the group sat beneath a fig tree after a sermon, Eliezar tore a piece of bread and spoke to James with feigned enthusiasm. "I think you should take your message into the Temple itself," he said. "…it would be powerful."

James' pulse began to race as he thought about the possibility. The Jerusalem Temple was a wonder of the ancient world. It rose majestically, its dazzling white marble and gold facade visible for miles. With walls ten stories high enclosing an area bigger than five of today's football fields, the outer courts were teeming with a constant throng of pilgrims and merchants. Beyond this bustling public expanse, the inner courts, reserved for purification and worship, were approached through towering gates. One of the most prominent, the Nicanor Gate, was crafted from gleaming Corinthian bronze. At its center, the Temple itself stood fifteen stories high and crowned with golden spikes. It was a beacon of faith dominating the ancient city's skyline.

Eliezar, sensing James' excitement, continued, " The Sadducees would hear it. The Pharisees, too. They could not ignore you." James hesitated, then said with a shaky voice. "It's sacred ground. I'm not trained. I never led a formal study."

"That's why it would matter," Simeon added. "You're a fisherman. One of Jesus's own. Many want to hear his message. Let them see who truly carries his voice."

Damaris smiled warmly. "You belong there, James."

Paul watched, silent. His heart pounded. His instincts screamed trap. But his voice would carry no weight. He was not known yet—just one of the crowd. His preaching would wait. He had come to observe. To see what remained. He could not intervene without exposing everything.

James agreed.

The Temple courtyard was packed that morning—more so than usual. Word had spread. The last known Apostle of Jesus would speak openly beneath the portico.

Paul stood in the outer crowd, his head bowed, heart hammering. James stepped forward, humble and clear. He spoke of the kingdom of heaven, of love and justice, of a resurrection that lifted not only bodies but burdens. It was the message of Jesus before the crucifixion. Strong. Powerful.

And the growing crowd listened.

Until they didn't.

It started with whispers.

Then came the stones.

Shouts erupted—"Blasphemer! Heretic!" Cries tore through the crowd as stones flew from hidden hands. The three men—Simeon, Damaris, Eliezar—stepped back, then forward again, now bearing the insignia of Temple guards.

They were not tradesmen anymore.

James was seized and dragged down the Temple steps.

Paul followed in the crowd, heart pounding, ducking between pilgrims and stalls. He heard the accusations. Watched the mockery of a trial unfold in a dusty chamber near the Sanhedrin court. Nothing had changed from years ago at his own trial. They still said it was the work of evil….of the devil. He saw the verdict in the eyes of the priests before it was ever spoken.

Death.

Execution by sword.

It happened the next morning, at dawn. Swift. Public. Brutal.

The crowd gathered outside the city wall, where the sentence would be carried out. Paul moved among them like a ghost, each step heavier than the last.

James knelt. Calm. Dignified. Unafraid.

The sword lifted.

And Paul's voice broke from his throat.

"No! You can't do that!"

It was not a shout of protest—but the sound of something tearing free inside him. A cry of grief. Of fury. Of betrayal.

The blade fell.

And the last Apostle was no more.

His outburst caught the immediate attention of Simeon, Damaris, and Eliezar. Their eyes locked on Paul. They recognized him—not from the Temple, but from James's gatherings.

Paul fled through the streets, hood drawn low, heart splintered. They were close behind. But he knew the back alleys better. He was faster. He didn't look back until he reached the house on the far hill, where the Roman road curved toward the western gate.

He had lost them. But now they knew him—and he had to leave.

In that moment, he also knew something else.

His message of believing in the crucifixion of the Messiah would never survive here.

Not in Jerusalem. Not among those still too afraid. Not among the heirs of the old law.

He had planned to commit five years to his ministry in Jerusalem—to rekindle the fire of Jewish Christianity. But the flame had already gone out. Or perhaps it had never truly caught.

Now, he needed to rethink his future. Where would he go? Where would he build his Church?

It was still too soon for Mary to join him—the children were not yet old enough, and his aging mother too frail. He would return to Gaul. And with Mary's help, decide what to do next.

That night, by a low oil lamp, Paul dipped his pen and began writing in the scroll—not only a message to the future, but also a present declaration:

From this day forward, the Church would not belong to Jerusalem.

It would belong to the world—to the Gentiles.

CHAPTER TWENTY-SIX

Alister and Susan leaned in close, silent, almost breathless, listening as Luca's eyes neared the end of the scroll, delicately unrolled in front of him. The sun had long since dipped beneath the sea, leaving the villa bathed in a warm, amber glow of lamplight. The only sound was the rustle of the cool evening breeze drifting through the garden from the Mediterranean.

Luca sat at his long wooden desk. He had been reading for more than two hours. He paused, then exhaled slowly as he finished the final words:

> *I returned to the hillside with a soul fractured by loss.*
> *Mary met me in silence. She had known. Perhaps always. That Jerusalem would not welcome me back.*
> *Maybe she had learned that early—the rejection from her own family.*
>
> *We sat quietly for hours on our favorite hillside bench overlooking our beautiful valley, the warmth of our love like a blanket.*
>
> *We did not speak of James. We let the olive groves mourn for us.*
>
> *We spoke of the vastness of the Empire and where I should look to ignite the fire of my Church. But whenever I spoke of going, her eyes became lonely and searched the horizon.*
>
> *I told her that I would bury this second scroll beneath the terrace stones beside the first before I left. She said no. Because this place—our place—where she sits every evening when I am away, was no longer only a sanctuary. It had become a recording—our Gospel. She would bury the scroll.*
>
> *I told her that in just two more years, she could join me.*
> *The children will be old enough to be left with my mother by then. In the*

meantime, I would send her messages with Lucius when he returned here to his vacation estate."

Alister broke the silence. "So that's where he went. Antioch."

Susan nodded. "He left her again."

"He had to," Luca said gently. "But Mary had changed. She was stronger. She stayed behind to raise the children and care for his mother. She would join him in Antioch when the time was right. Two years is what they thought."

It wouldn't be in Antioch. Instead, it would be a sparkling spring day at a harbor near Rome, much longer than two years from now, when they did meet again. But they couldn't know it then.

Luca paused, then translated the closing lines:

We decided that I will journey east, back to Antioch.
The city is teeming, layered with voices. Jews, Greeks, Romans, traders.
Believers and doubters both.

It will begin there.
Not inside temple walls that shadow my message,
but in the open air of teeming markets and public places.
With those not only willing to hear—but to listen.

Antioch is the home of Lucius. He will show me the city, provide some support, introduce me to his friends, and help to organize my ministry.

Luca leaned back. "That's the end…but only of what was written on the scroll. But, when he was in Antioch, he wrote two letters to Mary, and Lucius brought them to her during the next two years when he visited his vacation estate."

The room was quiet. The sound of the fire crackling in the hearth filled the space between them.

Luca carefully held up the two letters so Susan and Alister could see them, and said, "They're written on smaller pieces of Papyrus, and seemed to have been damaged by seawater…probably on the trip back from Antioch. Mary wrapped them around the scroll and sealed the jar before burying them under the terrace.

Reading them will take some work. Hopefully, they will help us locate the third scroll. I'll see what I can do tomorrow. Tonight, I'm too tired."

Luca carefully rolled the scroll with the two letters and placed it in its ceramic tube, sealing the lid with a soft tap of his palm. His hand lingered there for a moment—almost as if blessing it.

He walked to the far side of the room, opened the wall safe, and locked the scroll inside with the turn of the safe's key.

He turned and quietly said: "If the Silentii knew what we now know…"

Alister interrupted Luca in mid-sentence, "They already know it all from the writings they collected and destroyed since the fourth century. Their problem now is that they suspect we know some of that truth…but they don't know how much.

They don't know we have a first-hand account of Church history from Jesus and Mary. In their hand. Not copies but originals. If they learn that, they will stop at nothing to possess and destroy it. And us, too."

Susan glanced at him. "They're already trying to find us."

"Yes," Luca said. "And, so far, just a single agent? But when they learn he has failed twice already, they'll respond… by assigning more resources. They're an old order that's survived for almost two centuries. Discipline is their foundation. The Silentii do not tolerate failure."

Alister looked out toward the dark sea. "So what happens now?"

Luca didn't answer at first.

Then he turned from the firelight and said,
"Now… we must find that third scroll before they do…and be careful because they will begin escalating."

CHAPTER TWENTY-SEVEN

Far below the tourist eyes that gaze up at the grandeur of St. Peter's Basilica in Vatican City—beyond locked iron gates and false walls in the dim necropolis grotto—a stone corridor, carved from Vatican Hill two millennia past, winds deep into the bedrock. At its far end stands a reinforced titanium door, shielded against electromagnetic intrusion. Behind it, carved from ancient tombs that once held Rome's forgotten dead, the Ordo Silentii maintains its hidden headquarters: *Domus Silentii*—The House of Silence.

The architecture is a study in calculated contrast. Twenty thousand square feet of polished black basalt floors and arched ceilings of Greek marble stretch beneath uplighting so discreet it feels like moonlight. Fourth-century pillars bear the weight of it all, while fiber-optic bundles run inside the bones of Roman columns. Frescoes glow behind layers of protective glass. Offices that appear Renaissance at a glance reveal their true nature only under closer inspection—retinal scanners where keyholes once were, acoustic baffling embedded in the walls. This is no place for prayer. It is a fortress for control.

At the corridor's end, Cardinal Vittorio Vallente, Supreme Prelate of the Ordo Silentii, stood alone in his private office, rereading a report he had already memorized. Though his expression betrayed nothing, he was too furious to sit. The glow of his secure tablet illuminated the polished onyx surface before him. Three names glared back like a rebuke:

Susan Hale. Alister Duran. Corvus.

Only a week ago, he had descended via elevator from the corner of this very office—thirty feet down—to the Chamber of the Seventh

Seal to welcome Corvus into the Order.

"Was that only a week ago?" he muttered aloud, *"so much has unraveled since."*

The assignment had been simple. A minor test. An introductory errand. A suspicious shipment from Nice to the Metropolitan Museum in New York. Corvus was to trace it, assess its significance, and report back. Silent. Surgical. Controlled.

Instead, Corvus had failed to intercept the package in New York—and again in a small Provençal town. The object turned out to be a scroll. Papyrus. Possibly first-century. Definitely dangerous. Somehow, Corvus made a mistake. The Americans realized they were being followed. They vanished with the scroll. Their credentials—those of recognized experts in early Christianity—suggested they might have discovered something far more important than anyone had previously guessed.

Vallente shut off the tablet. As the screen went dark, his reflection stared back: gray at the temples, jaw clenched tight, the skin stretched taut over features too tired for their age. Beneath his close-cropped silver hair, rage simmered. But deeper still—he hesitated to name it— was fear.

He whispered to himself, "What if I have to explain this to him? To the Holy Father? What if the one man I can't control demands answers I don't have?"

This was never supposed to become anything more than a litmus test, Vallente thought bitterly, sliding a leather attaché across the desk. *Something manageable. Contained. Discreet.*

Now it had the makings of a disaster.

And in the Ordo Silentii, failure was not tolerated.

It was sanitized.

He had seen it himself. Brother Niklas, who cracked under pressure in Beirut, was found drowned in the Tiber—labeled a suicide. Sister Leva, whose digital trail nearly exposed the Lisbon breach, died of a heart attack at thirty-five. Mistakes weren't punished. They were erased. He had personally signed the orders.

And yet… not this time. Not yet. Corvus was too valuable. Too rare.

Ruthless. Loyal. Unpredictable. Vallente saw something of himself in the younger man.
Corvus had been born in Bucharest, the son of a diplomat and a Romani woman tied to a Balkan crime syndicate. He'd grown up between embassies and back alleys, fluent in six languages by age ten, a thief and prodigy by twelve. The scar—a jagged slash from brow to jaw—came from a failed hit when he was fifteen. He'd killed his attacker with a shard of mirror.

The Ordo Silentii had taken notice.

He excelled. Infiltration. Intimidation. Emotional detachment. Surgical precision.
He had never made a mistake—until now.

Vallente opened the secondary report, which included surveillance footage from St Cyr, thermal scans of the hillside, and evidence of excavation beneath a terrace. *They found two scrolls,* he thought. *They didn't consult anyone. Didn't turn them over. They ran. Why? Because they understood? Because they were afraid? Could they possibly know of Silentii?*

He tapped a secure app. A red screen appeared:
G-FALCON. Paris Site. Assemble: EU Command Tier.

He populated the manifest:

- Corvus

- Commander Riss – Digital Surveillance, Cologne

- Sister Eliane – Doctrinal Compliance, Lyon

- Matteo Varga – Field Operations, Trieste

- Dr. Eberhardt – Linguistic Forensics, Munich

As the Silentii Gulfstream fueled on the Vatican's private runway, Vallente slid the attaché into a titanium compartment beneath his seat. It was 6 am. The aircraft would be airborne within minutes and in Paris by 8:15.

The Silentii site in Paris lay far beneath the Institut Catholique, accessed through a disused Jesuit wine cellar, protected by papal exemption and French diplomatic immunity.
There, he would reassert control.
No more assumptions. No more delegation.

Failure was one thing.

But these Americans were not ordinary. They were connected. Academic networks. Major museums. Media platforms. Global reputations. If the contents of the scrolls surfaced unfiltered—this would not merely be an embarrassment.

It would be fire.

Some truths, Vallente thought grimly, as the jet climbed into the Roman night, *must remain buried forever.*

The secure satellite phone in his side pocket vibrated, interrupting his thoughts. "Yes," he abruptly answered. As he listened, his face relaxed for the first time this evening, and a slight smile crossed his lips.

CHAPTER TWENTY-EIGHT

From the window at the Hotel Ritz, Paris shimmered in the wet spring mist—lights blurred like brushstrokes, the Eiffel Tower blinking in the distance, cold and indifferent. It was 2:43 am. Corvus was not sleeping. He rarely did before meetings. Especially not one like this.

He stood barefoot on the carpeted floor, shirtless in the dark, facing the mirror above the dresser. The scar from brow to jaw caught a shard of light from the minibar. To most, it would be a wound to forget. But for Corvus, it was a mark of identity—one of many. A medal. A memory.

He stared into his reflection, unblinking, and spoke aloud the incantation his mother had taught him:
"You are not afraid. You are not weak. You are in charge."
Once in Latin. Once in Romani. Always in that order.

Dressing came next. Ritualized. Slow. Each motion precise. He pulled on a tailored charcoal combat shirt with integrated Kevlar lining, matte black tactical trousers, and soft-soled shoes that made no sound. His dual shoulder holsters came next—ceramic blade left, Glock 19 Gen5 right. The pistol, modified for silent recoil and trace-resistant ammo, bore the Silentii seal etched beneath the barrel. Around his neck, beneath the collarbone, he clasped a thin chain bearing a micro-crucifix—lined with RF shielding, illegal even within the Order. His mother had worn it always. It had not saved her, but he wore it still.

The raw scar on his right shoulder still burned—the brand from his induction—the vine-protected cross of the Silentii. A wound not yet healed. It itched with memory.

He sat on the bed's edge and retrieved a thin leather pouch hidden inside his jacket lining. From it, he slid out a fading photograph: he and his mother on the Dalmatian coast, sunlight behind them, boats in the harbor. He was smiling. She was not.

Behind him, the hotel phone lay in pieces on the desk—receiver casing peeled open, its circuitry exposed. Compromised. Someone had wanted to listen. Perhaps Vallente. Perhaps someone else. But his mother's rule remained:
Trust no one. Not even your own.

He stared at his reflection in the mirror across from the bed.
Lean. Surgical. Expressionless.
He spoke again:
"I am a weapon. I am not afraid. I am not weak. I am in charge."
But the voice inside whispered otherwise.
What if you're slipping? What if you're failing?

His mind drifted—back thirty years.
Sofia, Bulgaria. At the foot of Vitosha Mountain.
His father, Petru Drăghici—a mild Romanian diplomat—was rarely at home, barely present. Tiptoeing through life, apologizing more than speaking. Especially to Lenka. Corvus's mother.

Lenka was Romani. Raised on the streets of Craiova. Brilliant, brutal, untouchable. She taught Corvus to lie by four, steal by six, and recognize weakness by seven.

When Petru was killed in a 1990 car bombing outside the Romanian embassy in Ankara, Corvus watched from their apartment window. He was nine. Later, he would tell Silentii recruiters: *That was the day I became responsible for everything.*
But what he never said—not aloud—was the other thing he felt.
Relief.
I won, he thought. *I have her now.*

For three years, he was her shadow. Her shield. She let him believe he ruled her world. But she was shaping him, hiding his fragility behind silence and control.

She called him *vrajitor mic—little warlock.*
And her warlock he became.

Until at fifteen, when his world changed…forever. His mother, Lenka, had stolen from a rival underworld figure with connections and soldiers. It was a bad choice. Retribution was fast. He remembered that winter in Bulgaria—snow, deep and silent---when a man with a knife came for her. The apartment furnace had gone cold. Ice crusted the windows. Sitting in a dark corner of the room, Corvus sprang like a cat, intercepting the attacker, shielding Lenka. But the blade opened his face from brow to jaw, blood filling his eyes. His fingers closed around a jagged piece from a shattered mirror. His mother's voice surged in his mind: *Never hesitate when it's your life.* He didn't. He killed the man, then collapsed from blood loss.

He was arrested hours later.

The court called it murder. His mother vanished before the trial—likely paid to disappear. Corvus never saw her again, but he never forgot. He had just turned sixteen and was sentenced to two years in a crumbling Bulgarian prison near the Serbian border. It was more than punishment. It was humiliation. The rats. The cold. The flaking walls that reminded him of his father's impotence, his endless silences. And the inmates—older, predatory, vicious—who mocked his scar, challenged his toughness, smelled what they thought was weakness. He was assigned to clean showers. One morning, an inmate cornered him, taunting the jagged line across his face, making a crude advance. It triggered a rage that never announced its presence but was always close to the surface. Corvus snapped his neck with a single motion. No sign of that hidden rage. Just precision.

Solitary followed. Darkness. Hunger. But Silentii had been watching.

He had been identified at birth. His potential tracked as he grew. His skills now proven at seventeen. They had flagged him years before, and that episode in the shower only confirmed it. Now—with government help—they extracted him. Recruited him. His release was masked as a diplomatic transfer. He believed he was being offered a second chance. What he was given was a purpose.

The moment he heard the phrase "Mother Church," something locked into place inside him. Maternal. Absolute. Unquestionable.

And the Church's warlock he became, committing himself to protect and defend her, no matter what, even in death's grip.

As he sat on the edge of the bed, he remembered every scar from his Silentii training.

His right shoulder—Sarajevo. Infiltration failure.
His left forearm—Tbilisi. Exposed safehouse.
His ribs—Rome. Blade training.
Each a lesson. Each a line in the map of becoming.

A siren wailed below. A sudden reminder: Paris was awake. The meeting approached.

What if they turn on you?', he thought.
He had seen it before.
A vodka bottle left visible. An elevator door that opened at the wrong time. A smile from Vallente that said, 'You're already dead.'

'Would they do it to me? Would I see it coming?'

The hotel line rang once. The signal. It was 5:30 am.

Time.

Outside, a black SUV idled. Inside sat Commander Riss and Sister Eliane. Riss nodded. Eliane stared ahead, silent.

They would descend soon, beneath the Institut Catholique—through the old wine cellar, down the ancient shaft, into the Paris site. A sanctuary. A tribunal. Or a tomb.

Corvus looked at his reflection in the rain-streaked window one last time. Blurred. Pale. Almost spectral.

'You were the predator.' He thought, 'Now, you're the question mark.'

He didn't mind.

Predators evolve.

CHAPTER TWENTY-NINE

The villa was quiet.

Beyond the terrace, waves lapped against the base of the cliffs, rhythmic and soft in the night air. A distant lighthouse blinked across the water. Inside, the house had grown still, its guests finally retired after the day's strain. The second scroll had shaken them all—its revelations upending everything they thought they knew. Jesus returning to Galilee. Abandoned by the apostles. Assuming the identity of Paul. Spreading a new gospel under Roman noses. And now, hints of a third scroll, hidden somewhere, containing a history that could be even more dangerous.

Luca, seemingly deep in his own thoughts, had said little after reading the final lines. He had simply locked both scrolls in the concealed wall safe in his study, securing them behind steel and stone. The door had closed with a deliberate, echoing click—and a full turn of a key. He replaced the framed painting that covered the safe's location. Then, quietly, they had said goodnight.

The villa was quiet. Peaceful at last. But Alister couldn't sleep.

He lay in bed for nearly an hour, staring at the carved wooden beams overhead, the weight of the scroll's implications pressing down on him. A cold whisper crept into his thoughts. They were being hunted, and the air in the villa felt too still in the face of that knowledge. If he couldn't sleep, he might as well work on a plan. Think clearly. Strategize. Write. So that in the morning he could talk to Luca and Susan about next steps: decoding the letter fragments, retracing Paul's journey, and searching for the third scroll.

He sat up. It was 1 am.

Still dressed but barefoot, he crossed the hallway and quietly went down the stairs. He slipped into Luca's study.

The room smelled of sandalwood, old paper, and something fainter—dust, perhaps, or time itself. A small lantern glowed in the corner. Alister crossed to the desk and opened the top drawer, looking for paper and a pen.

He saw the paper he needed beneath a leather-bound notebook. As he lifted it out of the way, a key fell to the bottom of the drawer. It was gold-plated. Archaic in design. Its stem flared into a flat, round head, engraved with a symbol.

He picked it up and stared.

His mind didn't immediately register what he was seeing.

Then—his breath caught.

A cross
Protective vines
Curling from the base
Encircled by Ordo Silentii
And their sacred code 7777

The mark of the Silentii.

His fingers tightened around the key.

His mind reeled. That symbol was sacred. Secret. Even among the few scholars who whispered of the Silentii, none had ever claimed to *see* the emblem, let alone *hold* it. Why would Luca—of all people—possess such a thing?

Unless...

Unless he wasn't merely a scholar studying the Silentii.

He was one of them.

Alister's thoughts raced. The safe. Luca had used a key earlier. Could this be it?

He crossed the room and pulled aside the framed painting that concealed the wall safe. The steel door stared back at him, a keyhole beneath a digital pad.

He inserted the key.

It turned—perfectly.

The keypad blinked.

He hesitated, staring again at the engraved symbol.

Then he tapped in the number he had only ever heard in whispered rumors. The one no one dared write down.

OS7777

The lock clicked open.

Inside the safe sat the two ceramic jars. The scrolls. Untouched. But no longer protected.

The realization hit like a wave.

Luca Severin—trusted friend, mentor, his father's old companion—was one of them. Silentii.

The fragments of knowledge Alister had believed he pieced together from colleagues, debates, and obscure scholarship... they weren't his discoveries. They were breadcrumbs. Left by Luca.

Luca, who had invited him here that summer between semesters. Who had welcomed him so many times before. Offered guidance. Trust.

Had it all been for a purpose?

"Was I being groomed?" he thought. "Was Luca evaluating my suitability? Did he think I might become a hand-delivered prize to his masters at the Silentii?"

He quietly removed the scroll jars from the safe, then closed it carefully, turned the key, and returned it to the drawer. No trace.

As he turned to leave the study, he paused.

"No," he thought. "I have a better idea."

He set the two jars down on Luca's desk and gently removed the improvised cork seals. The original mud-and-resin seals used by Mary two millennia ago had broken when the jars were opened earlier that week. They couldn't be reused.

He unwrapped the scrolls and the letters from the ancient linen cloths in which they were protected. Then he opened the cabinet beneath Luca's printer, where he remembered Luca kept office supplies. Inside, he found printer paper. He rolled two sheafs tightly into cylinders, about four inches in diameter—close enough in shape to match the scrolls—then wrapped them in the same linen cloths and slid them carefully back into the jars.

He retrieved the key, reopened the safe, resealed the jars with a gentle tap, and returned them to their place.

No trace. It would look as if nothing had happened.

Luca would never know—until it was too late.

Now he moved quickly.

Back in his room, he packed what he needed. Documents. Gloves. Flashlight. He found an old Amazon box at the bottom of his closet, wrapped the actual scrolls in soft polo shirts, and secured them in the box, cushioned with a third shirt.

He padded down the hallway to Susan's room and knocked gently.

She stirred as he entered. "Alister?"

"We have to go," he whispered. "Now."

She sat up, frowning. "What are you talking about?"

He knelt beside the bed. "I'll explain everything in the car. But we can't stay here. Not another minute."

She stared at him. "Why? What's happened?"

"It's Luca," Alister said. "He's not a friend. Not *our* friend. Not who he pretends to be."

She read his face. Something in her shifted. Then she was up.

Five minutes later, she was dressed and packed. It was just after two am. They crept through the villa like shadows. Alister retrieved the car keys from the side table by the entry. The garage door opened with a faint shudder. Luca's battered Peugeot waited in the dark. The gardener's disguises from two days ago—hats and shirts—were still in the back seat.

They pulled out in silence, headlights off until they reached the edge of the private road.

It took more than an hour to navigate the twisting mountain path down from the cliffs. The sea fell behind them. By the time they reached the highway, the sky was lightening in the east.

Susan finally spoke, her voice low and tight.

"What happened?"

Alister didn't answer right away. His hands gripped the wheel. His jaw clenched.

Then, quietly: "We've been played. Luca's one of them."

On the far side of the villa, Luca woke early. It was 6 am. He stood by the tall window of his bedroom, watching the waning moonlight glimmer on the Tyrrhenian Sea. He hadn't heard the car leave 4 hours earlier. Hadn't known they were gone.

Not yet.

On a table beside him, an encrypted satellite phone blinked softly.

He stared at it for a long time before lifting it.

He dialed six digits. Slowly.

O…S…7… 7… 7… 7…

A pause.

"Identity?" came the clipped voice on the line.

"Severin. Priority relay."

"One moment. The Supreme Prelate is in transit."

Luca waited. His throat was dry. His thoughts crowded.

He had joined the Silentii decades ago—drawn in as a young scholar at the Gregorian Institute in Rome. He had believed then, and still believed, in protecting the Church from dangerous ideas. Heresies. Forgeries. False revelations that could tear the faithful from the truth.

That belief had never wavered.

But Alister?

He had known Alister's father. They had walked together through the ruins of Qumran. Argued theology under olive trees in Provence. When Alister came to study, Luca had seen himself in the young man—curious, bright, searching.

He had considered recruiting him. More than once. But in the end, he hadn't. Alister was too independent. Too unwilling to serve a cause he didn't fully trust.

And now, by some cruel twist of fate, it was Alister who had uncovered the scrolls. Who had come to him for help.

And he—Luca—had tried. Tried to protect him. Tried to buy time. Tried *not* to make the call. Hoping that the scroll they brought from New York would prove a dead end—like so many others before it.

But after reading the second scroll... he could no longer remain silent.

Some truths were too dangerous.

The phone clicked.

A voice came through. Cold. Commanding.

"Yes."

Luca swallowed hard. "Vittorio. I have urgent news."

While Luca spoke, he couldn't see Vittorio sitting in Silentii's Gulfstream G800 on the Vatican's private runway. He had just shut off his tablet, and as the screen went dark, his reflection stared back. It was gray at the temples, jaw clenched tight, and the skin stretched taut over features too tired for their age. It was 6 am, and they were awaiting takeoff clearance, headed for Paris and an emergency meeting with Corvuss and his Silentii senior team.

As Luca gave him the news that Susan and Alister were at his villa, the taut expression softened, and for the first time in days, a faint smile crossed his lips.

This was excellent news—and just in time.

CHAPTER THIRTY

The secure satellite phone inside the black SUV lit up as it slipped through the fog-draped streets of Paris. It was 6:10 am. Rain traced jagged paths across the tinted windows, blurring the morning into a gray smear of light and motion.

They were en route to the Silentii assembly chamber beneath the Institut Catholique—through the old wine cellar, down the ancient shaft, into the vaults below.

Commander Riss and Sister Eliane sat forward, silent, their reflections flickering against the glass.

Corvus took the call.
"Yes. Yes. Understood."

He hung up. No elaboration. Just a glance in the rearview mirror. "Change of plans," he said flatly. "Cardinal Vallente's orders. The meeting is canceled. I'll be proceeding alone."

Riss nodded once. No questions.

Twenty minutes later, the SUV pulled to a stop outside the Paris Silentii offices. The doors opened. Riss and Eliane stepped into the rain. Corvus stayed seated.

"Driver," he said, his voice low but sharp. "Le Bourget. The Silentii hangar. The Bombardier Challenger 350 is waiting."

The vehicle eased back into motion.

His new destination: Naples.
His new orders: Retrieve Professor Luca Severin and do anything

necessary to secure Dr. Susan Hale, Dr. Alister Duran, and two scroll jars. Return immediately to Silentii headquarters in Rome.

At 8:30 a.m., the Silentii jet touched down at Naples International Airport and taxied to the private jet terminal. Within minutes, Corvus was in a black Alfa Romeo on the Autostrada del Sole heading for the winding roads in the cliffs above Positano. The map on the GPS showed the way to Luca's villa, thirty-five miles ahead. He would arrive at the villa at 9:15 a.m.

He was thinking of Alister and Susan as his hands gripped the wheel tighter than necessary. "They won't get away this time," he mused quietly under his breath.

But he was wrong again. Six hours earlier, on this same highway, he would have passes Alister and Susan going the other way.

CHAPTER THIRTY-ONE

Alister kept his hands steady on the wheel as the Alfa Romeo accelerated to 130 km/h. The dark ribbon of the A1, the Autostrada del Sole, stretched ahead, quiet and slick from recent rain. It was 2:47 a.m. Behind them—wedged between suitcases in the back seat—sat the unmarked Amazon shipping box. Inside, about the size of two large rolling pins and wrapped in soft cotton T-shirts, were the two ancient, priceless, papyrus scrolls.

Susan glanced over her shoulder for the third time in ten minutes.

"We're not being followed," Alister said gently. "I've been checking the mirrors every minute since we left Amalfi. We made it through all the back roads."

"You're sure Luca didn't hear us leave?"

"I'm sure. The windows were closed. His study light didn't come on when we drove off. And I left the safe looking untouched."

Susan turned to him. "Looking untouched? What do you mean?"

"I just took the scrolls, not the jars," he said. "I found copier paper in the cabinet under his printer. Took about a dozen sheets—same size and weight as the scrolls—wrapped them in the original linen, put them back in the jars, and resealed the tops."

She exhaled, part shocked, part impressed.

"He won't suspect I opened the safe. So when he opens it, he'll see the seemingly untouched jars. He'll think we panicked and ran, leaving the scrolls behind."

Susan leaned her head back against the seat. "We did panic."

He nodded. "Yeah. But we took the scrolls."

They drove in silence for several miles. The autostrada at this hour was a wide, empty artery leading north.

"The problem is," Alister said softly, almost to himself, "we need someone who can read Aramaic. I only have basic skills. We need someone fluent. Probably in New York."

Susan was quiet, thinking. Then she said, "I think my brother Thomas can help. I'm sure he still has university contacts from his years with the Jesuits. I can ask if he can help us find someone fluent in ancient Aramaic. Someone we could trust. Thomas lives in New Jersey and commutes to his office in New York City when he's not traveling to client locations."

"But the problem remains… how are we going to get to New York when they'll be watching everything?" she said, frustrated. "Airports, tickets, passport control—every manifest, every border, every road."

"You're right," Alister said with a bounce in his voice. Given their situation, he sounded far too confident.

"That's why we're not flying from here."

She turned to him. "From where then?"

He glanced sideways, eyes dark and mischievous. "Sardinia."

She blinked. "What?"

"We're going to drive to the ferry port at Civitavecchia. It's about four hours north of here, just above Rome. We'll board a ferry for Olbia—the main port in Sardinia. Then…" He paused. "I'll call someone."

"Someone… who?"

"Remember I told you my father ran a global mining business? From a young age, I met many of his colleagues and the executives who ran his companies. One of them was just a few years older than me and became a close family friend—Leonardo Rossi. Leo. He's now CEO of Terra Nuova Resources, a major strategic minerals company based in Sardinia. We've stayed in touch. He'll remember me—and more importantly, my father."

He paused, shifting gears as the road curved.

"My father," he said quietly, "was a mining kingmaker. Harrison Duran. He didn't just build companies—he reshaped careers. Leo was one of his protégés. Dad is probably the reason Leo is where he is today."

Susan frowned. "And you think he'll help us escape?"

Alister nodded. "If he's still the Leo I knew—he will. Just last week, I read that his company just took delivery of a new jet, the Bombardier Global 8000. It's quite an impressive aircraft. They use it mostly for flying into remote mining locations in mountainous regions. But it also flies to New York often. And if we can reach him this morning, there's a chance we can be on one of those flights. Quietly. Legally."

Susan didn't respond right away. "Why is he mining in Sardinia? I thought the industry there collapsed decades ago."

Alister smiled faintly. "That's why Leo went there. While others abandoned Italian mining in the '90s, he did the opposite. He saw the future—not sulfur and lead, but lithium, fluorite, rare earths… essential for modern tech. He was ahead of his time. Now he's leading the charge—reclaiming old mines, reprocessing waste, building sustainable operations."

He glanced over.

"You'd love it, Susan. The geology, the history. Sardinia was the Roman Empire's third-largest metal producer. Lead, silver, zinc. Then the sulfur rush in Sicily—nineteenth-century hellholes, 90% of the world's sulfur at one point. Brutal work. But those resources shaped empires."

"And now?" Susan said.

"Now, Leo's rebuilding it. With EU backing, private equity from the States, and circular economy science. It's not extraction anymore—it's transformation. That's what makes his strategy for Terra Nuova different."

She looked out as dawn began to grey the sky. "And your friend Leo… he'll let us on his plane?"

"We're old family friends. That counts in the world my father built. And that'll be enough."

They reached Civitavecchia at 7:15 a.m. The sun was rising, and the port was waking. But Alister didn't drive into the dock parking area. Instead, he parked in a remote area two streets away from the dock, retrieved a pair of pliers from the glove box, and removed the Peugeot's license plates and put them in his backpack. He left the keys in the ignition.

As they walked to the ferry dock, Susan, who was quietly observing all of this, finally said, "What was that all about?".

"It's Luca's car," Alister answered. " If we abandon it in the parking area, within a few days, the police will identify it and Silentii will know we took a ferry from here…and they would soon figure out the rest. But on a side street, unlocked with the keys still inside, it's likely to be stolen…and wrecked or disposed of without a trace. And I will drop the licence plates overboard after we are on the ferry."

Yet again, Susan was surprised, but even more impressed.

They walked to the dock, backpacks over their shoulders and an unmarked Amazon box under Alistar's arm. Gulls wheeled overhead. The ferry for Sardinia would leave at 9 a.m. They had a long day ahead, so they had time now for breakfast at a café. A latte and a Cornetto, the Italian version of a croissant, were fast and easy options.

Their tickets, purchased in cash, had been easy enough to obtain. It was now 8:30. The Olbia ferry would board in ten minutes. Alsiter had been hesitating, but before boarding, it was time to call Leo. They needed to confirm that Leo would be there.

Standing by the terminal railing, Alister held his breath and dialed the number he'd found buried in his encrypted address book. "I hope he's there," he said to Susan. "We don't have a plan B."

"Leonardo Rossi," came the answer.

"Leo," Alister exhaled. "It's me. Alister Duran."

A pause. Then a familiar voice, bright with surprise.

"Well, well. I thought I recognized that American accent. Great to hear from you. What's going on, my friend?"

"I'm in Italy. I need a favor."

Another pause. "You're here?"

"I'm trying to get out. Safely. With a colleague. Can we talk in person?"

"I'm in Sardinia. Where are you?"

"We're ready to board the next ferry from Civitavecchia. It arrives in about six hours."

Leo hesitated. Then: "I'll have someone meet you at Olbia."

Their ferry departed the dock on time at 9 am, sailing out into the Tyrrhenian Sea headed for Sardinia. At that same moment —250 miles north at Luca's villa that overlooked that same Tyrrhenian Sea —Corvus had just arrived, expecting to find Susan and Alister. He couldn't know that, instead, they stood at the bow of a ferry, wind tangling their hair. And that the Peugeot's license plates that Silentii would soon be searching for were now sinking to the sea bottom, thirty meters below.

Six hours later, at 2:48 p.m., as the ferry cut through brilliant blue-green water, the jagged silhouette of Sardinia's cliffs emerged from the afternoon sea mist. As they approached the island, the air grew warm and fragrant with a breeze hinting of salt and distant pine. It seemed to stir the spirits of the vacationing passengers, who began moving to the bow. Families with boisterous children, couples seeking romantic escapes, and groups of friends eager for adventure lined the railings, their chatter a cheerful counterpoint to the rhythmic thrum of the engines.

Sardinia seemed to be a combination of wealthy vacation beach resorts and untouched wilderness. The resorts stretched for miles in both directions along the pristine shoreline—luxury villas with sparkling pools and private beaches. Beyond the shore rose a lush, rugged, timeless landscape. It was the heart of the island. Cork oak forests, granite mountains, and secluded villages, a vast expanse of untamed interior, far removed from the commercial shores.

The harbor unfolded: fishing boats, whitewashed buildings, small cranes swinging lazily.

Susan turned to Alister and squinted. "Is this…?"

"Olbia," Alister said. "Sardinia's commercial gateway. Just about everything to and from the island passes through here. And those hills beyond—that's Leo's mining empire. The Iglesiente region."

For now, Alister thought, it was perfect. A place no one would think to look.

At the dock, Terra Nuova's black SUV was waiting.

After two hours on winding cliffside roads, they arrived at Terra Nuova Headquarters. As they entered the glass-and-stone atrium, their nerves were tight. This plan had to work.

A receptionist looked up, nodded, and pressed a button.

"Dr. Duran. Dr. Hale. Signor Rossi is expecting you."

The hum of servers and filtered air pulsed as they were led through silent corridors.

And then, the door opened.

"Alister," said a deep, commanding voice.

Leonardo Rossi stood against the floor-to-ceiling windows, silver hair haloed by sunlight and the jagged Iglesiente skyline. His face had aged—but not the eyes.

"Every time we meet, you look more like your father," he said, gripping Alister's hand. "You've inherited more than you know."

Alister introduced Susan. Leo shook her hand warmly, but his gaze had already sharpened.

"Tell me," he said, "what brings you here so urgently?"

CHAPTER THIRTY-TWO

The villa was quiet.

No noise or footsteps were coming from the guest bedrooms.. After last night's tense and lengthy discussion of the scroll's contents, Luca Severin assumed Alister and Susan had collapsed for a much-needed rest and were still asleep in their rooms.

He stood alone in the tiled foyer, sipping a lukewarm espresso. His linen shirt was buttoned and tucked, but the nerves beneath it wouldn't settle. The call from Cardinal Vallente had come less than three hours earlier—brief and unambiguous. It had rattled him.

"Corvus will collect you at 0900. You, the scrolls, and the fugitives. You will all return to Rome. Headquarters will decide their fate."

No discussion. No opportunity to protest. Luca had simply replied, "Understood," and hung up.

It had never occurred to him that Susan and Alister might have left the villa. They were fugitives with nowhere to go. All was secure. The scrolls were locked behind steel and stone. The guests were asleep.

At 8:57 a.m., the roar of an engine and the crunch of tires on the gravel driveway shattered the calm.

By the time Corvus descended the final bend, the Alfa Romeo was howling. It shot through the gate like a missile and skidded into the courtyard, tires slicing white dust into the air. Luca winced as stones ricocheted off the walls.

The car hadn't fully stopped before the door flew open. Corvus emerged in all black—tactical boots, close-cropped white hair, jaw locked. His pistol was holstered but visible. A matte earpiece pulsed blue in his ear.

"We're running late. I need to move quickly," he said flatly, striding past Luca without a glance or handshake.

Luca blinked. *He's exactly on time.*

"Welcome to Villa Severin," he said dryly. "You must be Corvus."

"I'm here for the prisoners and the scrolls," Corvus snapped, scanning the foyer like a soldier clearing a kill zone. "Where are they?"

"Asleep. In their guestrooms," Luca replied coolly. "They've had a difficult few days. I didn't think it wise to wake them."

Corvus didn't answer. He turned and marched up the central staircase, boots pounding the ancient wood. Luca followed, irritation building with every step. *I've worked with five Cardinals. Cleaned up Vatican messes on three continents. And now I'm taking orders from this psychotic Boy Scout?*

"Which rooms?" Corvus barked.

"Alister took the west room," Luca said, gesturing down the hall.

Corvus moved like a predator. Without hesitation, he kicked open the door—gun drawn, arms steady.

Empty. But the bed had been slept in. Pillows askew. Curtains drawn. Window latched.

Corvus spun. "Susan?"

Luca, equally surprised, pointed to the next door. Another kick.

Same result. The bed was slept in, but the room was also empty. No suitcase. No shoes. No sign of recent use. The bathroom was dry. Towels folded. Silent.

"They must be hiding somewhere," Corvus growled.

He shoved past Luca, storming through the hall, flinging open closets, scanning corners. He tore open the linen cabinet, then thundered down the stairs. Luca followed, heart now pounding.

"Where's the car?" Corvus snapped.

"In the garage," Luca said automatically.

But when they stepped inside, the garage was open—and empty.

"They've gone," Luca said, voice tight. "But I don't understand—"

Corvus's face hardened. "How many cars do you own? What kind?"

"Only the one. A black Peugeot." He reached into his wallet and handed Corvus the registration card.

Corvus pulled out his secure phone, stepped away, and spoke quietly into the encrypted line.

"Vallente Protocol Seven. Tier-two alert on a black Peugeot, Italian plates—SCO-1437. Primary suspects are Susan Hale and Alister Duran. Likely exited Salerno province within the last six hours. Possibly armed."

He hung up and took a deep breath.

"Let's get the scrolls."

They moved to the study. Luca removed the framed painting that covered the safe, inserted the key, and entered the code—OS7777. With a smooth hydraulic hiss, the steel door opened.

Two scroll jars stood where he had left them. Lids sealed, wrapped in ancient linen. Undisturbed.

Corvus dialed again—this time, the cardinal himself.

A minute passed. Then the secure channel clicked open.

Corvus spoke three clipped sentences. Then stood still, listening.

Luca couldn't hear the voice on the other end, but he saw its effect. Corvus's jaw tightened. His eyes narrowed. His thumb tapped once against his thigh.

Then came the final word:

"Yes, Eminence. Understood."

Corvus turned and snapped the phone shut.

"We're leaving. Now. Bring the scrolls."

"Where?" Luca asked.

Corvus opened the front door.

"To Rome."

In Vatican City, twenty minutes later, Cardinal Vittorio Vallente sat alone in Silentii's subterranean library beneath the Apostolic Palace. The line had gone dead. He hadn't moved since.

The ancient shelves around him stood like witnesses—volumes of canon law, centuries of doctrine, the quiet burden of power. A tarnished crucifix hung above the hearth, its corpus darkened by smoke and time.

The Holy Father, his oldest and dearest friend, was on his deathbed.

Vallente had visited him the night before. A faint blessing. A trembling hand on his sleeve. The Pope had recognized him—barely—and whispered something about trust.

And now, this. Another failure.

The fugitives had escaped again. They were more resourceful than he'd allowed for. More connected. The press. The universities. Research networks. The scrolls may be recovered, yes—but they already knew what was inside.

Vallente clenched his jaw.

They had to be found.

He could not risk a scandal—especially not now, with the papal seat about to fall vacant. The next conclave loomed. And rumors swirled of an American cardinal being groomed—someone with financial savvy, but no loyalty to the old ways. No respect for *Silentii*. No knowledge of the invisible scaffolding that had preserved orthodoxy for over a thousand years.

Corvus was a weapon, yes—but even weapons misfired. And Luca? A relic. Sentimental. Weak.

Vallente rose and crossed the chamber. From a lower drawer, he withdrew a narrow black folder, stamped with three embossed sigils: Rome. Jerusalem. Antioch.

Inside were contingency files. Names. Coordinates. Protocol chains. Dormant accounts masked by global aid networks. High-grade forgeries. Sleeper agents.

A single phrase was stamped across the inner cover in deep red:

Orbis Clavium — The Keys of Silence.

It was the last fallback. A doctrine of narrative manipulation and institutional pressure. If the story within those scrolls ever surfaced—truly surfaced—Orbis Clavium would activate.

Not with blood. Not at first. But with control.

It would begin with seeded stories, planted documents, counter-forgeries. Media contacts. Academic pressure. Discreditation.

And if that failed—if containment crumbled—there were other pages in the folder.

Tiered hit lists. Forced conversions. Capture-and-convert protocols for those, such as Susan and Alister, who may still be of use.

Vallente hadn't opened the file in nearly a decade.

He did not want to open it now.

But he let his fingers rest on the seal. Just once. To remind himself it was there.

Then he closed the drawer and stepped back into the shadows.

This was not a moment for prayer.
It was a moment for preparation.
It was a moment for control.

CHAPTER THIRTY-THREE

Leonardo Rossi studied them, arms resting on the carved stone table that doubled as his desk. They sat in silence for a moment. The low hum of air circulation and the distant clicking of office doors gave the CEO's office at Terra Nuova headquarters a suspended calm. Behind him, the Iglesiente hills shimmered in the hot late-afternoon sun—studded with wind turbines and half-restored shafts of Sardinia's mining past.

Susan felt it immediately—this wasn't a man who wasted words. But he wasn't cold, either. His eyes were warm, veiled by the practiced calculation of someone who'd spent decades managing risk.

There was no need to ease into pleasantries. Leo has asked why they were here so urgently. Alister answered his question directly.

"We need to get out of Europe. Fast. Quietly. I think you're the only one who can help."

Leo nodded slowly. "And what are you running from?"

Alister didn't answer.

Leo waved a hand. "Don't worry. I'm not asking for details. I know you well enough to know it's not about gold or greed. You've always been a researcher at heart—digging into hidden truths. I suppose Dr. Hale is the same."

He leaned forward.

"Let me guess—you uncovered something someone wants for themselves. Or wants to keep buried."

Susan met his eyes. "Exactly."

Leo's expression remained serious. "Loyalty matters to me. And it was one of your father's hallmarks. He once pulled me out of a near-disaster in Montenegro. I've never forgotten. But understand—Terra Nuova is under scrutiny. We're sitting on Europe's most valuable remaining rare earth deposits. Everyone's watching—governments, investors, even competitors posing as regulators."

He paused.

"Whatever you've uncovered, it better not drag this company into a storm. I'll help you get back to the States. But if anything threatens this operation…"

The silence finished the sentence.

Susan met his gaze. "We're not bringing a storm, Leo. We're escaping one. It has nothing to do with mining or minerals. Just early first-century historical artifacts. Critically important, but not to anyone in your business. "

That, finally, seemed to satisfy him.

Leo sat back, fingers steepled. "Our plane leaves from Cagliari Elmas tomorrow night for a joint venture planning meeting in New York. A group of my top executives from different divisions of Terra Nuova are working on he deal. I'll have you on it."

Relief swept through Susan. Alister exhaled.

"But," Leo added, "once you're on that plane, you work for me."

Alister blinked. "What do you mean?"

"You will be identified as geological consultants—rare earth specialists—part of my joint venture due diligence team. Your credentials make it plausible…you work for me at headquarters."

Leo paused for several seconds and then added with a quiet, confidential voice, " One more thing I need to mention about the flight you will be joining. You may have read in recent press about China being the world's leading producer of rare-earth minerals. But what you probably haven't read is that they also produce more than 90 percent of the world's supply of rare-earth magnets. These magnets are an essential part of the technology in everything from cars to smartphones to missile systems. China has begun using its virtual monopoly as a stranglehold on Western technology giants, forcing the United States and the EU to the negotiating table for favorable trade talks. However, the deal we are negotiating with NQ Materials in Texas will include billions of dollars invested by the US Pentagon and NATO, and will become the largest source of rare-earth minerals and magnets in the Western Hemisphere. In just three years, it will leapfrog us ahead of China.

However, if they discover what we are planning, they will do anything to stop us. And I mean anything. We are certain that they have hacked passport control databases in both the EU and the United States to identify those involved in this deal, as well as to track our travel history. Therefore, when we fly internationally for meetings related to the joint venture, our countries have agreed to issue anonymous passports to our executives and not record the Terra Nuova jet in flight databases. For all the world, our flights and everyone on them are ghosts."

"And by the way, " Alister added, " speaking of the trip to New York, I told Susan about your new jet we'll be flying on. The Bombardier Global 8000. I read about it in the Journal two weeks ago, and I thought she would enjoy hearing about it…from you."

Leo smiled, a note of pride in his voice. "Susan, before I begin, let me clear up the usual misunderstanding. Everyone fixates on the price—over eighty million dollars—and assumes it's an indulgence. It isn't. For a mining company like ours, it's a business weapon, a strategic necessity. Competition today is brutal. Problems need to be solved on-site, fast. The G8000 can fly 8,000 miles nonstop at nearly the speed of sound. At just under 105,000 pounds, with twin GE Passport engines, it cruises in ultra-smooth air at 51,000 feet, far above commercial traffic, and can slip into Terra Nuova's mining runways as short as 2,200 feet, where no other jet aircraft can land. Inside, it seats more than twenty executives and engineers across four zones for work, meetings, and rest—with beds and even a shower, so they arrive clear-headed after fifteen hours in the air. Compared to that, your six-hour hop to New York will feel like nothing.

He pressed a button on his desk. When Francesca's voice answered, he said, "Make arrangements to issue two new US Passports and two temporary ID profiles under new names for Dr. Alister Duran, Dr. Susan Hale. Consultants. Add them to tomorrow night's flight manifest to Teterboro."

Alister almost couldn't control a broad smile. Silentii will think we are still in Europe. That was even better than he expected. Teterboro Airport is also a quiet, discreet destination used by most private and corporate aircraft traveling to New York City. It avoids the tourist crowds and the advanced facial recognition surveillance systems commonly found at airports like JFK and Newark. And it's only 12 miles from Midtown Manhattan. Perfect.

"Yes, Signor Rossi."

Leo turned back. "You'll also receive company-issued burner phones and briefing packets tonight. Read enough to pass general conversations on the plane."

Alister nodded. "Thank you. Truly."

Leo was quiet, thinking, and then said cautiously, " I don't want to know what you've discovered here, or whom you are running from, but if, for some unexpected reason, going to New York doesn't solve your problems, the plane returns with our team in about two weeks. You are now part of our team, and if necessary, you can be on that return flight. Just call my office here, and Francesca will give you the return flight details."

Alister said, " Thanks, Leo. But I don't think we will need that. You've already done more than we could have hoped for." Alister didn't know it yet, but he was wrong…in two weeks, they would be on the return flight.

He stood. "Francesca will show you to our photo studio, where they will take passport pictures. Then you'll sleep in the secure guest suites here on the compound. Shielded. No signals. No eyes. A driver will take you to the jet tomorrow evening. He will have your new passports. Until then—lie low. This island forgets easily…but it also remembers who it shelters."

He offered his hand to Susan, then to Alister. "Welcome to Terra Nuova."

As they walked to the guest suites, Susan said, "As soon as it's 6 a.m. in New Jersey, I'll call Thomas. If he agrees—and I think he will—he can pick us up at Teterboro when we arrive."

CHAPTER THIRTY-FOUR

Thomas Hale sat at a small round table inside the café at Teterboro Airport, nursing a too-hot coffee in a biodegradable cup. The arrivals board flickered above him in muted LED green, listing corporate jet landings with the cold precision of a spreadsheet.

But the Terra Nuova flight his sister had mentioned on her call wasn't listed. Not at all.

He frowned and took another sip. Susan had been specific—Terra Nuova Resources, departing Cagliari, arriving around 8:20 a.m. at Teterboro.

He flagged down a security officer passing near the café and gestured toward the screen. "Quick question. Any chance that the Terra Nuova jet from Sardinia is still en route? It's not showing on the board."

The man squinted, then shrugged. "Probably a software hiccup. We get ghost glitches on charters sometimes—especially international. But hold on."

He pulled a clipboard from a podium nearby and flipped through the printed manifest. "Yeah, here it is. Bombardier G8000 inbound from Elmas. Arrived six minutes ago. Hangar 4. Should be at the gate now."

Thomas nodded, but his questions lingered. He was a seasoned traveler. Paper manifest and digital board out of sync? That almost never happened.

He glanced at his watch. 8:29 a.m. Still on time.

He lived just ten miles away in Ridgewood, but commuter traffic on Route 17 had been unforgiving that morning—nearly an hour from his driveway to the terminal. When not on a field assignment for Covenant Partners International, his usual commute was even worse—train from Ridgewood to Hoboken, transfer at Secaucus, then Penn Station, and finally a cab to CPI's Park Avenue office in New York. A daily battle with movement.

After a long career in the field with UNESCO, Thomas was recruited by Covenant Partners International (CPI), a nonprofit organization formed in the 1990s that focused on preserving religious artifacts at archaeological sites in Turkey, Jordan, and Syria, which were being plundered by illicit artifact trafficking. Thomas had been with them for three years. They had worked with and been impressed by Thomas during their partnership with Unesco, where they had seen him co-ordinate the post-earthquake restoration of the St. Pierre Church in Antakya and advise on the Antioch Renaissance Initiative.

The CPI was a major eye-opener for Thomas, as he witnessed a life-style of wealth that was previously unavailable to him, yet was not incompatible with his religious beliefs. He saw this firsthand with the board members and executives who led CPI, as well as with the finan-cial package that accompanied his employment.

His workload was large, but today, family mattered more. So, after Su-san's early morning call yesterday, Thomas had cleared his schedule for today and took a day off. No questions.

As he stirred his coffee and watched the glass doors, the scent of the coffee and the warmth of the air pulled up a memory from long ago. She was eleven, packing for their family trip to Cape Cod. As usual, she'd filled her bag with notebooks, colored pencils, and a half-doz-en stuffed animals—but no socks, no toothbrush, and no underwear. Thomas, three years older, noticed and quietly added the essentials that night. When she found out, she was furious. But she needed his help. She knew it. And so did he. From the urgency in her voice last night, nothing had changed much.

He smiled faintly, but his mind wandered further back, to the years he spent becoming a Jesuit. Few people knew any about the Jesuits, except for their name. It wasn't just another sect, another seminary. Becoming a Jesuit was a distinct kind of Catholic commitment—longer, deeper, and different. After university, he had entered the novitiate, a two-year immersion in discernment, silence, and service. Then came philosophy studies, a pastoral assignment, theology training, and finally, ordination. He took four vows—poverty, chastity, obedience, and a special vow of obedience to the Pope, particularly in matters of foreign mission. Jesuits weren't parish priests. They were scholars, diplomats, teachers, and scientists—missionaries of mind and soul. And for years, it had been enough. Until…the glass doors slid open, breaking his train of thought

It was 8:34, and there they were.

No announcement. No crowds. Just a sudden presence: Susan and a man Thomas assumed was Alister Duran, walking calmly through the arrival terminal. No sign that anything was out of the ordinary.

Susan tried to appear composed as she introduced Alister, but Thomas saw it instantly—in her eyes. And in the way Alister's body never fully relaxed.

Something was very wrong.

"There was no record of your flight," Thomas said as they walked toward the short-term parking lot. "It's like your plane never existed. How is that possible?"

Alister glanced at Thomas as they unlocked the car doors and entered. "That wasn't accidental. We'll tell you about that later."

Susan sat in the front, her bag in her lap. The jet-black Mercedes-AMG S63E moved like a shadow through the thinning commuter traffic, its 791-horsepower V8 engine growling, but almost unheard in the quiet of the padded interior beneath its polished frame.

"This car," she said, smiling faintly, "is a little more than I expected from a man who left the Jesuits with a one-foot box of books and a vow—no, a belief—in poverty."

Thomas grinned without turning. "Everything changes. Sometimes even the beliefs that once defined your life."

Susan glanced at Alister, who raised an eyebrow. They didn't say it aloud, but the irony hung between them.

Thomas's house sat on a quiet hill on the west side of Ridgewood—a classic 1950s two-story brick colonial with white trim, black shutters, and a slate-gray roof. Symmetrical windows framed by boxwood hedges. A flagstone path led from the wide circular driveway to a broad front porch. The lawn was professionally manicured, the grass freshly mowed, and the flower beds at full bloom with June roses, lavender, and pale yellow coreopsis. An American interpretation of an old-world order.

On crisp winter mornings, you could see all the way to Manhattan—the new Trade Center buildings and the glass towers along Billionaires' Row sharp against the sky. But on this misty late spring morning, only a faint silhouette of the skyline shimmered on the horizon.

The three of them sat in comfortable chairs on the front patio. It was cool in the shadow of the house, but warmth was rising steadily with the sun. Behind them, trees leaned unevenly over a crumbling stone wall, where moss and wild ivy competed for ground. The air smelled of cut grass and honeysuckle.

Thomas sat with one leg crossed over the other, sleeves rolled, collar open, hands still on the table. His eyes—always kind, always skeptical—were fixed on his sister.

Susan exhaled. "Thomas, we have a problem. A big problem. Something I can't share with anyone else. Not friends. Not colleagues. Not even people I've trusted for years. We didn't come for a favor. We came because you're the only person we know who might understand what this is."

As she spoke, Thomas caught a glimpse of the old Susan—the obsessive detail-keeper, the relentless digger. But this wasn't a childhood crisis. This was different. And he was about to find out just how different.

Over the next thirty minutes, Susan and Alister told him everything.

A clean, efficient account. The scrolls buried in the terrace at St Cyr. Jesus's escape from Jerusalem with Mary and his mother. His years in Gaul. His family and children. His evolving ministry, no longer focused on death but on resurrection. His Roman benefactor, Lucius Aurelius Barrius. His meeting with Paul—and the decision to assume Paul's identity. The scrolls. Silentii. The murder of his doorman. Luca…the betrayal. The escape. Everything.

Thomas didn't interrupt. His Jesuit discipline held.

But as their story unfolded, his face, at first a mask revealing nothing, slowly began to change. At the end, Thomas finally leaned back and turned toward the trees. His initial disbelief was beginning to show cracks. And his belief was starting to surface, rattling his calm composure.

"That flight," he said quietly. "No record. No broadcast. No announcement. But it arrived…like the security guy said…a ghost glitch. How was that possible?"

He paused.

"And Silentii… I remember hearing rumors. Thought it was just internet drama—Vatican ghost stories for the postmodern age." He paused for a long moment, then said, "But seven years at UNESCO and CPI taught me something important: powerful change always creates powerful enemies. And not all of them are on government lists."

No one spoke.

Until this point, Susan and Alister had not told Thomas that they had the scrolls with them. The used and tattered Amazon box with them looked like it contained some random travel supplies. They didn't want to show the scrolls until they were sure that Thomas would be willing to help. Now that they were comfortable with Thomas's response, they looked at each other with a quiet nod. Alister opened the Amazon box at his feet and slowly removed two scrolls, wrapped in soft cotton T-shirts. He placed them on the table with reverence. Then, folded parchment tied with a thin leather cord—the letters from Antioch.

Thomas didn't move.

He just stared.

The color drained from his face.

"Are these what you were just talking about? You have them? Here?" he said softly.

Susan nodded. "And they're not copies. Not apocryphal. Not Gnostic. These are the originals. Eyewitness accounts from Jesus and Mary, in their own hands, from two thousand years ago."

Alister leaned in. "And these are just the first two. We believe more are hidden—possibly in Antioch. We know what was in the scrolls. Luca translated them before we realized he was part of Silentii. But the letters…those haven't been read by anyone."

Thomas ran a hand down his face slowly, like a man absorbing a blow.

"Do you realize how dangerous this is?"

Thomas didn't continue his thought right away. He leaned forward, elbows on the table, eyes drifting toward the window as memories stirred—years with the Jesuits, years spent preparing for questions meant to shake the foundations of belief. Their mission had always been to carry Christianity and the word of God to the far corners of the world. But what he'd just heard was more unsettling than anything he'd faced in all those places.

"This isn't just dangerous because it might be true," he said at last. "It's dangerous because it pulls a thread tied to everything else."

He turned back to Susan, his expression sharper now. "You know that phrase—'Judeo-Christian values'? People toss it around like a bumper sticker. But it's not. It's an architecture. And the Church—capital C— built the scaffolding for almost everything we think of as moral order. Not just for believers. For everyone."

"Christian orthodoxy shaped the world's spine," he continued. "Reli- gious codes became moral codes. Those became behavioral norms—

what's right, what's shameful, what's forbidden. From there came laws. And from those laws, punishments. Legal codes, penal codes, entire systems of justice—all rooted in what the Church said God wanted. And layered on top of it all, the saints—echoes of pagan gods—are assigned to guide us, protect us, inhabit our daily lives."

He paused. "And then there's sex. That's the part the Church feared most—Jesus and Mary, married with children. If Jesus could leave off-spring on earth, even if they were adopted they, might wield more power than the clergy. So they spent centuries controlling that narrative, inserting themselves into the most private space between two people, and claiming it for God. Just think about it…since God is omnipotent, then he could certainly allow his son on earth to have children.

They went even further to secure their grip on power. They defined who could love whom. Who could lead. Who could be pure. To make sure only men could climb the ladder to God, they locked women out of the clergy and kept the divine gate in the hands of men and the Church. Not the family, not the feminine, just them."

Thomas ran a hand through his hair. His voice dropped, quiet but steady.

"Do you see? If what's on this scroll spreads, it won't be the faithful who collapse. It'll be everyone around them. The cynics. The atheists. The angry. The disillusioned. The young. They'll seize it like a weapon. And the ones already questioning—already half out the door—this will shove them the rest of the way."

He drew a breath, then softened.

"But here's the part that stays with me, Susan. Life is governed almost entirely by what we can't see or touch. We pretend to live in an age of proof. 'Show me the science,' we say. And yet—time, gravity, love, loyalty, grief, prayer, meditation, the feeling of a child's hand in yours, the flash of enlightenment—none of it fits in a vial or under a microscope. But those are the things that structure our lives."

He looked at her again, eyes calmer now, almost tender.

"We are defined more by what we can never prove than by what we can. That's not a flaw—it's a feature. And whatever these scrolls contain, we'd better approach them with that in mind."

Susan met his gaze. "That's why we need you."

"How can I help?"

Alister said, "Someone who is fluent in Ancient Aramaic. Galilean dialect. Someone you trust."

Thomas was quiet. The shadows on the patio stretched like fingers across the stone.

"I know a man," he said finally. "Close friend. Professor Emeritus from Columbia's Middle East Studies department. Brilliant linguist. Lives right here in Ridgewood, actually. After I left UNESCO, I visited him for a weekend—I fell in love with the neighborhood, bought this house, and never left."

He smiled briefly. "Retired last year after a mild stroke. But his mind is still sharp. Used to date a Chaldean priest's daughter. Speaks Aramaic like it's still the imperial tongue."

Susan gave a soft, tired smile. "And he's discreet?"

Thomas nodded. "As a grave."

But after the experience with Luca—someone he'd trusted like family—Alister said nothing. Trust, for him, would take more than words.

CHAPTER THIRTY-FIVE

The traffic north from the Amalfi Coast was a slow, grinding purgatory. A drive that should've taken just over three hours was creeping toward five, bogged down by late-summer congestion and the Roman bottlenecks that never seemed to move.

Corvus gripped the wheel of the armored black Audi so tightly his knuckles had gone white. He hadn't said a word since they left the villa. The silence wasn't relief—it was diagnostic. He was unraveling.

He wove between lanes with surgical aggression, tailgating German-plated minivans, laying on the horn at distracted tourists in rental cars. His lips were pressed into a pale, rigid line.

Luca sat beside him, hands locked on the armrest, watching the blur of highway and wondering if he should have seen this coming. Corvus wasn't angry—he was afraid. And truth be told, Luca was, too.

This wasn't how it was supposed to unfold.

Corvus's first mission—intended as a low-risk trial under the Silentii's watchful eye—had detonated into something far larger. And Luca? He'd been confident, even smug. He had complete control of the villa, the guests, and the scrolls. He'd gone to bed certain the mission was secure.

Now, Susan and Alister were gone. And no one knew where.

Corvus barked into the encrypted handset. "Operations. Update. Hale and Duran."

A pause. Then a static-cracked reply: "No movement detected. No hits on road cameras. All known egress points are under observation. Nothing."

Corvus slammed the handset back into its cradle. "Impossible."

Luca said nothing. The worst part was—it was impossible. And yet it had happened.

He still couldn't make sense of it. The night before, they'd talked calmly about the scroll's implications. Nothing in their behavior suggested they felt threatened. Before bed, they even discussed plans for the next morning.

Then they vanished.

Worse, Vallente seemed rattled. Not his usual cold control. He'd dispatched a volatile novice—Corvus—without a proper briefing. Luca, who had served the Order longer than most of them had been alive, was treated like an afterthought.

By late afternoon, the Audi cleared Vatican security and slid into a private access road leading to the Via Triumphalis Necropolis. The vehicle stopped near an unmarked tomb. On its lintel: a faint Aramaic symbol.

The number seven.

They descended through a narrow accessway, its walls damp with centuries of condensation. The corridor opened onto a vaulted chamber flanked by two Silentii guards in matte black uniforms. Retinal scans. Ring authentications. The stone door slid open.

They entered the Chamber of the Silentii.

It had once been the mausoleum of Gaius Varius Marcellus, but centuries ago, it was repurposed as their secret meeting chamber beneath Vatican Hill. The white-veined ceiling soared above them, echoing with the hush of marble and memory. Bronze statues lined the alcoves—saints, martyrs, forgotten gods. At the center: a gleaming slab of polished Numidian marble. The table.

The inner circle of the Silentii sat in silence.

No one rose as Corvus entered. No greetings. No acknowledgments.

Luca followed. Only Cardinal Vallente, seated at the head, gave the slightest nod, indicating a chair beside him. His white-gloved hands were folded like a tomb effigy.

To Vallente's left, the Keeper of the Archives spoke first. Her voice was dry, surgical.

"Report."

The words struck like a slap. Luca bristled but did not respond. The inner circle was unaware of his true rank, nor the closeness of his decades-long alliance with Vallente. That relationship was hidden by design.

He had infiltrated universities, derailed academic careers, and seeded disinformation into archaeological journals. Not for power. But for belief. One truth, one order. If everything became relative, nothing would stand.

He cleared his throat and began.

He reported on Hale and Duran's arrival, the first scroll, their departure to recover the second, and the letters they had brought back. He confessed he had read the scroll, but not the letters. He detailed their disappearance and the failed surveillance.

As he began describing the scroll's contents, Vallente raised a gloved hand.

Luca stopped.

Without looking at anyone else, Vallente said, "Leave us."

Corvus flinched but obeyed. The others followed without a word. The door sealed shut.

Vallente turned to Luca.

"Proceed."

Luca resumed. As he spoke, Vallente's face went still. His color drained.

When Luca finished, Vallente leaned forward. "You hold senior Silentii clearance. But not the highest. There is only one level above yours. Three people currently hold it—the Pope, his chief advisor, and me."

He paused.

"Now you are the fourth."

A beat of silence.

"In the late fourth century, during the formation of the New Testament canon, a gospel surfaced in a remote olive-farming village in Gaul. It was the Gospel of Mary Magdalene, written in her old age. Its contents, if true, contradicted everything…the very foundations of Church history. It was simply too dangerous to continue existing. "

"We destroyed it. Or so the world believes."

Vallente stood, walking slowly around the table.

"A partial copy resurfaced in Cairo in 1896. We delayed its publication by decades. When it finally emerged in 1955, we had already discredited it. We reshaped Mary's reputation—made her a prostitute, erased her authority. Claimed she died alone in a cave near Aix-en-Provence."

He looked at Luca.

"But the original Gospel? We preserved it. Locked in the deepest vault of the Vatican Apostolic Library. Hidden even from the Secret Archives."

Luca's eyes narrowed. "It exists?"

Vallente nodded. "Bound in leather. Guarded by mechanisms only known to the Pope, his lieutenant, and me. And now…you."

He continued, his voice lowering.

"The Vatican Library contains nearly 50 miles of shelving—Renaissance halls, climate-controlled vaults, manuscripts from the fourth century, papal correspondence, Galileo's letters. But beyond all of it—beneath the Cortile del Belvedere—is a chamber seismically reinforced, fireproofed, and secured beyond anything else in the Church."

"In that chamber lies the Magdalene Gospel."

Luca was stunned.

Vallente stepped closer.

"But these scrolls? They are far more dangerous. They are not written in hindsight. They are contemporary. Firsthand. Written by Mary— and by Jesus himself. It is the only direct account we've ever seen. And if it spreads…"

He didn't finish the sentence.

"They must be destroyed."

The words hit like a stone.

"Destroyed?" Luca's voice cracked louder than he intended.

Vallente didn't flinch. "We open the jar. We burn the scrolls. Tonight."

Luca stood frozen.

This wasn't guardianship. This was annihilation. He remembered something a professor had once said during a long walk through the gardens at Cambridge:

"You start believing the cover-ups are for the good of the people. Until you realize they're for the good of the powerful."

He reached into the bag and placed the two ceramic jars on the marble table.

He hesitated.

Then, slowly unsealed the first.

A linen-wrapped scroll emerged. He laid it gently on the stone.

Vallente stepped forward and peeled back the cloth.

The copy paper unfurled like wings—twenty-four pages stretching across the polished surface.

He stared. Gasped.

Then fell silent.

They both sat for a long while, stunned.

At last, Vallente spoke, barely controlling his growing rage, "They've outsmarted us again… our best people, our complete surveillance network. We've been following. Now we need to get ahead. Find out where they are going next and be waiting".

"What these two scrolls tell us," Vallente said slowly, "it's only the beginning. The Magdalene Gospel tells us that there are more scrolls. If Hale and Duran have read these first scrolls, they'll also realize there are more scrolls — and probably learn where to look for them. There must already know…"

He paused in mid-thought, as if remembering something long forgotten, then spoke slowly, "You're fluent in ancient Aramaic. I will clear you for access to the Magdalene Gospel. You'll study it—for clues to where the remaining scrolls are hidden."

Luca nodded, his mind racing.

Vallente continued, his voice lower now. "I'll arrange access. You'll descend into the sealed archives, into the quiet, climate-controlled depths beneath the Cortile del Belvedere. There, you will find a document bound in ancient leather, locked behind fireproof vaults, known only to a handful of men alive."

He fixed Luca with a final stare.

"This is the Church's most dangerous secret. And you will use it to stop what has begun."

Luca said nothing.

But something inside him had already shifted.

CHAPTER THIRTY-SIX

It was late morning, but the heat hadn't yet risen. A soft, cool breeze moved across the stone terrace, carrying hints of rosemary, salt, and jasmine. Luca Severin sat motionless at the edge of his shaded patio, elbows resting on the weathered table, his gaze locked on the sweep of silver-blue clouds casting shadows over the Tyrrhenian Sea. Fishing boats bobbed like commas in a sentence too long to finish. The horizon blurred—sea dissolving into sky.

It was beautiful. God's creation. Perfect.
And it felt like a betrayal.

He hadn't slept. Not really. His bed—carved walnut, hand-restored—might as well have been marble. Sleep had fluttered just beyond reach, as if repelled by the thoughts he couldn't silence. The meeting in Rome had shattered whatever fragile threads still tethered him to the Order.

He sipped his espresso. It had gone cold.

He couldn't erase the image of Vallente's face—not merely furious but pale, drawn, sweating—twisted into something nearly unrecognizable. The Cardinal had insisted on opening the sealed scroll jar himself. And when rolled blank copy paper was suddenly released, fluttering through the air onto the tabletop and floor, his expression wasn't rage. Luca had seen that look before—on the faces of men who knew death was seconds away.

It wasn't anger.
It was fear.
Pure, unadulterated fear.

Vallente had recovered quickly, but not entirely. His voice, when it came, was stripped to its bones—clipped, cold, irreversible.

What Luca couldn't know was that just one day earlier, Cardinal Joseph DeProssimo of Cleveland—just last month elected as Pope Leo XVII by the Conclave—had been fully briefed on the Ordo Silentii. As with every new pontiff, knowledge of the Order was passed on in private. But Leo XVII was not like his predecessor. Educated in the United States, trained in finance and digital systems, he had been selected as a modern reformer —a man capable of addressing both the Church's moral and financial crises—and dismantling its older, expensive machinery.

The Prefect of the Holy See's Directives, Father Carlo Verano, had met with Vallente behind closed doors. The message was clear. While the defense of orthodoxy remained vital, the Holy See didn't believe that an aging, opaque organization like the Ordo Silentii was still the best tool for that mission. His sharpest complaint, Verano said, was their spiraling costs. With barely suppressed anger, he singled out Silentii's newest indulgence—a Gulfstream G800 purchased just the year before for $85 million.

He reminded Vallente that the aircraft, weighing over 103,000 pounds and powered by 36,000 pounds of thrust from twin Rolls-Royce Pearl 700 engines, was more than half the size of a commercial Airbus A320, which could carry over 100 passengers. By contrast, Vallente's extravagant jet had a cabin usually designed for nineteen, but rebuilt to Silentii specifications for no more than eight—complete with hidden compartments and private living quarters. Why, Verano demanded, did he need such raw performance? To cross oceans nonstop at nearly the speed of sound? To allow landing on only 3,100 feet of runway? To fly from Rome to any capital on earth without refueling, in a level of comfort that bordered on obscene? A two-man crew operated the cutting-edge Symmetry Flight Deck, while agents traveled in the lowest-altitude, freshest-air cabin in the industry. Verano all but sneered: Why should men sworn to silence and humility require a machine more suited to billionaires and global empires than to priests?

He concluded the meeting, noting that the Holy See believes new technologies—such as AI surveillance, algorithmic monitoring, and psychological profiling—could achieve better results with greater precision, less liability, and at a fraction of the cost.

Vallente was given six months. Prove the Silentii's value or begin its controlled dismantling.

At first, Vallente left the meeting in a state of fright. But suspicion soon reared its ugly head. Perhaps, with the election of a new Pope, he has become a pawn in a bigger game. And why so much focus on the G800? Was it something visible that could damage his reputation? Or were the Holy See's top officials jealous and wanted to have it for themselves?

With growing rage, he finally concluded, it wasn't about cost at all; it was about power. It always is!

Luca and Vallente had known each other for decades; he knew him well. But when the flutter of copy papers settled onto the meeting table, he recognized something he had never seen before…a deep crack beneath Vallente's mask. The fear wasn't about the missing scrolls. Luca could sense it was Vallente's fear of losing power.

Luca remembered that after telling him to read the Magdalene Gospel in search of clues, Vallente had reconvened the meeting. It was short.

Vallente barked, "I don't care how," his voice echoing through the chamber. "Use every channel. Every asset. Every shadow. *Find them.*"

No one dared speak. Corvus nodded once and disappeared.

It wasn't anger, Luca realized again. It was panic. Vallente didn't just want to erase the scrolls—he *needed* to. It wasn't that their existence threatened the scaffolding on which the modern Church was built. It threatened him and his power.

If the meeting with the Pope's emissary had never happened, Vallente would have ordered the scrolls stored quietly in the Vatican archives—alongside other heretical texts that had been buried, not burned. But now, with his authority in question and his future on the line, he was no longer acting for the Church.

He was acting for himself.

Luca's hands tightened around the espresso cup. He thought again of the scrolls—their weight, the dryness of ancient papyrus, the steady, reverent script in Aramaic. The voice on the page had not been heretical. It had been *human*. Wounded. Wise. Hopeful. Perhaps dangerous—but not in the way Vallente claimed.

This wasn't protection. This was obliteration.

And if they succeeded, they would destroy the only firsthand testimony of Jesus and Mary Magdalene known to exist.

He stared at the sea, his chest rising with something molten and unfamiliar. Not fear. Not regret.

Anger.

He had given the Order everything. His scholarship. His silence. His loyalty.

And now?

Now he wasn't sure they deserved any of it.

A gull screeched overhead. Below, a child laughed from a small patch of beach hidden on the shoreline beneath the cliffs.

Luca reached into the pocket of his linen jacket and pulled out his phone. For a long moment, he just stared at the screen. His reflection stared back in fragments.

He opened the call history. Scrolled. Stopped.

There it was—the number Alister Duran had used to contact him last week. The call that had started everything.

He hadn't deleted it.

He stared at the number for a long time.

Then he tapped "Save."

CHAPTER THIRTY-SEVEN

Their roast chicken dinner was simple, the scent of garlic and lemon hanging in the air. The evening breeze drifted through the open doors of Thomas's Ridgewood dining room, quietly brushing aside the linen curtains. Soft jazz played from a speaker near the window. For the first few minutes, they ate in silence—the kind that signals mutual exhaustion and too many thoughts to count.

Finally, Alister broke the quiet. He looked up from his plate, his voice low but clear.

"We need to talk about the scrolls."

Thomas nodded slightly, as if he'd been waiting. Susan looked up, her brow already furrowed.

Alister continued. "We've been running since Positano. Even before that. One step ahead of that thug with the cropped white hair, the Silentii, and whoever else is watching. We've relied on clever moves and travel routes. But this won't keep the scrolls safe much longer. We need a plan. If something happens to us—if they're taken—then it's all gone, lost forever. We need to store them somewhere. Off-site. Safe. Out of reach."

Thomas wiped his hands on a cloth napkin. "I've been thinking the same thing."

"I was considering something basic to start," Alister said. "A safe deposit box. Maybe in a neutral country. Switzerland. Austria. Even Malta. Somewhere discreet and stable."

"That could work short-term," Thomas said. "But we're not just dealing with burglars or amateurs. These people rewrite history for a living. If they want to erase something, they won't worry about collateral damage. If we put them in a bank vault somewhere, they'll erase the whole bank."

Susan looked between them. "So what can we do?"

Thomas leaned back in his chair and took a slow sip of red wine. "To put it in one sentence: we digitize them and store the data on the blockchain."

Alister and Susan turned and stared at him. He let the thought hang for a beat, then continued, sensing their hesitation.

"I know. You've heard the word 'blockchain' before—usually in stories about crypto crashes, Bitcoin theft, or billionaires buying digital art. But forget all that press garbage. Remember, they treated the internet with the same hype just twenty years ago."

He set down his glass.

"Think of the blockchain as an unbreakable, super-secure record book. Once something is written into it—like a timestamped copy of the scroll—it's there forever. No one can erase or change it. And there's more: only we have the secure codes that permit access to add new information. It's like having a special pen that only authorized hands can use to write in this permanent book.

"That means Silentii can't access, change, delete, or destroy it. And that's exactly what we need."

Alister sat back, arms folded. "Okay. But how does that actually work—in practice?"

"Let me simplify," Thomas said. "We don't just scan the scroll once and put it on a drive. We break it into pieces—frames, really—like zoomed-in sections. Each section gets a digital fingerprint: an image, plus details like ink composition and parchment texture. Those are stored as 'blocks,' each one linked to the next, forming a chain. If someone tries to alter even one frame, the system detects the change immediately."

Susan frowned. "That sounds... intense."

"It is," Thomas said. "But I've done it before. At CPI and during my time with UNESCO. We were dealing with artifact smugglers and forgery rings—people who produced Ottoman manuscripts and papal bulls so authentic they fooled major museums. We stopped them by creating what we called 'digital twins'—exact, high-resolution replicas embedded with forensic data. Even if the physical object was stolen, destroyed, or modified, we had the original digital twin—and could prove it. The digital twin was the insurance policy."

Alister leaned in, intrigued. "How detailed were these twins?"

"We used multispectral photography, captured every fiber and ink bleed, and documented any historical repairs. Then we timestamped and anchored the transaction on the blockchain. Once sealed into the chain, it was impossible to fake or modify."

Susan stared at him. "You did this with sacred manuscripts?"

"Dozens," Thomas said. "And often, we didn't even need heavy protection for the originals. Just documenting their existence securely made them harder to sell on the black market. Destroying or forging copies became pointless—because the digital twin would always remain."

Alister nodded slowly. "So we do that for the scrolls."

"Exactly. We scan them. Map every fold and stain. Layer in historical references—maybe even carbon-date a fiber or two if we're careful. Then we lock that data into the blockchain."

"But," Susan added, "the scrolls are huge. Fifteen feet long. And there are two of them...maybe more later."

"Which is why we don't scan them in one piece," Thomas said. "It'd be technically impossible without a Vatican-grade imaging lab. We'll digitize them in high-resolution overlapping frames. Someday, if we need to, we can stitch them together into full images."

Alister looked around the room. "So, where do we do it? We can't risk sending them anywhere."

"I've got a local option," Thomas said, rising from his chair and taking out his wallet. He removed an edge-worn, wrinkled card and handed it to Susan.

Stillwater Imaging & Archival
East Ridgewood Avenue, Ridgewood, NJ

"She's the real deal. I've worked with her on and off for years," Thomas said. "Clara Ionescu. She was an archival photographer for museums in Bucharest before immigrating to the United States. Now she mostly scans heirlooms and land records for Bergen County families—but she still has professional-grade gear. Zeiss lenses, full-spectrum lighting, calibrated sensors. She knows how to capture texture and depth."

Susan studied the name. "And the content?"

Thomas shrugged. "To the untrained eye, Aramaic looks a lot like ancient Hebrew. No one except a first-century scholar would notice the difference. We tell her it's a research project—early Jewish history in Ridgewood. Maybe a 19th-century Hebrew school or long-lost rabbinic correspondence."

Alister looked at Susan. "It sounds like a good plan."

"And our only option," she said.

Thomas gave a tight nod. "But there's one more layer. The real safeguard."

He waited until both of them were looking at him.

"If we're compromised—if none of us logs in to the blockchain system after sixty days—a second contract activates. A dead man's trigger. It's a high-tech version of what blackmailers used to do in old cop-and-robber movies. Remember? They'd hand off a sealed envelope to a trusted friend with instructions: if anything happens to me, mail this to the press. Instead of the post office, we now use a smart contract linked to our blockchain record."

"A what?" Susan said.

"A smart contract with a countdown. If we go silent, the system assumes we've been killed or captured. It begins distributing the scroll contents automatically—across media networks, academic archives, and social platforms. No one can stop it."

"You're saying," Alister said slowly, "if we disappear, the scrolls go public?"

"Immediately. That's the point," Thomas said. "It's the only thing that stops them. If we vanish, the Silentii lose control of the narrative."

Susan exhaled. "That changes the game."

"It forces them to keep us alive—and guessing. And if they try to force someone to access the files early, it won't work. Final decryption requires either biometric verification or a custom phrase embedded in a pre-recorded video. Without both, nothing unlocks."

There was silence again at the table—heavier now.

"We're not just protecting the scrolls," Thomas said quietly. "We're protecting the future ability to prove they ever existed. They won't be able to repeat what they did with the original Magdalene Gospel—or any of the others. This time it's not just check, it's checkmate."

Alister stared down at his plate, then nodded. "When do we start?"

"I already booked time with Clara," Thomas said. "Tomorrow morning. Early. We'll bring the scrolls. She'll roll them out and digitize them in sections. No names, no records. But one of us should stay behind for security."

Susan looked out the window, where the last blue of dusk was fading into black. "I'll do it. I'll be an admin working for you. Just doing my job. Nothing unusual."

She stood, already planning.

"Then tonight," she said, "I'd better get some sleep."

CHAPTER THIRTY-EIGHT

The diner was already half full when they arrived. A tangle of booths, chrome, and thick accents, it sat just off Route 17—far enough from Ridgewood proper that no one would recognize them, but close enough for a quick return. A waitress with a bun like a cinnamon roll poured coffee before they even asked.

Thomas added cream and sugar with the kind of practiced rhythm that suggested he was buying time.

"I have second thoughts," he said finally.

Alister looked up from the menu. "About what?"

"About involving my old friend, the Professor Emeritus from Columbia's Middle East Studies department."

"You mean to translate the letters?"

Thomas nodded. "Like I said yesterday, he's brilliant—best Galilean linguist I've ever known. Retired now, but still sharp. It would be convenient for us because he lives right here in Ridgewood. And I've worked with him for decades."

"But...?" Alister prompted.

"But if I hand him those letters—even one of them—he'll know what he's reading. And when he does, a letter from Jesus to Mary, he will lose control of his promises to keep it quiet. The heart of a professor will take over, and he will need to tell someone. He associates with many highly connected scholars and researchers. All we would need is a whisper to reach someone at the Vatican or one of their academic proxies. At that moment, he becomes a target, and so do we."

Alister folded his hands. "So what's the alternative?"

Thomas pulled out a folded napkin and began sketching boxes as he talked.

"In the twilight before dawn today, another thought just popped into my head. It's slower, and more complicated—but safer. Through my contacts at CPI, we can gain access to a state-of-the-art AI Aramaic language translation model. They are training the model and searching for material in the Galilean Aramaic dialect. Aramaic material is scarce, and they will be anxious to use the training texts we provide. We will have the digitized letters by this evening. Tonight and tomorrow, we'll read them through, line by line—me and you, together. We sanitize them and then feed the rest into the model."

"We read them, you and me?" Alister raised an eyebrow. "We can barely order lunch in Aramaic."

"We don't need fluency. Just enough to spot the landmines—names, places, dates. Anything specific that would make the letters suspicious or valuable to anyone training the translation AI."

" We strip out every sensitive detail and replace it with generics. Instead of 'Sepphoris,' it says 'that town.' Instead of 'Mary,' it says 'a woman.' It reads like a bad breakup letter with half the nouns blacked out. No real context. No theological flags. Just ink and grammar."

Alister nodded slowly. "So to anyone else, it looks meaningless."

"Meaningless *enough*," Thomas said. "Then I feed the sanitized text into one of the academic AIs we've tested at CPI. The one from Cambridge or the joint Hebrew University program. They're still training their Galilean dialect model—they want sample inputs. I give them two."

He took a sip of coffee. "Short ones. Uninteresting ones."

"And they translate them?" Alister asked.

"They do. Basic output, not perfect, but close enough. We should be able to spot any location references, personal meanings, or geographic cues."

"If anyone at CPI questions it, I say I was testing new tools for future artifact work. That's true enough."

Thomas added, "Without names. Without context. To anyone else, they're just two broken letters from one anonymous villager to another. And besides..."

He paused.

"...no one else is looking for what we're looking for."

A waitress came by and refilled their mugs without a word.

Alister leaned back and looked toward the window at the traffic on Route 17. Somewhere, a few miles down that road, Susan was sitting in a quiet imaging lab, watching history turn into pixels.

CHAPTER THIRTY-NINE

Thomas Hale's home office was lit only by the soft glow of the computer screen. Outside, Ridgewood slept quietly under a moonlit midsummer sky, but the hush inside the house was not calm—it was anxious.

Digitization had taken two days. After careful scanning under high-resolution lenses, advanced lighting, and blockchain tagging, the scrolls were now secure, at least in digital form.

From their time at Luca's villa, they already knew the story.

But what sat on the screen before them tonight was new: two personal letters, translated through the world's most advanced AI linguistic engines—thanks to Thomas's academic contacts.

The results had come in just an hour ago. The translation word count indicated that the first letter was very long, but the second was very brief.

Now, Susan, Alister, and Thomas leaned forward in their chairs, the quiet punctuated only by the soft hum of the desktop fan and the occasional creak of 75-year-old oak floorboards.

Thomas scrolled to the first letter. " It's dated *Antioch, AUC 7971. That would be 797 years since the founding of the city of Rome…or what we call 44 CE today.* It appears that we have successfully sanitized the original we sent to the AI engine. The translation begins, *To you, my beloved.* The rest contains no names or dates. Excellent. And the translation is fascinating. The linguistic markers, the phrasing—this is unmistakably first-century Galilean Aramaic. And the voice…" He looked over his glasses, pausing to catch his breath. "It's Jesus himself. It's hard to believe I am the first person, besides Mary, to read this."

Then, vivid images of Jesus arriving in Antioch all those years ago emerged as he began to tell the story written in the letter.

The Mediterranean sun blazed overhead as the merchant vessel—one of the trading ships owned by Lucius Aurelius Barrius' company, Domus Lucullus et Filius—rounded the final bend of the Orontes River. The harbor of Antioch unfolded before Jesus, and he could feel its presence, the Empire's third-largest city after Rome and Alexandria, a shimmering crown on the eastern edge of Roman control.

Antioch in 44 CE was no outpost—it was a capital in its own right, alive with commerce, movement, and ambition. To a visitor from the 21st century, it would have felt uncannily familiar: gridded, multilingual, constantly under construction, and pulsing with reinvention. In spirit and scale, it echoed New York, Singapore, or Dubai—the great global gateways of a later age.

Calling it a "city" hardly did it justice. Antioch was a strategic hinge between Rome and the Eastern empires. In this central import-export hub, spices from India, glass from Sidon, and scrolls from Alexandria moved along colonnaded boulevards. Traders and scholars spoke in a chorus of Greek, Latin, Syriac, and Aramaic. Its seaport at Seleucia, just eighteen miles downriver, kept the markets busy day and night, fed by caravans and river barges in a constant churn of goods.

Across the Empire, it was known as Golden Antioch—a name that spoke not just to wealth, but to appetite. This was a marketplace of ideas as much as of commodities. Mystery cults and Stoic philosophers, Jewish scribes and Roman magistrates—all found space here. Its population was a blur of classes and origins: retired soldiers, Phoenician merchants, Roman engineers, Nabataean couriers, all moving through the same crowded streets. This was not a city built on tradition. It was built on ambition.

Even the entertainment had its own scale. Just outside the walls, in the famed groves of Daphne, fountains and temples gave way to more indulgent pursuits. The phrase Daphnic morals had already become shorthand for Antioch's reputation, but something deeper was at play—a cultural boldness, a willingness to blend piety and pleasure, ritual and risk. It was this restless, layered spirit that made Antioch fertile ground.

Jesus could feel it as he stood at the bow, gripping the rail; if his message took root here, it could spread along trade routes, across borders, and deep into the Empire's arteries. It was what he dreamed of. He had entered many cities before—Galilean villages, the courts of Jerusalem, the ports of Gaul—but none like this. Antioch had no edge, no center—only motion.

As the ship approached the dock, he could see white limestone walls rise in tiered brilliance from the river's banks. Eight hundred thousand people were pressed within those walls, more than ten times the size of Jerusalem. From the harbor, the city climbed the slopes of Mount Silpius in layers of red-tiled roofs, catching the sun like rubies in marble. It felt alive. Breathing. The perfect place to reignite his mission.

Palm trees lined the port, their fan-shaped leaves stirring in the May breeze. The air carried cumin, sea brine, and smoke. Traders shouted. Amphorae clinked. Camels groaned. Sailors cursed. Commerce never stopped.

His ship, the Pax Antiochia, docked between Egyptian grain ships and Greek transports. Longshoremen barked orders in Greek, Latin, and Aramaic as cranes swung cargo from hold to wharf—wool from Sardinia, ginger from the Indus, boxes marked with unknown scripts. An Arabian caravan master cursed his camels as they slipped on the planks.

Jesus stepped down the gangplank onto the sunbaked quay, knees unsteady from two months at sea. A harbor clerk glanced at his papers—a letter from Lucius Barrius identifying him as Paulus of Tarsus, merchant and scribe. The man barely looked up. Tarsus was a provincial backwater to him. The name Paulus raised no flags.

As he walked from the quay, the city swallowed him whole.

He moved with the crowd toward the cardo maximus, the great colonnaded road that ran through the city like a spine. Four deep marble columns shaded a covered walkway. A narrow water channel ran down the center, draining to the river.

No one noticed him. He expected that. The apostles had scattered, abandoning their missionary promises almost six years ago. So, outside of Jerusalem, no one had yet heard his words. And that was fine. He would bring the message of Jesus Christ to Antioch using Paul's name. His intent was not to deceive the people of Antioch, but to avoid the wrong eyes. Soldiers often transferred from Judea, and even though

Jesus was a very common name, there could be officers who might have heard of him, seen him preach…or watched crucifixions on the hill outside Jerusalem nine years ago.

He kept to the shaded edge of the walkway, listening.

Latin. Aramaic. Persian. Egyptian. But mostly Greek—the language of the street. He understood them all. He silently thanked the merchant who had taken him to India as a child and, for 14 years, taught him survival, languages, and customs.

He passed bakers selling barley loaves, girls with baskets of dyed thread, soldiers in polished leather, and perfumers blending oils. He passed shrines to strange gods— bulls, faceless idols, women with wheat. A Roman woman muttered before a statue of Fortuna, rubbing its feet for luck in childbirth.

No single god ruled here. No single truth. Antioch thrived on layers of belief.

It was overwhelming.

He wandered for hours. In the early afternoon, he came to the central market. Pipes and flutes echoed. Smoke drifted through the square. A festival had begun.

Drums. Chanting. Then movement.

Cybele.
The Great Mother of Anatolia. Her cult had survived Rome—and here, it thrived.

Her priests, the Galli, danced in saffron robes. One whipped his back, blood streaking his skin. Others spun, eyes closed, hair flying. Tambourines clashed with the crowd's cries. It was wild. Ecstatic. Unrestrained.

Not sacrifice. Something else.

Men wept. Women tore their sleeves. Coins and petals littered the stones.

Jesus stood still. He had seen passion. He had seen madness. But never both together.

Then another procession.

Dionysus.

God of wine, release, and frenzy. Men draped in ivy carried a carved phallus. Half-naked women danced beside them, laughing, tossing grape leaves, pouring wine into mouths and onto the ground. The scent of wine clung to the air.

Two boys watched nervously from the temple steps.

Jesus turned away. He felt the hunger in the crowd—not for gods, but something deeper. Something older. Freedom, maybe. Or forgetting.

They needed more. Not ritual. Not blood. Salvation.

They would hunger for what he carried.

He moved again, past temples to Apollo and Artemis, past gymnasia and stoic philosophers debating under cloaks, past an amphitheater casting long shadows, and the great imperial baths rising behind it.

It was late afternoon now, and he had seen enough. He was tired. And hungry.

It was time to find Lucius.

He remembered the instructions: the house of Lucius Aurelius Barrius. Senatorial Enclave. Eastern Decumanus, just beyond the Temple of Jupiter.

He asked directions. Shopkeepers pointed. A potter offered a shortcut. A water-carrier led him partway.

The road climbed.

Stone walls. Cypress trees. Less noise. Fewer people. The city receded. Quiet settled over him.

At a bend, the view opened—and there it was.

A Roman mansion. Domus Urbana. Elevated, balanced. Its travertine façade glowed in the softening light. Corinthian columns framed bronze doors that opened to a courtyard lit with lanterns swaying beneath linen drapes.

The roof sloped gently to an open atrium with a mosaic floor more beautiful than any he had seen. Blues, golds, and yellows rippled in the stone. The border held intertwined ropes and acanthus scrolls, with sacks of coins in the corners. At the center, a fish-filled lagoon held a merchant ship, anchor stowed, ready to depart. And the words on the ship's unfurled sail

FORTUNA FAVET OFFICIO
Fortune Favors Commitment

He paused. The colors. The designs. Those words. They revealed a duality in Lucius that Jesus hadn't seen before.

Clearly, he was a merchant. Possibly a Stoic. A successful businessman, but not bound to commerce alone. The ropes and anchors marked him as a trader. The fish recalled the secret gatherings of the faithful. The coins might suggest wealth—or the duty to give. And the motto? It could serve faith. Or profit.

Lucius seemed layered. Like the city itself.

Why had he visited the chapel in Gaul? Why had he listened? Why had he stayed? Come back so often?

Why was he helping me?
Jesus wondered if Lucius believed. Or if he had simply learned to use belief to build his business.

Jesus turned away from the mosaic, and his train of thought broke as he noticed two marble plaques flanking the main entry, each bearing a carving of an olive tree. One stood above a bronze basin for ritual washing, the other above a votive shelf with myrtle and a single clay lamp—still burning, even in the master's absence.

He couldn't know that time would soon erase this house and almost everything in it. Deep in the earth beneath the atrium's mosaic floor, three fault lines slowly shifted. Unseen. Continuous. Silent. In less than seventy years, Antioch would fracture. Earthquakes would bury the city and kill thousands. It would be rebuilt—only to fracture again four centuries later. The rubble of Lucius's mansion would wait centuries to be discovered, still buried under still larger mansions. And during those waiting centuries, the city's name would slowly fade, evolving into Antakya as the Arab language and culture gained dominance.

But for now, the house stood whole.

Leaving Jesus in the atrium, Paul stepped onto the portico as a servant appeared at the entrance gate. He bowed, then led him into the house of Lucius Barrius.

Lucius was waiting.

"That's where the letter ends," Thomas continued, " It sounds like he just wanted to let Mary know that he arrived and how his first day went. Let's read the second letter to find out what happened when he met with Lucius."

Thomas scrolled to the second letter. They each scanned the first few lines. It was very different.

"It sounds like he's afraid," Alister said quietly. "Genuinely afraid."

Susan leaned past Thomas, closer to the screen, and read the lines aloud, slowly, hoping to catch any hidden messages.

I am leaving this morning. They are searching Antioch for me. They've already been through the city. And the port. They'll be here soon. My house is too exposed, too near to Barrius. I must leave now. I have packed some basic supplies, but the scroll jar is too large and fragile to carry on my journey.

It contains the record—my own words, my complete account of how I built my Christian Church throughout Asia, Galatia, and other provinces during these six years. There is a statue in my atrium, a god with no chains and one raised hand. I've hidden the scroll jar in a cavity hollowed out in its base. I carved it myself, lined it with gold leaf, and sealed it with wax. It's behind the plaque that identifies the sculptor.

Hidden beneath the heel of his forward foot is the mechanism to open it. Press, turn, and slide left. You'll hear the latch. If it's still there, the scroll is waiting. When it is safe, I plan to return and retrieve it. However, if I am unable to do so, I want you to know how to access it.

I will send for you when I am settled in Rome.

The room fell into silence. Susan finally asked the questions that were on everyone's mind. "What did he talk to Lusius about? What is he afraid of? Who is searching for him? Why? And Rome, why go there?

Thomas exhaled. " I don't think this is a letter to Mary. It's a map—for Mary to retrieve the scroll if he couldn't do it himself."

Susan whispered, "We need to find that scroll…it will answer all our questions about what happened in Antioch after that first day?

"It's hidden in the base of that statue," Alister said. "Greek, male figure, no chains, one hand raised. Who is that?"

"Prometheus?" Susan guessed. "Maybe Asclepius, the healer?"

Thomas leaned forward. "Antakya sits atop the ancient city of Antioch—one of the most important centers of the Greek East and later a major Roman metropolis. Archaeological excavations have been ongoing for decades. Their museums house many of the discoveries, especially mosaics from Roman villas in Antioch and surrounding towns like Daphne and Seleucia Pieria."

He continued, voice steady. "I have strong personal and professional connections with construction and shipping companies, archaeological dig sites, and museums from my work with UNESCO and CPI. During my time there, a massive mosaic was uncovered during a hotel construction project, which led to the creation of the Museum Hotel Antakya—built right above the site."

He paused. "The earthquake three years ago damaged several heritage sites, including the museum itself. But if that statue that Jesus talks about, or the mansions mosaic, were recovered, they'll be somewhere in their collection—or in their workrooms."

Susan nodded slowly. "And you think we can get access?"

Thomas smiled faintly. "With my contacts, we'll get in. Somehow."

Susan turned toward him, still uneasy. "What about Silentii? What do we do to keep them off our trail?"

Alister's worried expression curled into a grin. "I've got the answer. We mislead them. Again. Let them chase ghosts."

He laid out the plan: He would contact Terra Nuova to confirm the jet's return to Sardinia from Teterboro. Leo had said they could catch a ride back if needed.

Then, the day before the flight, he and Susan would leave a noisy, trackable trail across Manhattan—ride-shares, lunch in Midtown, a stop at Bloomingdale's, maybe even a night at the St. Regis. All paid for with traceable credit cards.

Then they'd each purchase tickets to Israel, departing in three days.

Thomas smiled. "They'll be here the next morning, trying to follow our trail in New York, and then when they can't find us, they will wait at the departure gate for our flight to Israel. And they will think the next scroll is there."

"They'll have no idea how we're going back to Sardinia," Susan added, admiring Alister's foresight. "And if they think we're still in New York. They'll lower their surveillance in Italy. Maybe even pause it."

"Exactly," Alister said. "We'll be in Sardinia by then. And from there, we ferry back to the mainland. Then drive to Rome. Then fly to Antakya. We'll use our new passports. The ones the State Department issued for our Terra Nuova trip. With our new identities and our burner phones, they won't be able to track us. "

"They'll blame each other for failing to stop us from leaving Italy," Alister said. "…and they'll focus their anger on that guy with the white hair."

Susan turned to Thomas. "He broke into my apartment in New York, roughed up my husband, and trashed the place while looking for the scroll. Then he murdered Alister's doorman. And last week he tried to kill us in St Cyr. By now, I would guess that he's not only angry…but desperate. That's a dangerous combination."

Thomas stood, suddenly resolute.

"Then let's stay ahead. I'll finish locking the scrolls to the blockchain this week. And I'll contact my sources in Antakya—give them our credentials. When we arrive, they'll introduce us to the museum teams and dig operations. That's where we'll begin."

He glanced at them both, then added with a wry smile, "CPI's summer vacation starts Friday. I'll take the month. I'm in."

Three faces lit by one screen.
Three minds, now in motion.
And a third scroll waiting in stone silence beneath a forgotten god.

They didn't speak again that night.
They didn't need to.

CHAPTER FORTY

An ochre fog clung low over New York Harbor, turning sunrise into a smoldering yellow and orange haze. The city was already sweating. By 7:00 a.m., the National Weather Service had issued excessive heat warnings—triple digits expected by midday, with a heat index higher still.

Approaching Teterboro Airport in New Jersey from the southeast like a ghost cloaked in shadow, the Silentii Gulfstream G800 emerged from that steaming morning mist. Corvus sat in the rear seat, arms crossed, jaw tight. He hadn't spoken since they left Rome. The two agents across from him—older, more seasoned, their faces carved by years of silent work—offered no small talk. They weren't here to comfort. They were here to clean up a mess. His mess.

Three escapes. One from the Met. One from St Cyr. And now one from Italy itself. No one could explain how Alister Duran and Dr. Susan Hale had made it to New York. All surveillance, all checkpoints, all data trails had come up empty—until yesterday.

Silentii Center had picked up a flare of activity: credit card charges, ATM withdrawals, phone pings. All in Manhattan. Restaurants, cafés, taxis. And then their airline reservations. Flight LY0081. El Al Airlines. JFK to Ben Gurion Airport, Tel Aviv. Scheduled departure: 11:15 p.m. tonight.

"We will get them now. We have a string of their steps and plans traced with precision." Corvus told Vallente"

"You'd better get them," the Cardinal had said, each syllable clipped like a blade. "At JFK. Before their flight departs. Bring them back, with the scrolls."

The pilot received landing instructions from Tederboro Tower.

"This is Teterboro Tower, good morning, Gulfstream OS7777, prepare to turn to heading Three-Zero-Five and proceed to ILS Runway One-Niner. Wind one-zero at seven, cleared to land."

Corvus' thoughts were jolted back to the present as the pilot banked sharply to heading 305, a maneuver required to avoid densely residential areas to meet noise control regulations.

Cleared to land Runway One-Niner, Gulfstream OS7777

Its dark fuselage black on black—military-grade silence for a different kind of war--shimmered as it touched down gently and taxied to an unnamed private hangar on the east end of the airfield. Just a tail insignia. No callsign. The only identification was the jet manufacturer, model, and serial number imprinted inside the entrance door.

Corvus clenched his fists as the aircraft braked to a halt.

Inside the hangar, the air was still and muffled as they stepped down the stairs from the plane and walked through to the hangar's private arrivals lounge.

At precisely 7:14 a.m., a sleek black Mercedes sedan with bulletproof windows and diplomatic plates pulled up. The same car. The same driver. Two weeks ago, it had carried Corvus to the Metropolitan Museum of Art to intercept Susan Hale.

That felt like another life.

Corvus ducked inside without a word. The two agents followed. As the driver pulled away and exited the airport's main exit into the thinning commuter traffic, Thomas Doyle's jet-black Mercedes-AMG S63E moved like a shadow, its 791-horsepower V8 engine growling, as it slid into a parking spot fifty feet behind them.

Alister Duran stepped out into the humid morning.

He paused for a second.

Across the tarmac, the black Silentii Mercedes was vanishing through the service gate. Something about it stirred him—an echo of another morning just two weeks ago at Morton Street, a flash of polished chrome, a sense of threat. But he shook it off.

No need to make Susan nervous wth his ominous feelings. Not now.

She climbed out of the passenger seat, adjusting her sunglasses. "Feels like Sardinia already," she muttered.

"Much cooler there," Alister replied.

Outside the private terminal, the Terra Nuova G8000 was already fueled and waiting. The Terra Nova pilots nodded as all the executives on the manifest boarded, including Susan and Alister, who presented their new passports and identities.

By 7:45 a.m., they were airborne. Their destination: Cagliari Elmas Airport, Sardinia. Arrival time: 2:40 p.m. local.

From there, a short drive to the Port of Cagliari, where they'd take the overnight Grimaldi ferry to Civitavecchia, arriving at the mainland by dawn. They'd booked a small hotel nearby—walking distance from the ferry dock. Just one night, they would wake early and have the hotel car drive them to Rome Fiumicino for their morning flight to Antakya, Turkey. All payments in cash. Booked under their new identities. Untraceable. Invisible. They were ghosts.

As the jet reached its cruising altitude, high above commercial traffic over the Atlantic, Alister settled into his seat. He mused that the day before, they'd been anything but ghosts, going everywhere.

Lunch at Via Carota, Greenwich Village. Dinner at Le Zie Trattoria, Chelsea. A gallery walk in the East Village. A riverfront stroll in Battery Park. Every stop paid with their real cards, real names. Every server tipped in cash with a warm smile and a heartfelt thank you. Alister even visited a Chase branch on 79th and Broadway, withdrawing nearly

$25,000 in cash—enough to move across continents without leaving a trail.

The purpose was camouflage and noise in plain sight. And their plan was working. At this moment, back in Manhattan, the Silentii team was already retracing their steps.

They entered Via Carota and showed the manager photographs of Susan and Alister at the same time they were on the Grimaldi ferry, watching the blue curve of the sea stretch out toward the Italian mainland.

"Oh yeah," the woman said brightly. "They were lovely. Acted like lovers on a date, I think? Sat by the window. He ordered the cacio e pepe. She had the frittata."
"You're sure it was them?"
"Positive. They left a thirty-dollar tip."

Next stop: the art gallery. Then the taxi garage. Then the Chase branch. By late afternoon, they had a perfect trail. Their prey had been there, or so they thought.

At 9:20 p.m., while Susan and Alister were already asleep on the overnight ferry to Italy, the Silentii team arrived at JFK Terminal 4, flashing diplomatic credentials to bypass security. The El Al flight was boarding at Gate B36. They took seats in scattered positions—newsstands, wine bars, charging stations—awaiting visual confirmation.

They waited.

At 10:50 p.m., the gate closed.

At 11:17 p.m., LY0081 lifted off, bound for Tel Aviv.

No Susan. No Alister.

At midnight, in a quiet corner of the JFK terminal, Corvus raised the encrypted Silentii phone and pressed the black seal emblem.

"Report," came the voice on the other end.

Corvus's jaw moved once, twice. Then he spoke.

"They weren't on the flight. I repeat—they weren't on the flight."

A long silence followed.

"Then they've slipped away again."

Corvus's throat clenched. "We believe they're still in New York."

"No," the voice replied. "They've outmaneuvered you. Again."

A final pause. Then the line went dead.

CHAPTER FORTY-ONE

The Turkish Airlines Airbus A321 banked gently to the west, its polished wing catching the morning light as it crested the outskirts of Rome. Below, the tangled urban sprawl gave way to the timeless symmetry of Vatican City—its domes and gardens gilded by the sun. Alister glanced down through the window and gave a faint, almost irreverent smile.

"It's still beautiful, every time I see it," he muttered.

Susan looked up from her seat beside him, eyes following his line of sight. The dome of St. Peter's glowed like a molten crown.

"Right now," she said softly, "I bet it's not so beautiful down there… they've probably realized we're not in New York."

Alister leaned back, exhaling. "And not coming back."

Susan turned to him. "And getting very angry and very desperate."

The jet banked northward, engines humming steadily as they climbed above the Apennines. During the past two days in those labyrinthine stone corridors beneath Vatican Hill, Susan had been proved right. Cardinal Vallente had discovered empty scroll jars, and Corvus and his agents had chased a series of digital ghosts. They were angry and desperate.

But in their first-class seats onboard the Airbus, there was—for the first time in days—stillness. With a short stopover in Istanbul, they would arrive at Antakya's Hatay Airport in seven hours.

They had done it. Somehow.

The scrolls—both of them—were no longer in reach of the Silentii. Not physically, not intellectually, and certainly not digitally. The originals were hidden in a Midtown Manhattan safe deposit box, accessed only with their forged passports under false names. Their contents had been scanned, encrypted, and sealed within a blockchain-secured dead man's switch. If they failed to log in every sixty days, the documents would auto-release to journalists, scholars, and a distributed list of anonymous custodians worldwide. Silentii didn't know that…yet. It would provide negotiating leverage if they were caught.

Susan folded her arms, letting her head rest against Alister's shoulder. "Feels like we're finally ahead."

Alister didn't answer right away. He let the quiet hum of the cabin answer for him. It wasn't a triumph. Not exactly. It was more like altitude—like they had risen above the reach of the Silentii agents who had hunted them from New York to Positano to St Cyr.

They didn't know it yet, but they would only be ahead of Silentii by a few days.

It began in a basement room of the Pontifical Intelligence Wing, hidden within the archives of a disused library annex beneath the Vatican Library. The air smelled of old vellum and ozone.

Her name was Clara Sorrentino—a Silentii junior surveillance analyst, third rotation, assigned initially to digital anomaly tracing for Latin American dissident clergy. She was meticulous, underutilized, and hungry to be noticed. This was her chance.

After reviewing the blank travel logs and dead-end IP trails left by Susan Hale and Alister Duran, Clara expanded her parameters. She ran a secondary linkage sweep—not on the couple, but on their relational web. Family. Academic contacts. Old employment records. The search turned up nothing—until it didn't.

One name.

Thomas Doyle.

She ran it twice. Then a third time.

His background pinged on several indices: Jesuit education, former UNESCO consultant on religious antiquities, currently senior director for CPI's Near East compliance division. He lived in Ridgewood, New Jersey.

Six days ago, he had booked a commercial flight to Antakya. Then two rooms under his own name. Who was the other room for? It must be for Susan Hale and Alister Duran. But how would they get there without any trace? He departed the next day and had now been on the ground for three. If she moved quickly, Clara thought, their agents could be there tomorrow—giving Hale and Doyle only an one-day-head start.

Antakya.

Clara's hand hovered over the alert button. Was her logic sound? If he was going there, it wasn't a vacation. And if Thomas Doyle were going, then Susan Hale and Alister Duran would almost certainly follow—somehow quietly, invisibly.

She took a deep breath and keyed in the alert code: OS7777 – SHADOWTAI

Within minutes, the silent network lit up across Vatican intelligence. Notifications rippled across three continents. Cardinal Vallente's eyes narrowed as he read the report in his private chamber.

"They didn't escape our tracking and fool our agents because of luck," he whispered. "They're strategists. And good at it. They even had us convinced that the scroll was in Israel, and they we going there to find it."

But now, they were going to Antakya. Antioch in the time of Jesus. Of course, the birthplace of Christianity. They must know where the third scroll is hidden…and we have no idea.

Before nightfall, he issued strict orders: " Identify and track the fugitives. Do not apprehend until they have the scroll jar".

Two new agents, older, colder, were reassigned…he kind who didn't lose. Corvus—still smarting from the Vatican humiliation—received the instruction while in New York, still pursuing leads to the fugitives' whereabouts.

Their new destination: Antakya, Republic of Türkiye. The clock was already ticking.

Susan, Alister, and Thomas had no idea that they would have only a short time to find what they came for…and get out.

The arrivals terminal at Hatay Airport was half-lit and humid, its ceiling fans barely keeping pace with the heat. A few rusted baggage carts leaned together near the rental desk like tired old travelers themselves. But Thomas Doyle stood straight as ever, arms folded, waiting near the customs barrier as the doors hissed open.

Susan and Alister emerged from the narrow glass chute moments later, faces travel-worn but clear-eyed.

Thomas raised a hand. "You made it."

Susan hugged him first. Then Alister, clapping his shoulder.

They moved quickly through the lot and out into the hot light of the city's southern fringe. A driver with a faded cap loaded their bags into a waiting car.

As they drove into town, Thomas gestured through the windshield. "Brace yourselves."

Antakya was still raw from the twin earthquakes that had torn through it the year before. Whole sections of the old city had collapsed—Ottoman stonework crushed into beige dust, narrow alleys widened into rubble. Restoration had begun, but it was uneven—modern cranes rose above ancient Roman streets, while refugee tents dotted old Byzantine courtyards.

"Over twenty thousand dead," Thomas said. "And half the city still sleeps in prefab shelters. But look around."

They passed scaffolding-wrapped mosques, open-air bakeries, and a caravan of schoolchildren walking in single file beside a broken aqueduct. Life was returning. Dusty, defiant, and loud.

"But beneath it," Thomas added, "Antakya is still Antioch."

He pointed north, toward the foothills. "That ridge? That's where the original theater stood—Jesus would have seen it. The forum was just east of it. And the colonnaded road—the Via Tecta—ran right through where that hardware store is now."

Susan looked out the window as a veiled woman on a scooter passed, balancing two bags of cement between her knees.

Thomas continued, "Two thousand years ago, this city was the third jewel of the Roman world. Silk, spices, gold, and ships from Egypt and India. And here…right here…is where they first called them Christians."

Alister leaned forward. "And the statue?"

Thomas gave a slight nod. "Museum Hotel is just ahead. You've had a long day, and it's late. Get a good night's sleep, and we'll talk in the morning. I've got us set up to meet with the people running the dig sites and the two museums in the city."

The car turned onto Kurtuluş Caddesi. Ahead, the hotel rose from the ruins—modern, discreet, and built atop a layer of history even earthquakes couldn't shake.

And buried somewhere beneath their feet—or perhaps already recovered and mislabeled in a museum—lay what they had come for.

CHAPTER FORTY-TWO

Luca Severin had visited the Vatican dozens of times—invited lectures, private consultations, and theological summits in domed salons where Latin echoed beneath Michelangelo's frescoes. But he had never been here.

This was different.

This was the real Vatican. The one tourists never saw—the one that required silent approval from a pope—and three layers of armed guards to enter.

The marble hallway leading to the *Biblioteca Secreta* was cool and echoing, lined with ancient statues and quiet menace. Guards in dark uniforms stood every twenty paces, their expressions as impassive as their weapons were visible. No ceremonial halberds today—these men carried compact rifles and biometric scanners.

The final checkpoint was a narrow steel door flanked by two guards in earpieces. Luca held out the sealed credential envelope he had been given the night before, marked with the seal of the Holy Father himself.

The taller guard scanned it, paused, then glanced at the other with raised eyebrows. "You're the first in a decade to come with this level of access."

The other man nodded silently and turned, unlocking the door with a retinal scan and a hidden keypad. It slid open with a hiss.

Luca stepped inside.

The transition was almost cinematic: from modern security to ancient reverence. The chamber beyond was dim, temperature-controlled, and heavy with the scent of dust, leather, and ink that hadn't breathed fresh air in centuries. Marble gave way to wood. Vaulted ceilings disappeared into shadow. The silence was total.

In this most secure and secret chamber, Luca had always heard rumors: that it housed the true contents and location of the Holy Grail, ancient prophecies predicting the end of civilization, and even the real Third Secret of Fatima, which foretold a coming global chaos. There were also reports, started by the international publishing community, that the original manuscript of *The Scrolls of Provence* was confiscated before publication and locked away from public release.

Those rumors might not be true, Luca thought. But the implications of the Gospel he was about to read were. And that made this place more sacred—and more dangerous—than any vault on earth.

It was the first time in years Luca Severin felt small.

A robed archivist approached from a far aisle—ancient himself, hair like paper ash. He said nothing, only bowed slightly and gestured for Luca to follow. They passed rows of codices, vaults of forgotten languages, and iron-bound reliquaries. Finally, the archivist stopped at a locked glass cabinet inset into the stone wall. Inside was a single volume, wrapped in velvet the color of dried blood.

He unlocked it with a brass key he wore around his neck. Reverently, he lifted the book and placed it in Luca's hands.

The *Gospel of Magdalene.*

The most dangerous document the modern world had ever known. If revealed, it could fracture the foundations of civilization itself—and the eight billion people who depended on the illusion of unshakable moral order. That illusion had stabilized the world for two thousand years.

Its cover was blackened leather, so old it felt like cloth. The pages were papyrus, handwritten in a Greek-Aramaic hybrid. The script was delicate, flowing—unmistakably feminine.

But it wasn't a complete book. The first part was intact, but it appeared that about a third of the book, all the back pages, were missing. Destroyed or torn out. He couldn't tell. He would ask Valentii later.

Luca sat alone at a carved reading table under a cone of warm lamplight. He started to read.

And time stopped.

For hours, he read, eyes devouring every faded line. The narrative was familiar—painfully so. As he read, it mirrored the story he had already traced through the scrolls: the aftermath of the crucifixion, the forty days in hiding, the journey to Gaul, the adoption of children, the reimagining of ministry.

But it was nothing like the scrolls.

This was only a recollection—a memoir, written from distant memory—reflective, reverent, faded by time. The details were imprecise. Scenes blurred together. Locations lacked definition. Conversations were reduced to summaries.

And besides the back pages, another thing was missing entirely: Jesus's voice.

The scrolls had it. Clear. Personal. Inscribed by Jesus in his own hand. The Magdalene Gospel didn't. This was Mary's remembered past—but the scrolls had been their shared present. Fresh. Urgent. Immediate.

Luca paused at the end, just before the missing pages. It paralleled the events of the second scroll. He gently closed the volume and let out a slow breath.

Now he understood. Why the Silentii were panicked. Why Cardinal Vallente behaved like a man holding a lit match.

The scrolls were far more dangerous than this Gospel ever had been. They weren't just memories. They were evidence.

And they were alive.

He set the volume back on the velvet with trembling fingers. It was late afternoon when he left the chamber. Now, he would brief Vallente. Ask about the missing pages.

The guards nodded as he passed, one even stepping aside with a trace of deference Luca had never experienced—not at Harvard, not even at that state dinner in Washington. Here, he wasn't just a scholar. He was a vessel of something powerful.

He walked slowly through the bronze door into the shadowed garden walkway that led back to the administrative wing. The sun had dipped, casting long golden fingers across the marble.

Vallente was waiting.

The Cardinal's office was dark-paneled and spare, lit only by a floor lamp and a narrow window that framed the dome of St. Peter's in profile. A bottle of wine stood open on the credenza, half a glass already poured.

He looked more relaxed than he had during the Silentii council meeting. His face was composed. Almost cheerful.

"Sit, Luca," he said, gesturing to the chair opposite his desk. "How was your day in the vaults of the Empire?"

Luca sat. He hesitated. Then: "The gospel overlaps with the first and second scrolls."

"And?"

"It matches," Luca said carefully. "The Magdalene Gospel contains the same story as the first two scrolls, clearly written many years later and in far less detail. But it goes no further—no clues about where the next scrolls could be hidden. You must know that the last pages of the

Gospel are missing. Maybe what we are looking for was there. What happened?"

Vallente nodded. " In the fourth century, a rogue bishop decided to destroy the original Gospel. He almost succeeded. The Church Fathers heard about it and stopped him at the last minute, just as he was ripping out and burning pages. Most concerning now is that we have no record of what was on those burned pages. However, I fear that the scrolls contain that record."

Valentii paused for a long moment and then continued, "And that could be a threat far greater than the Gospel."

"Why is that?" Luca asked.

 "Because the Goapel is tame." Valentii responded, " Distant. Aged. And damaging if released, yes—but survivable. We've already rewritten and released a sanitized version centuries ago. Another version claiming to be the original could be dismissed as apocryphal nostalgia. We've already cast her as a prostitute, then a penitent living in a cave."

He leaned forward, resting his forearms on the desk. "The scrolls are the real life of Jesus—as it happened. Immediate. Undeniable. In his own hand. Not that of an old prostitute. With devastating implications."

Luca met his eyes. "Not only that, but they may contain what was written on those missing pages. And in Jesus's own hand. The only known writings of Jesus ever found."

"Yes," Vallente agreed. "That's why I haven't changed my mind…they must be destroyed."

Luca said nothing.

Vallente studied him. "You look pale."

"Must they be destroyed?" Luca said suddenly. "Perhaps they could be secured in the Vatican Library—with the Gospel. Preserved for the future. For—"

"We do not protect truth," Vallente interrupted, his voice calm but absolute. "We protect order."

Those words—*Protect order, not truth*—hit Luca like a brick.

Vallente continued, "Doctrine is a wall that holds back madness. If you let the flood through, you cannot control what it washes away."

He stood, walked to the window, and clasped his hands behind his back.

"I understand your conflict, Luca. I truly do. But you must trust that the preservation of faith sometimes requires the burial of fact."

Luca looked down. His voice, when it came, was steady. "I'll return to the Gospel tomorrow. So far, I've found no hints as to where the third scroll is hidden."

Vallente turned back toward him. "Good. But that may not be necessary…"

He reached for his glass and raised it slightly. "because we've found them."

Luca froze. "Found who?"

"Her brother," Vallente said, sipping. Confident. "Thomas Doyle. He's in Antakya. So they are too."

He smiled now, thin and certain.

"Corvus and two of our best men are en route. They'll arrive tomorrow. They don't yet know where the third scroll is hidden—but they'll follow Susan and Alister. Watch where they go. Once it's located, we'll recover everything. Quietly. Permanently."

Luca stood slowly, nodding. He turned, walked calmly toward the door. He didn't speak again until he was outside, alone in the corridor.

Then, under his breath:

"No. I can't… won't… let that happen. Now, I call Alister."

CHAPTER FORTY-THREE

The burner phone rang from somewhere across the room.

Alister blinked once, then again. Through the windows, he could see a blazing sun awakening the city from another hot and muggy night. Even from his air-conditioned bedroom, he could imagine the morning heat, the kind that clung to you before you even moved. The air outside would be thick, metallic, laced with the dust rising from Antakya's cracked streets.

He rolled onto his side. Sunlight spilling through the sheer curtain reminded him of old black-and-white film reels—soft and grainy. He looked across the room to the empty bed where Susan had been. From the bathroom came the faint sound of running water.

The phone rang again. Three seconds. Four.

He stared at the ceiling, still half-lost in a dream he couldn't recall. But the mood lingered—*Casablanca*. That's what it was. Black and white. The haze outside the window. The heat. The fan ticking uselessly above. That feeling of something slipping away.

And Susan…

Ingrid Bergman.

A grim smile tugged at the edge of his mouth.

That would make him Victor Laszlo, wouldn't it? And this dusty hotel room—Rick's Café Américain.

A quote surfaced uninvited.
Of all the gin joints in all the towns in all the world

He exhaled and finished it aloud to the empty room. "She walks into mine."

The phone rang again.

He threw off the sheet, crossed the room barefoot, and picked up the burner from the desk. No name. Just a number. European.

He answered.

"Alister," said the voice on the other end. Breathy. Urgent. Familiar.

He froze. "Luca?"

A pause.

"Yes."

Silence fell like a dropped curtain. Alister's grip tightened around the phone.

"You have thirty seconds before I hang up."

"I deserve that," Luca said. "But I need you to listen."

"Why would I? You lied to me. You put us in danger."

"I know." The voice cracked slightly. "I'm not asking for forgiveness. Just trust—just this once."

Alister said nothing. He could hear a kettle in the background, whistling faintly. Somewhere in Rome, the world was waking up.

"They're coming for you," Luca said. "Tomorrow. Two agents. Experienced. Silentii has issued explicit orders—observe you, let you search, wait for the scroll to surface. Then act."

"Define *act*."

Luca hesitated. "They're not there to negotiate."

Alister swallowed. The room, already warm, suddenly felt smaller.

"The one with white hair and the scar," he said. "Is he with them?"

"They call him Corvus. And yes—he's with them. Which means if they get what they want, there won't be a trial. There won't be questions."

Alister walked to the window. The street was waking. Dust swirled in the morning light like smoke. Vendors shouted across the square. A boy on a motorbike weaved through an alley, vanishing into shadow.

"How do I know you're not still working for them?" he asked. "That this isn't a trap?"

"You don't," Luca said. "But you knew my father. And there's something he told me—something you need to hear. It may change your mind."

That stopped him. He hadn't thought of Luca's father in twenty years.

"You stayed with us that summer in Florence," Luca continued, gently. "The year he died. Three weeks. Remember?"

Alister blinked. Slowly.

"You brought him espresso every morning, even as he got weaker," Luca said. "You sat with him on the veranda while he told you how proud he was of your dissertation—even though he didn't live to see it finished. You were the only person outside our family there in his final weeks. You think I forgot that?"

Alister closed his eyes.

"I loved your father," he said quietly. "He's one of the reasons I stayed in academia. Didn't follow my father into business."

Luca exhaled. "He once asked me to protect you—if anything ever happened. His exact words: *If Alister ever struggles with people on the wrong side of scholarly research, make sure someone still knows the truth.*"

Another silence. Longer now. "Now, after all these years, I've found that Silentii is on the wrong side of truth. I didn't know it until two days ago. I can't be part of it. Alister, we can work together, as my father said, 'to make sure that someone still knows the truth'."

The noise from outside crept in—construction, traffic, distant horns. But inside, the room had gone still.

"I read the original Gospel of Mary Magdalene yesterday," Luca continued. "It's in the Secret Archive of the Vatican Library. It tells the same story that's on the scrolls. But it's...different. It's from memory. Told by an old woman. Not when it happened. And not in Jesus's hand."

"We have to preserve the scrolls," Luca said. "Protect the truth."

Another pause.

"Vallente doesn't care about the truth. He said it himself: *We do not protect the truth. We protect order.'* That's what the Silentii believes now. Not truth. Order."

Alister's voice dropped. "By calling me, you're gambling with your life."

"I know."

A breath, then: "If you and Susan can leave Antakya without being seen, my villa is still secure. They still believe I'm loyal. You'd be invisible there."

Alister didn't respond right away. But the implications were immediate.

If they knew *Thomas* was here, then they knew where Thomas *lived*.

His house wasn't safe anymore.

"And if we stay?"

Luca didn't answer.

The silence was its own answer.

Finally, Alister spoke. "No more messages. No calls. No texts. If we come, we come. If we don't...you'll know why."

"I understand."

A pause, then Luca added, "Remember—they think you're unaware. Use that."

The line went dead.

Alister lowered the phone and stood at the window for a long moment. The street below looked unreal. A movie set. A place where fate arrived in a trench coat, cigarette in hand.

Behind him, the bathroom door creaked open. Water shut off. Susan's voice floated out.

"Who was it?"

Alister turned.

"Miss Bergman," he said. "Casablanca just got a little more complicated."

CHAPTER FORTY-FOUR

The elevator glided down in silence, cool and dimly lit—a cocoon insulated from the already intensifying June heat outside the hotel. Alister stood beside Susan, his hair still damp from the shower, his collar open. Neither had slept well.

As the doors slid open into the hotel lobby, Susan slowed her steps, taking in the space for the first time in daylight. She let out a quiet breath.

"Good God," she said.

The lobby was not a lobby in any traditional sense. It was glass and steel suspended above time itself—above a vast open field of ancient stones, columns, and tessellated color. A massive Roman mosaic stretched below them like a painting pinned to the earth, untouched and nearly whole, its faded reds and golds shimmering in the filtered sunlight.

They followed the ramped walkway toward the restaurant, their footsteps echoing faintly in the cathedral-like space. The bones of ancient Antioch were everywhere—bathhouse foundations, marble walls, statues, even the partial remains of an aqueduct. It was as though the past had never left, only rearranged itself, waiting.

Thomas was already seated near the edge of the dining terrace, a strong Turkish coffee in front of him, back to the mosaic field. He looked up and waved as they approached.

Susan slid into the seat across from him, still looking over her shoulder.

"This place is unreal," she said. "I've never seen anything like it. Who builds a hotel on top of a Roman city?"

Thomas grinned faintly. "That's the punchline. They didn't mean to."

He set down his cup and leaned back. "It started as a luxury hotel project back in 2009. The Asfuroğlu family, a major developer here, began digging the foundation. Within days, they hit stone, then mosaics, then more. Eventually, they realized they'd uncovered one of the more exclusive neighborhoods of ancient Antioch—a place where the wealthy built their mansions. Beneath their planned hotel lay more than 2,000 years of history. No one saw it coming."

Susan raised an eyebrow. "And they just… stopped construction?"

"More like forced to. The government stepped in—the Cultural and Natural Assets Board. You don't bulldoze the largest Roman mosaic ever found just to add a parking garage."

Alister leaned forward. "So how did this…" he gestured around them, "actually happen?"

"They got creative. Brought in Emre Arolat, a Turkish architect with a flair for impossible briefs. He designed a floating hotel—sixty-six steel columns drilled only where there were no ruins. The whole thing hovers above the site. The hotel rooms, the restaurant, the lobby—everything is suspended. Not a single ancient stone was moved."

Susan's eyes swept across the floor below. "It feels sacred. Like we're walking over someone's memory."

"In a way, we are," Thomas said. "There's a bathhouse from the fifth century just below the elevator shaft. And the big Pegasus mosaic—you can see it from the southern wing. Plus marble statues, bits of city wall, and thousands of artifacts. Thirteen civilizations, give or take."

"And the museum?" Alister asked.

"Fully legit. The Ministry of Culture took it over in 2019. A full staff of archaeologists and curators runs the site. This restaurant is part of the museum complex—officially the Necmi Asfuroğlu Archaeology

Museum. Most of the movable finds are stored off-site, but what you see here? It's original, just as it was uncovered. No tricks."

Susan shook her head. "It's like staying on a dig site. Except with breakfast and linen service."

Thomas smirked. "Exactly. Welcome to Antakya—where history refuses to stay buried, even after two centuries of earthquakes."

Susan glanced at Alister, her smile fading. "Speaking of buried things… we need to tell you about the call."

Alister shifted in his seat and leaned in, lowering his voice. "It was Luca. He used the burner. Called just after sunrise."

Thomas straightened. "He called you?"

Alister nodded. "Said he was sorry. That he'd read the original Magdalene Gospel in the Vatican Library. Even though it was written years later, when Mary was old, it matches the scroll's story almost word for word. But ours—written in Jesus' own hand—are far more precise. He's convinced they're real. And Silentii thinks they're dangerous."

Thomas frowned. "And you believe him?"

"I'm not sure I believe everything," Alister admitted, rubbing his temples. "But I believe he's conflicted. Luca and my father went back decades. He was one of the most principled scholars I ever met—obsessed with truth, rigorous about ethics. I think helping the Silentii made sense to him, for a long time. He thought he was protecting the Church from chaos. But now? Now he sees it's not about truth. It's about control."

Susan folded her arms. "He said they're coming. That maniac with the scarred face and clipped white hair—Corvus. He's leading the team."

Thomas went still. "Then they know where I live. We can't go back to Ridgewood."

"No," Alister said. "Luca was clear—they're tracking us. Your house is compromised. We're out of options. But Luca offered us something we may not get anywhere else."

"His villa," Susan said softly.

Alister nodded. "He says it's still safe. The Silentii don't know he's turned. They trust him—for now. It's isolated, defensible. And if—when—we find the third scroll, he can read it. Fluently. No risk of leaks from translation software or your professor friend. We keep the circle tight."

Thomas exhaled. "So you're willing to trust him?"

"I'm willing to take the risk," Alister said. "Because here's the truth—we're already exposed. But they don't know how much we know."

He held up a finger. "We're in a tough spot, but I think we have the advantage... at least until they believe we've found the scroll."

He began ticking off the points on his fingers.

"First—they don't know Luca has turned. Second—they don't know he warned us. Third—they don't know we know they're arriving today. Fourth—they've been ordered to follow, not act. Not yet. Fifth—they have no idea where the scroll is. Sixth—they don't know we know any of this. Seventh—we're traveling under new identities. Eighth—those identities are clean. No digital trail. Ninth—we can still return to Luca's villa."

Thomas leaned back, impressed. "Then we use their ignorance to our advantage. That buys us time."

"Exactly," Alister said. "The key is not to run. Not yet."

"So what do we do?" Thomas asked.

"We start by meeting your contacts working on digs around the city. We'll find out if they are digging in areas where there were Roman villas—estates large enough to match Lucius Barrius's mansion. Then the Hatay Museum. It's here in the city, collecting antiquities since the

1930s. We'll also look into any ancient land records that mention his or Paul's name. Finally, we return here to explore more recent discoveries," Alister said."

"We know the scroll is hidden in a secret compartment at the base of a statue in his entry hall," Susan added. "If we can ID any likely dig sites, museum exhibits, or storage areas where that statue might have ended up, we can move."

She looked between them. "If we find it, we'll stage a ruse—make them think it's somewhere else. Then we get the scroll. And maybe we can get out of even here before they find us."

None of them noticed the man sitting across the terrace.

He looked like any other hotel guest—mid-40s, clean shave, neutral suit, sipping his coffee and scrolling his phone. But he wasn't here for breakfast.

He'd arrived in Antakya ninety minutes earlier. Alister had been on the phone with Luca at the time—when the walls and floor vibrated faintly, not from traffic outside but from something deeper. The distant roar of thrust reversers on a landing jet. Six miles away.

It was a polished black Gulfstream landing in the morning mist, contrails streaming from its wingtips as the late-morning sun shimmered off its fuselage. It was unmarked but for its tail number OS7777.

It rolled to a stop on the private runway at Hatay Airport.

Corvus stepped out first.

No briefcase. No handshake. Just a nod to the waiting driver, who stood beside a black Mercedes-Benz V-Class van with diplomatic plates and tinted windows. Two agents followed—one male, one female, both in tailored dark linen suits.

The driver opened the door. Corvus didn't speak. He slid into the rear seat and closed his eyes, already calculating.

The van pulled away smoothly, headed for the Hotel Anemon Antakya—a discreet, business-class property just outside the old city walls, where Susan and Alister wouldn't see him. It was three minutes from the Museum Hotel. Close enough, but not to be seen.

Alister and Susan had never seen the other two agents before. So they continued to the Museum Hotel, where they could track their prey without being noticed.

The lookout—now across from them at breakfast—was already in place. And his partner had moved faster.

Disguised in a borrowed hotel server's uniform, she had quietly taken a master key and slipped into their rooms. She searched Susan and Alister's first, then Thomas's. No scrolls. Not yet.

She placed a GPS tracker—disguised as a shirt button—into each of their backpacks. The devices had a range of 125 miles and would update via satellite ping every thirty seconds.

As his targets stood up from the table, the man across from them tapped his earpiece and spoke quietly.

"Get out. They're coming up."

CHAPTER FORTY-FIVE

The alarm shrieked without warning.

A piercing, high-pitched wail erupted overhead, echoing off the metal-framed security checkpoint. Lights flashed red above the scanners. Everyone in the dig site entry hall froze—security guards, researchers, interns, and laborers—all now staring at Susan, Alister, and Thomas.

Two guards raised their hands. "Step back! Away from the line."

Thomas raised both palms in mock surrender, trying to keep his tone calm. "It's all right. We're authorized visitors."

"Still need you to step over there, sir," one of the guards said, pointing toward a glass-walled office just off the security screening area.

Inside, a gray-bearded man with olive skin and kind, sharp eyes waved them in.

"Thomas Doyle," the man said, smiling tightly as the door closed. "You always know how to make an entrance."

Thomas let out a breath of recognition. "Rami. Thank God."

Rami Mardelli—former UNESCO field officer, now head of security at the central Antakya dig zone—stepped forward and embraced Thomas briefly.

"I'd say welcome back, I haven't seen you in what…eight years…but this isn't that kind of visit, is it?"

Thomas motioned to the others. "Susan Hale. Alister Duran. My friends. Trusted."

Rami nodded but remained serious. He reached to the counter behind him and held up a sealed evidence pouch.

Inside was a small, metallic disc—no bigger than a shirt button.

"We found this in your backpack," Rami said. "And identical devices in theirs."

Susan's jaw tightened. Alister said nothing, but his eyes flicked toward Thomas.

"They're GPS trackers," Rami continued. "Not the kind metal detectors catch easily. But dig site scanners are built differently. You'd know that, Thomas. We scan for contraband, smuggled devices, and anything that could be used to tag shipments or track trucks leaving the site. We've had entire crates intercepted that way—small GPS tags sewn into packing foam."

Thomas's mouth was dry, but he forced a nod. "Yes. I remember." He hesitated for only a second, then said smoothly, "We use trackers as a precaution. We often carry sensitive documents, such as draft manuscripts and rare source material. If we're ever separated from our bags, we can locate them. It's an old habit. I guess we forgot to remove them yesterday after we arrived."

Rami studied him a moment, then nodded. "Well, in that case, I suggest retiring the habit. You're lucky I was here when our staff caught them. Otherwise, they might have called the local police and detained you."

"We'll remove them immediately," Alister said quickly. "Thank you for catching it."

As the conversation turned to the dig site, Thomas mentioned that they were interested primarily in residential artifacts from the early first century. Rami said, "Most digs in the city focus on temples and commercial roads. Nothing from domestic spaces."

Susan frowned. "No mansions?"

"Not a priority, usually," Rami replied. "Too fragmented. But you know what was built right on top of Antioch's old mansion district?"

Thomas turned his head sharply.

"The Museum Hotel," Rami said. "You might find what you're looking for there."

They left the dig site within minutes, still shaken by the discovery of tracking devices in their backpacks. The moment they were clear of the crowd, Susan turned to Thomas, "They were in our rooms. During the night or this morning."

Thomas didn't respond—he didn't have to. They all knew.

Silentii was already tracking them and watching everything.

Thirty minutes later, they walked into the employee wing of the Museum Hotel. An older man, dressed in a pressed shirt, was waiting by the staff elevator.

"Father Mateo," Thomas said, his voice softer now. "You look the same."

"You look tired," Mateo replied, eyes twinkling. He pulled Thomas into a brief embrace. "But you have a reason…such a long trip to get here. Let me take you down to see our ancient treasure."

He led them down two levels to a quiet, climate-controlled archive adjacent to the subterranean display halls. They passed crates, drawers, and labeled fragments. The air was cool and dry, with a faint scent of clay dust and oiled wood.

"This hotel stands on the site of a fourth-century mansion," Mateo said. "That mosaic floor in the lobby? From the main hall. And beneath that, we found traces of an even earlier estate—destroyed in the second-century earthquake…in the year 105."

Susan stopped walking. "There was something before?"

"Yes," Mateo said. "Fragments of foundation stones, mosaic debris, and an intact statue base. The statue itself was broken, but still attached to the base—the legs and feet were intact, but only a partial torso and one raised arm remained. We think it was originally located in the entry hall of the earlier home. But the location is not easily identifiable. It's all here, waiting for us to study it, after 2,000 years."

He stopped before a wide storage shelf lined with unremarkable crates.

"That base, and the statue," Mateo added quietly. "It's all in this crate."

Susan looked at Thomas. Her throat tightened.

Alister stepped forward, staring at the dark crate in front of them.

It was real.

But was it from the house of Lucius Aurelius Barrius?

And was the scroll still there?

CHAPTER FORTY-SIX

The bar was dimly lit and mostly empty, save for a pair of Turkish men nursing beers near the door and a table of university students dissecting archaeology in fluent French. A haze of cigarette smoke curled beneath the ceiling fan, mingling with the low hum of foreign music and the faint clink of glassware.

In the far corner, three Silentii agents—freshly embedded that morning—sat in a booth beneath a flickering wall sconce.

Gabriel Moreau, wiry and sun-creased, had the dry stillness of a man who'd seen too many operations go sideways and survived each one by standing very still. Across from him sat Leila Kazan, composed and alert, her dark hair pulled into a tight knot. Her slate-gray cargo pants and sleeveless blouse revealed a faint tracery of old scars—quiet trophies from years in the field.

Beside her, Corvus sat stiffly, his jaw set. His arms were crossed over his chest, and though he hadn't touched his drink, his right leg bounced under the table with a low, caged energy.

They raised their glasses of Yeni Rakı.

"To local camouflage," Moreau said, tipping his glass toward the white work van across the street. The logo *Hatay Klima & Elektrik* flaked slightly under the bar's yellow light.

"To discipline," Leila added.

Corvus raised his glass a beat late.

Moreau noticed. "That includes patience," he said, letting the words hang just long enough to sting.

Corvus forced a tight smile but said nothing. His eyes stayed fixed on the screen in his hand, where three blinking dots drifted across a satellite map of Antakya.

"All three trackers still active," he muttered. "They've stayed between the Museum Hotel and the Kurtuluş dig compound. No side trips. No erratic behavior."

"Amateurs," Moreau said. "They have no idea they've been tagged. If they did, those bags would be in shreds."

He turned to Leila. "Excellent work gaining access and planting the trackers this morning. Smooth. Quiet."

Leila shrugged modestly. "They left their rooms for breakfast. Nothing was even locked. Fifteen minutes, tops."

Corvus's lip curled. "Lucky. Could've done it faster myself."

Moreau raised an eyebrow but didn't look at him. "You've had your chances."

Leila glanced toward Corvus—neutral, unreadable—but said nothing.

Corvus sat up straighter. "They're relaxed. No indication they suspect anything. If they did, we'd have seen signs—looping paths, nervous glances, split formations."

"Unless they're better than we thought," Leila said mildly, her eyes flicking toward him.

"They're not," Corvus snapped. "The man's a scholar, not a tactician. The woman's emotional. The brother's Jesuit-trained, still thinks in rules."

Moreau exhaled through his nose, unimpressed. "You've had two chances to capture them. And now you're profiling."

Corvus's voice tightened. "This is field work. Not library chess. I know how they think."

"Good," Moreau said flatly. "Then prove it tomorrow."

A silence settled over the table.

"They'll resume casing," Leila said after a beat. "Today was recon. Two sites only. But there's another dig south of town. A museum annex near the river. Private archives. If the scroll's here, they're hunting for something buried. Hidden."

"We'll know when they find it," Moreau added. "They'll return to the same site. More than once."

Corvus finally nodded. "They won't get far."

Moreau unlocked his phone, opened the secure Vatican relay app, and typed a short encrypted burst:

> S48T active. All targets tagged. No discovery activity yet. Confidence high. Standing by.

He watched the confirmation flash, then closed the app.

Outside, the van's hazard lights blinked once—then went dark.

Six blocks away, in the Museum Hotel's upper wing, another light flickered—this one beneath the frame of Room 212, where a Do Not Disturb placard hung like a shield.

Inside, the mood was quiet but electric.

Thomas Doyle sat at the desk, his laptop open in front of him. The screen mirrored the same Antakya city map the Silentii agents were seeing at that moment—but without the three blinking GPS location dots. They had just finished using the map to finalize their escape plan.

Alister stood beside the desk. Susan sat on the edge of the bed, her hands laced, her gaze steady.

"Tomorrow, they'll still be watching us," Alister said. "Mainly through the GPS trackers, backed up with eyes from here." He tapped a mark on the map. "Their disguised work van. Parked there all day. South curb. Two streets away."

"They'll follow from a distance until they think we've found the scroll," Thomas said. "Then they'll close in."

Susan looked up. "So tomorrow we put our plan into action."

A quiet beat.

Then the beginning of a smile. "We'll give them an Academy Award performance... creating the illusion that we're still searching..."

Thomas finished her sentence. "...while we find the scroll and get out of here."

The room fell still as they each considered the plan that had taken shape over dinner, ordered in from room service: grilled lamb köfte, stuffed eggplant, lavash bread, and small bowls of ezme and hummus. Antakya on a plate.

It was a risky plan—one that would require discipline, coordination, and perfect timing.

But above all, it would require luck.

Susan rose and walked slowly to the window. Below, the lights of Antakya glittered like a city trying to forget its past.

Behind her, Alister whispered, "They have no idea we're about to disappear."

No one replied. But in their shared stillness, tomorrow had already begun.

CHAPTER FORTY-SEVEN

It was past two in the morning, but the air still hung thick and muggy—eighty-three degrees and not a whisper of breeze. The lights of Antakya shimmered faintly through the Museum Hotel's high, dew-glazed lobby windows. But down here, in the sub-basement, it was cool, dry, and black as pitch.

They were in. Somehow. Unseen. Undetected.

Or so they thought.

The storage room was quiet—too quiet. Susan, Alister, and Thomas crept cautiously across the stone floor, a fine layer of dust blanketing everything like ash. Between rows of crates and cataloged remnants, even the air felt ancient.

Now they froze—backs to the wall, listening. A faint skittering echoed from somewhere ahead. Claws on stone. Rat? Cat?

They held their breath.

In the silence, their minds replayed the plan they'd crafted the night before in Thomas's room. So far, it was unfolding exactly as intended. Luck, it seemed, was on their side.

Earlier that day, Susan and Alister had made themselves highly visible—posing at the Hatay Archaeological Museum, a collapsed Roman drainage site near the Asi River, and the Antakya land records office. Thomas's GPS tracker had traveled quietly in Susan's bag, making it appear the trio was still moving as one. At each stop, their cab dropped them on crowded side streets, allowing them to slip unnoticed into museums and dig sites—making it difficult for any observer to notice that one of them was missing.

The missing one —Thomas—had spent the day executing the more dangerous half of the plan.

He left the hotel in disguise: an oversized Galatasaray hoodie, mirrored sunglasses, and a surgical mask. Unremarkable in an era of outbreaks and urban anonymity. He weaved through Antakya's back alleys to avoid surveillance, then met with Arda Sancar, a veteran UNESCO shipping contractor who owed him a favor. Years ago, Thomas had falsified documents to help free Arda's nephew after a smuggling sting in Aleppo. Now it was payback time.

Thomas kept it simple: he and two colleagues were Interpol operatives. A powerful trafficking ring was closing in. They needed to vanish— quietly.

Arda didn't hesitate. "Tomorrow. Ten a.m. I'll be waiting," he said. "It won't be easy. A difficult plan. But they'll never see it coming."

Later that afternoon, while Susan and Alister were at the records office, Thomas focused on phase two. He had lunch under the fig trees with Father Mateo on the hotel terrace. They reminisced about Nabataean architecture, Jordan, and the dangers of Turkish wine. But Thomas kept an eye on the museum's side door.

Each time Mateo returned from his office, he used the same keypad code: 4-1-2-6—no retina scan. No fingerprint. Just four digits. It was all Thomas needed for access to the museum storage room.

Back in the sub-basement, the scratching sound ceased. Silence again.

So they pressed forward.

Twenty meters ahead, the crate stood like a sentry: *Barrius Villa Artifact, 2017 Excavation*—nearly a meter tall, chalk label fading.

This was it.

Thomas knelt, crowbar in hand. He looked up. Alister nodded.

The wood groaned softly, then gave. Inside—wrapped in linen and stabilizing foam—was a partially fragmented marble statue. Its legs and feet still intact. And its base.

Alister remembered the letter from Jesus to Mary:

A god with no chains, one raised hand. I've hidden the scroll jar in a cavity hollowed out in its base. I carved it myself, lined it with gold leaf, and sealed it with wax. It's behind the plaque that identifies the sculptor. Hidden beneath the heel of his forward foot is the mechanism to open it. Press, turn, and slide left. You'll hear the latch. If it's still there, the scroll is waiting.

Susan leaned in. "That's Liber Pater," she whispered. "Roman god of freedom. The raised hand, no chains—it fits."

"But why would it be in Barrius's house?" she asked.

"Because if Jesus never returned," Alister said, "Barrius probably handled the sale. Back then, before online marketing, that meant managing everything personally. He must've moved the statue to his own villa. Then came the earthquake sixty-five years later, in 105—and it was buried under the rubble of time."

The statue's foot extended forward, just as described.

Alister crouched beside it. "Press… turn… and slide left."

He tried.

Nothing.

Again—nothing.

Thomas handed him the crowbar.

Alister struck the base. A scraping, grinding sound echoed through the dark.

Then—click.

A latch released. A small brass plaque dropped to the floor with a sharp *clink*.

Behind it, a cavity—lined with flaking gold leaf. Inside: a wax-sealed scroll jar and a blackened leather folder, about the size of a small book. The string that once bound it had crumbled.

They didn't move.

Then Susan stepped forward, snapping photos of the crate, statue, scroll, and pouch.

"For the record," she whispered. "Blockchain later."

Thomas gently lifted the scroll jar and leather folder. He placed it in his padded backpack.

"Let's go."

They moved quickly back through the archive, slipping out the keypad door. A quiet breath of relief passed between them.

They had the scroll.

The plan was working.

Or so they thought.

What they didn't know was that Leila Kazan—the third Silentii agent—hadn't trusted Corvus's smug conclusions about how naive their targets were. She'd quietly paid the hotel janitor 200 euros to watch Room 212 and text her if there was movement. When he saw them leave, he alerted her. She followed—silent, patient, armed—into the museum's sub-basement. Unable to open the code-locked door, she waited in the shadows for their return.

"Stop right there."

They froze.

Leila stepped from the dark, raising a matte-black Jericho 941. Her finger hovered just outside the trigger guard.

"I knew it," she said. "You're a lot more clever than that idiot Corvus gives you credit for. Drop the bag. Now."

Their hearts sank.

Alister tightened his grip on the backpack. Thomas slowly stepped forward, hands raised.

But before anyone could speak—

"No. *You* drop the gun."

A sharp click.

Leila froze.

Father Mateo stood behind her, steady hands holding an old Beretta 84.

"I don't like people hunting guests in my museum," he said calmly.

"You're making a mistake," Leila hissed.

"You already made yours," Mateo replied, stepping closer.

Thomas exhaled. Then turned to Mateo.

"She said she was following her husband," Mateo said. "Room 212. Suspected an affair. But the janitor saw Thomas leave and remembered him from yesterday—with me. He put it together. Called me."

Thomas nodded. "I couldn't tell you—for your safety. We're Interpol. That crate held key evidence. She's part of a trafficking ring. Her team plans to destroy it before prosecutors can act."

Mateo studied them for a beat—then nodded.

"So what now?"

"We need to disappear," Thomas said. "Quietly. If her team finds out she's compromised, they'll scatter. Or retaliate."

"Storage chamber," Mateo offered. "Twelve hours?"

"Perfect," Thomas said.

Leila didn't resist. As they led her to the conservation room, wrists bound with plastic ties, she hissed under her breath:

"Corvus was wrong again. They're not amateurs."

Upstairs, halfway through the stairwell, no one spoke.

Finally, Susan broke the silence. "Now?"

Alister nodded. "Now we start the next part of the plan—and vanish."

Thomas added, "Let's get our bags packed. Be ready to leave by 6 a.m. We'll meet at the lobby's side door—where we can slip out without anyone noticing.

First, I'll speak to the concierge and get the next phase moving."

CHAPTER FORTY-EIGHT

Corvus was feeling very confident. Their mission was going well. They would have the scroll soon…he could feel it. Vallente would be impressed, and his two failures to capture the fugitives would be forgotten. It had only been two days, but he hated waiting. Yesterday, the fugitives spent the whole day casing possible sites where the scroll could be hidden. He was sure today would be different.

He stood in the corner of his hotel room at the Anemon, wound up like a predatory cat, ready to spring. It was 8:03 a.m. He had been fully dressed for two hours—black tactical trousers and a gray linen blazer concealing his weapon.

Finally, his earpiece buzzed.

"They're on the move," said Gabriel Moreau, his voice clipped. He was two miles away at the Museum Hotel. "Three GPS signals. All active. They've left the hotel. Two are heading east toward the city center, and one is northbound. I'm going to the lobby now to meet Kazan."

Corvus grinned. "The hunt begins… again. But this time…"

The elevator doors opened into the lobby of the Museum Hotel. Moreau walked quickly to the same quiet corner of the lobby where he had met Kazan the past two mornings. His dark blue suit blended with the tourists and academics trickling through the lobby.

Five minutes later, Corvus's voice crackled in his ear. "Where the hell is Kazan?"

Moreau exhaled. "I just checked her satellite phone records. Offline for five hours."

Corvus snorted. "Hungover or careless. Typical."

Moreau scowled. "We go without her."

As they were about to get into cabs to follow the GPS trackers, an alert appeared simultaneously on both screens.

[ALERT: Three Turkish Airlines tickets purchased. Departure: 1:05 p.m. IST. Names: Hale, Doyle, Duran.]

Corvus's jaw tightened. "I knew it. They found the scroll. They're retrieving it now, then heading for the airport. It's nine a.m.—we've got five hours. They'll need to be at the terminal by eleven. We intercept when all three are there."

Moreau nodded. "I'm going to Kazan's room. We need her now."

Less than a minute later, he kicked open the door. Empty. Bed untouched.

"Gone. No trace."

"Screw her. We don't have time. We move," Corvus said. "Track them to the airport."

But Moreau had a bad feeling. So he stopped at the Museum Hotel concierge desk. The clerk shook his head—no sightings. Outside, the cab stand manager gave the same answer. Nothing. Ghosts.

"Just minutes earlier," he thought, "they went through the lobby and got into cabs… without anyone seeing them?"

He tried to chalk it up to chance. But the feeling shook his confidence as it lingered longer than it should have.

9:11 a.m.

They drove separately. Two hotel cabs. Two trackers in one. The other alone.

Their dashboards showed the two blinking dots arriving at the Hatay Archaeological Museum. The other one pulsed and went to Hatay Airport, entering the domestic departure lounge.

10:04 a.m.

"Two of them have left the Museum. Moving toward the airport," Moreau radioed. "They must have the scroll."

"I see it," Corvus said. "ETA in 51 minutes. All three will be at the Turkish Air terminal. We intercept there."

Corvus adjusted his lapel, revealing a Turkish Intelligence Services badge—one of three false credentials sanctioned by the Vatican Office of Internal Affairs. Clean-shaven, pressed collar, dark blazer over tactical gear—he looked every bit the operative. Moreau wore an Interpol windbreaker with a forged pass and concealed body armor.

"We move at eleven sharp," Corvus said. "Nice and tidy."

10:59 a.m.

Hatay Airport hummed with midday departures. Families stood in slow-moving lines. Children clung to animal-shaped backpacks. Flight attendants glided past in navy skirts.

Corvus and Moreau stepped through the sliding doors, their secure phones in hand, guns holstered beneath their coats, and GPS locators open.

The three blinking dots had merged—Turkish Air ticket counters.

"Let's finish this," Corvus muttered, cracking his neck.

They moved in.

Two young men—clearly cab drivers—stood near the counter, nodding to music only they could hear. Oversized sunglasses. Polos. Each with a brown paper bag at his feet.

Corvus paused for a moment, thinking that the fugitives had seen them coming and had run, not having time to retrieve their bags from the cab drivers. Perhaps, in their panic, they had left the scroll behind.

Corvus drew his weapon.

"Step away from the bags. Now."

The two froze, their earbuds falling out, their sunglasses hitting the floor, their eyes wide.

"What's going on? We were told—"

Moreau shoved one against the wall as airport security closed in.

"The hotel concierge sent us here and to the Hatay with these bags… gave us each 50 euros and promised 50 more when we returned. Said to deliver it to someone who would give us the code words—' fooled again.' That's all we know!"

Corvus ripped open the first bag. Inside: a terracotta jar. The right size for a scroll. His pulse jumped.

He pulled off the stopper.

Two button-sized GPS trackers bounced to the floor.

"No scroll," Moreau said.

Corvus turned to the second bag. A thick envelope.

He opened it. A third GPS beacon dropped and rolled.

Around them, a silent ring of staff, guards, and travelers stared at the bouncing GPS trackers spinning across the polished floor.

In that embarrassing moment of silence, had they paused to listen very carefully, in the distance they would have heard the deep throaty roar of twin Volvo Penta D8-600 engines, powering a 42-foot Marex 375 fast cruiser named *Veritas*, as it rocketed westward up the Orontes River. Susan was gripping the boat's railing. A ruddy-faced veteran captain who had grown up on this dangerously silted and shallow river helmed the wheel. Thomas and Alister watched the ancient Antioch docks fade into the late morning mist. It was dead calm, humid, and 93 degrees.

If their plan had worked, they knew what would be happening now. Silentii would be locking down every highway, bridge, tunnel, and airport. But not the river. Except for locals in rowboats fishing for their dinner, no one ever thought of the river.

The Orontes dockyards—where Jesus once arrived—hadn't seen real marine traffic in centuries. Earthquakes had changed the land. The river was shallow and silted, with only a few deeper channels…all unmarked and constantly shifting. Only locals who had grown up navigating it could do so now. The captain at the helm of the *Veritas* was one of those rare locals.

It was twelve miles to the Mediterranean. Then 120 more to the port of Mersin.

Veritas could reach 65 knots on calm seas. They'd be there in three hours. The sea in July was warm and glassy. The boat could outrun anything—police, pirates, patrols.

A launch from the freighter *Aquila Maris* would meet them offshore. No port entry. No customs. Rome in one week.

They were already gone when the GPS trackers bounced across the terminal floor.

CHAPTER FORTY-NINE

It had been thirty-three days since the escape from Antakya. Thirty-three days without word. Without a sign. Without certainty.

From his terrace high above the cliffs of Positano, Luca Severin watched the morning unfold. The effortless beauty of sailboats catching the sun and the faint echo of laughter rising from the small patch of sandy beach below did little to quiet the unrest inside him.

Still no trace. No leaks. No intercepted signals. No sightings.

Only silence—and questions that refused to let go. Had Alister believed him? Had they escaped safely…or had something gone wrong in the chaos of their flight? The region was dangerous—riddled with smugglers, highwaymen, and factions as ruthless as the Silentii. And the scrolls—did they still have them? Had they survived? Was he still part of their plan, or had they found sanctuary elsewhere?

These doubts had become his constant companions. Not even the sun-drenched calm of the Amalfi Coast could still them.

And then there was Vallente.

His old friend was unraveling. Once a pillar of control, now a man driven by paranoia. He still trusted Luca completely—confided in him often, almost compulsively. The fugitives, he kept repeating, had outwitted his most seasoned agents three times. How? How had they discovered the GPS devices so quickly?

Corvus, Gabriel, and Leila had begun to turn on one another. Their unity dissolving into suspicion.

Vallente had told Luca everything. And when they last spoke, his voice was stretched thin, edged with quiet panic. With each call, Luca felt the weight of betrayal pressing harder.

But what Luca didn't know—what Vallente hadn't shared—was the deeper reason for his unraveling.

Just days after the Antakya disaster, Father Carlo Verano, Prefect of the Holy See's Directives, had met with Vallente behind closed doors. The message was simple and final: the Vatican was losing faith. One month gone. One failure down. Five months left for the Silentii to prove their worth. If they failed, the Holy See would dismantle them.

Luca exhaled slowly and reached for his coffee.

He couldn't have known it, but the silence was about to break.

Just yesterday—at this exact hour—a Turkish freighter named *Aquila Maris* had slipped quietly past the Amalfi Coast, bound for the Port of Civitavecchia. From its upper deck, a pair of binoculars might have captured Luca seated exactly as he was now—coffee in hand, eyes locked on the horizon.

He hadn't seen them.

But he was about to.

He set the cup down, the ceramic ticking gently against the mosaic tabletop.

From the far side of the villa, he heard the crunch of tires on gravel.

He stood.

And walked inside to open the door.

CHAPTER FIFTY

The next morning dawned bright and cloudless over Positano. From the stone-floored terrace—where they had last stood six weeks ago—it felt as though time had both flown and frozen. When Susan, Alister, and Thomas arrived the day before, there had been hugs, handshakes, and a deep, unspoken relief.

They had made it. Against all odds. And, in the end, thanks to Luca.

He had repeated his apology. It wasn't long, but it was heartfelt. And after that call he made—the one that saved their lives—they had believed him.

They sat late into the afternoon, reliving every twist and turn since the night they'd fled the villa. Thomas described how they'd fooled everyone by escaping Antakya by boat. They recounted the three-hour high-speed run across the Mediterranean to the Turkish freighter *Aquila Maris*, docked near Mersin. Uneventful, they said, smirking—except for the gunfire as they outran a pirate vessel.

Alister handed Luca a flash drive with the AI-translated letters Jesus had written. Susan filled in the story of the third scroll hidden in the Museum Hotel's storage room—and their narrow escape from the Silentii agent.

Luca listened quietly, taking it all in. He'd already heard the Silentii's version of the Antakya incident—how Leila Kazan was overpowered and locked in a sub-basement storage room at gunpoint. But Susan gave him the other side. Silentii had underestimated Thomas's experience and personal network in Antakya. That had been their mistake—and it changed everything.

They shared dinner and wine on the terrace as the sun dipped behind the Lattari Mountains. For the first time in weeks, they slept in real beds.

Luca did not.

He stayed up for hours, reading through the second scroll and the translated letters. But fatigue overtook him before he reached the contents of the leather pouch. That would have to wait until morning.

When he finally joined the others at breakfast, the brilliant midsummer sun had already climbed high over the cliffs. He looked pale but alert— like a man who had seen something he couldn't unsee.

Over strong coffee and fresh figs, he began.

"It starts in Antioch," Luca said. "But the tone—it's different from the earlier scrolls. Raw. Unfiltered. Jesus—now Paul—is disillusioned. His letters to the apostles go unanswered. He's cut off. Alone. And then something shifts."

He looked up. "His relationship with Barrius changes everything."

Alister nodded. "The merchant from Gaul. Mary met him at Olea Vallis."

"Jesus thought he came to hear the message," Thomas added. "But Barrius saw a business opportunity."

"And after no one except the dockworkers in Antioch responded to his preaching," Luca said, "Barrius made him an offer: help him build loyal, disciplined, and more hardworking crews by becoming their spiritual guide. In return, if successful—a full partnership. Profits. Land. A villa. A share in the Roman Empire, so to speak."

"Jesus said yes," Luca continued, "and over twelve years, he succeeded beyond anything he expected."

Susan pointed to a passage. "He writes, *'There is no shame in this if the message reaches further than I could carry it alone'.*"

Luca nodded. "The scroll describes him walking into Lucius's mansion for the first time. He has written a letter to Mary about what he has seen since his arrival that morning, and he gives it to Lucius to bring to Mary on his next trip to his vacation villa in Gaul."

"But as he sees how Lucius lives, he notices things he had never allowed himself to admire before: the mosaic floors, the silence of trained staff, the order of it all. And he begins to imagine a life—not just for himself, but for Mary and their children."

"A daughter educated, not bartered. His son clothed in Egyptian cotton. A mother cared for in dignity," Luca said quietly. "He begins to see wealth not as betrayal—but as strategy. A tool to build something lasting."

They sat in silence.

Thomas spoke next. "He always believed suffering was a requirement for truth. But this scroll suggests otherwise. It reframes resurrection—not just as spiritual endurance, but as a structural rebirth of his message. Wealth, used with purpose, becomes infrastructure."

"Lucius taught him that," Luca said. "He ran his shipping empire with discipline. For Jesus, the men with the talent to carry his message became his disciples. Commissions paid to reward success incentivized loyalty, hard work, and outcomes."

Alister leaned forward, realization dawning. "Of course," he said. "The Church rewrote it all. Barrius became Barnabas. The ship crews—rebranded as Apostles. Jesus's instructions became the Epistles. And the trade routes—the very network that carried his message—were erased and replaced with the myth of missionary wanderings."

He ticked off cities on his fingers. "Ephesus. Corinth. Galatia. Philippi. Thessalonica. Rome. All coastal trade hubs—established through Barrius's shipping routes, not Paul's miraculous travels."

Luca nodded. "Eighteen prosperous years pass. He works relentlessly—preaching to crews, managing the network of commissioned church builders in the port cities. He has little time for leisure. And not enough to bring Mary from Gaul."

He paused. "Then the scroll shifts. The final section is frantic. Clipped sentences. Slanted script. There's panic."

Susan leaned in. "Why?"

"Because Barrius's business was booming," Luca said. "And his competitors grew envious. They went to the Roman authorities and accused Jesus of stirring unrest. They claimed the problem wasn't the religion—it was this man. This foreigner is inciting dockworkers and sailors, creating disruption. And the governors…"

"Only cared about order and taxes," Thomas said. "Belief was irrelevant."

"Exactly," Luca said. "Jesus found himself in trouble again. He knew what could happen, so he planned to flee to a bigger city—one where he wasn't known. Where he could continue managing the partnership quietly. Before he left, he sent that final letter to Mary, entrusted to Barrius."

He sat back.

They were quiet, each absorbing the implications.

Susan broke the silence. "Take us through it. From the beginning."

CHAPTER FIFTY-ONE

For the next two hours, as the morning light deepened across the villa terrace, they became the first to hear the words of Jesus from two thousand years ago—unfiltered, undistorted, and almost lost—telling the untold history of his Church.

Luca began to read.

I stepped from the mansion's atrium onto the portico as a servant appeared at the entrance gate. He bowed, then led me inside.

Lucius Aurelius Barrius stood smiling in the golden light of early evening. His arms extended, not with Roman stiffness but with an almost Galilean warmth.

"Jesus," he said, approaching. "You've arrived at last."

Jesus returned the smile and stepped forward. They embraced briefly—a touch more formal than friendly, though not without affection. Lucius smelled faintly of myrrh and sea salt.

"Your journey?" Lucius asked as he led him toward the impluvium.

"Long," Jesus replied. "But on a good ship and with good company."

Lucius nodded. "I had the guest chamber prepared two days ago—just in case the winds were favorable. Clean sheets. Warm bread. Tolerable wine. Stay as long as you like."

Jesus thanked him, but inside, he remained cautious. The mosaic floor had already told him more than Lucius realized—this was a man of dual allegiances. Commitment, yes—but to whom? To what? Commerce or God? Jesus would wait and see.

They sat briefly in the triclinium, sipping watered wine. The conversation danced along safe edges—coastal weather, crew behavior, the state of trade in Seleucia. Jesus spoke of his first impressions of Antioch.

"As you've probably noticed," Lucius said, "Antioch is a sponge. It soaks up everything—languages, cults, habits. But what it can't digest, it spits out. Loudly."

Jesus raised an eyebrow. "And what do you think it cannot digest?"

Lucius smiled as he refilled their cups. "We'll find out soon enough."

That night, Jesus slept lightly. He dreamed of olive branches, of the chapel in Gaul. Of Mary, and of their children.

Morning sunlight angled through the latticework window. At breakfast, Jesus sat across from Lucius, sharing dates, flatbread, and goat cheese. The air smelled faintly of lemon blossoms and lamp oil.

"I should tell you something," Jesus said quietly. "I'm not the man you met in Gaul."

Lucius looked up, but said nothing.

"Six years ago, I preached in the temple at Jerusalem. I challenged the orthodoxy. They turned on me. They took it to the governor, and I was sentenced to death. Crucifixion. As a criminal—not as a man of God. But I escaped. Fled to Gaul with Mary and my mother."

He paused. "Some Roman soldiers here in Antioch may remember my name. They may have seen me speak. Maybe worse. I can't risk being recognized."

Lucius's eyes narrowed—not in suspicion, but in understanding.

"At one of my services in Gaul, I'm sure you remember meeting my Roman friend, Paul. He knew I planned to come here, but he fell ill. Before he passed, he offered me his name. So I, Jesus, became Paul. And Paul…is who I must remain."

Lucius chewed slowly, then nodded. "And the man you are now?"

"Carries a message. One that might save many."

Lucius leaned back. "Then, Paul it is."

A silence passed—difficult, but not hostile.

At length, Lucius stood, and as they headed for the docks, he said, "Then let us find out how this Paul speaks."

The shipyard smelled of pitch, sweat, and salt. Lucius led Paul to one of his ships—Domina Fortuna—moored along a weathered dock.

"She's been unloading for three days," Lucius explained. "The crew's grown restless. They listen better when their hands are idle."

Dozens of men—freemen mostly, some shirtless, others in torn tunics—lounged nearby, eating, sharpening blades, or dicing for coins. Lucius whistled sharply, and heads turned.

"This man Paul is a guest in my house," Lucius called out. "He speaks of the Christos… in a way you may not have heard before."

Lucius knew the risk. His crew came from every corner of the empire, with vastly different beliefs.

For those with Jewish backgrounds, Christos meant Messiah—a warrior king who would restore Israel's sovereignty.

To the broader Greek-speaking crew, the concept was unfamiliar, even absurd. One god? A suffering savior?

To the Romans, it was worse. A potential political threat. A challenge to the emperor's divinity.

Lucius continued, "You will listen as you like—no coin required, no record kept. It is a message you have not heard before."

Paul stepped forward and stood on an overturned barrel. The crew fell silent.

He spoke in Greek—the empire's common tongue.

He spoke of resurrection. Of belief not rooted in temples or sacrifice, but in faith. Of love—not just for the divine, but for one another. Of a man who healed without payment, who wept and bled and returned from death not to judge, but to forgive. Of a world not divided between master and servant, but between those who love—and those who do not.

Some blinked. A few crossed their arms. One man laughed, but was quickly hushed.

By the end, several had stopped chewing. One clapped. Another muttered, "The Christ Man speaks true."

Word spread.

In the following weeks, Lucius rotated him through the dock crews of three ships. Each morning and evening, Paul preached—before meals, after the day's labor. His voice grew stronger. His stories sharper. He began to see which words lifted eyes.

One captain invited him back. Another crew asked for him by name.

Down by the riverfront, they began calling him "the Christ Man." At first mockery, then habit.

He tried to bring the same message to the city. The agora. The Temple of Apollo. The gymnasiums. The baths.

But there, the response was ridicule, or worse.

At the agora, a trader shouted, "Your god died like a criminal! Why follow such weakness?"

At Apollo's temple, a Stoic sneered, "Pain is illusion. Don't glorify it."

At the baths, a sculptor snarled, "You're ruining my business. People whisper your words—but stop buying my statues."

As months passed, he was shouted down, chased off, mocked again and again.

Each night, he returned to Lucius's house. They dined in the triclinium over fish and bitter wine.

"They call me Paulus, the Christ Man now," Paul said.

Lucius chuckled. "Started as a mockery. Now? They come early just to hear you."

"Do they believe?"

"Some do," Lucius said. "Some hope you'll bless their voyage. Or forgive their debt. Or bring luck."

Paul smiled faintly. "Maybe they just like the sound of hope."

Lucius shrugged. "Does it matter why they come? They quote you. Repeat your stories. That's how ideas spread."

Paul nodded. "I came hoping to reach thinkers, the powerful, the philosophers…"

He hesitated.

"But it's only the laborers. The crews. They hunger. They listen."

Lucius tapped the table. "Then feed them. Let them carry your bread—to distant shores."

He poured more wine, then added, "You wondered, back in Gaul, why I helped you?"

Paul looked up.

"I saw your teachings as useful," Lucius said. "Life here is brutal. The gods are many. People pick one—or five—for survival. But you…you offered purpose. Discipline. Hope beyond today. That matters."

"You used me," Paul said softly.

Lucius didn't flinch. "I believed in the benefit—even if not the message."

He continued, "I let you try the city. I hoped you'd surprise me. But it didn't work. Too many gods. Too much noise. But the docks? That's where your power lies."

Lucius leaned in.

"What if we formalize this? A partnership. You preach. I fund. You become the face of my crews. My rivals won't know what hit them. And if it works—well, we both profit."

Paul stared at him. Not angry—just stunned.

He thought of the apostles, scattered. The temple leaders who condemned him. The trial before Pilate. The silence since.

He realized he was alone—and failing.

Except for Lucius. And Lucius's empire.

Lucius sat back. "You want to change the world. I want to survive it. Maybe we do both."

Later that evening, on the docks, a young deckhand whispered to another, "Is Paulus the Christian talking again tomorrow?"

Neither noticed how Christ Man became Christian.

A blurred phrase became a label. A nickname became an identity.

Paul heard it. And paused.

Christian?

It wasn't what he planned.

But it seemed to fit.

And that sound—first heard that night in Antioch—would travel to every port of the Mediterranean.

And one day, reshape the world.

CHAPTER FIFTY-TWO

Sophie's eyes were fixed on Alice, her hands loosely clasped in her lap, as if afraid to look away and lose the thread of the story she was hearing.

Then the clink of porcelain broke the spell.

The waiter moved briskly between tables, clearing lunch plates and coffee cups from the few guests who lingered longer than they should have. Alice Hale sat back, letting the interruption wash over her, though her mind was still inside the story she'd been telling.

It was past mid-afternoon now. Time to go. A faint chill was sliding in with the light, the way it did in the shoulder seasons here—winter not yet gone, spring not yet certain.

They left the café without a word.

The walk down from the village was steep but familiar, the stone path bordered by old houses and weathered barns, many with sagging shutters and terracotta roofs mottled by centuries of weather. Some foundations reached back to the earliest days of St Cyr, over a thousand years ago.

Alice's pace slowed near the bottom of the road, where it bent to the right and climbed toward her mother's house.

They passed the small, pale-yellow stone Chapel of St Cyr. Alice paused.

"This," she said quietly, "was the spot. The original place. It started as just a pile of stones—Jesus's first chapel."

Sophie turned to look at her.

"She came every Sunday," Alice went on, "and she swore the earth spoke to her—from somewhere deep below. When you hear the rest of the story, you'll know why."

The road widened into a gentle upward slope.

When they reached her mother's stone house—the one she had lived in for the past five years—they settled into comfortable chairs on the terrace out back.

In the distance, the tiled roofs of the neighboring town glowed warm under the lowering sun. Sophie didn't expect it, but her breath caught as she saw Colume du Roma as if for the first time. Centuries ago, it had been built from stones and broken terracotta roof tiles salvaged from a collapsed olive farmer's hut. But after what she had heard this afternoon, the column seemed alive, breathing.

In places, she could still make out the patched stones from the old earthquake repairs, their edges softened by time but still distinct—a quiet record of what had started the story she was hearing today.

Alice poured two glasses of pale rosé, the same ritual her mother and Bob had shared here decades earlier on the afternoon just before the tremor that changed everything—and where, centuries before, Jesus and Mary had once sat imagining their future.

Sophie held her glass, watching the play of light across the rim, and felt the weight of ancient moments pressing together on this terrace—past and present, before and after—all on this very spot.

In a voice softened by those same feelings, Alice quietly continued the story, "My mother and Alister, after it was all over, suddenly realized that somewhere along the way they had fallen in love."

She smiled faintly. "They never married, but wow, were they in love."

Sophie tilted her head, surprised. "So that's why…".

"Yes," Alice said. "She met her soulmate." Alice paused for a long moment, then went on. "I never understood why my parents divorced so suddenly—not until I heard the story over these past two weeks. Mom said that sometimes your kindred spirit appears in the most unexpected ways. Sometimes you only get that one chance in life, so you either go for it…or always regret *that which might have been.*

Alice continued, "They kept this as a vacation house, and moved into Alister's apartment in New York and lived there happily for years. Mom loved her role as Curator of Ancient Near Eastern and Christian Antiquities at the Met. Just yesterday, she told me that the position had proved more useful than she ever imagined, connecting her with artifacts and scholars from across the Mediterranean. I sensed there was more to that story, but now I'll never have the chance to ask.

"Alister returned to his professorship in Classics and Early Christian Studies at Columbia University. Mom said he loved researching arcane linguistic mysteries and theologies, but the position also deepened his ties to colleagues and archives abroad. Again, I got the feeling that was also part of a bigger story."

Sophie and Alice had met in their first year of college in California and connected immediately—two teenagers away from home for the first time. By their second year, they were inseparable.

Sophie remembered how adrift Alice had seemed when her parents separated, how much sadness she carried without explanation. And now, with the story still unfurling between them, she understood.

Alice took a sip of wine, her gaze fixed on the evening horizon. "The next part," she said softly, "will explain even more."

The sun slipped lower, touching the western mountains with molten light. Shadows stretched across the terrace, and the first cool breath of evening rose from the valley.

They settled in, neither in a hurry, as if both knew that what came next would continue to change the foundation of everything they had ever believed.

Alice leaned forward, her voice almost conspiratorial.
"Do you remember," she said, "when I told you I thought I was being followed by dangerous-looking people? Two men and a woman, never together, but in different places… the grocery store, the luncheonette, the movie theater".

"It was just a month or so before I learned my parents were going to divorce. We talked, and you convinced me it was just my imagination. Then it stopped as suddenly as it started, so I figured you were right and chalked it up to study nerves."

She let the pause stretch.

"What I'm about to tell you," she said, "is the real story. And yes—back then—I was being followed.

CHAPTER FIFTY-THREE

The hum of the tires on the A1 southbound was steady, almost hypnotic, but Luca Severin's mind was nowhere near the road.

Just after noon, he had left the villa, still replaying in his mind the final words of the third scroll he had read aloud to Susan, Alister, and Thomas. They'd sat in the library, the air scented with cool sea air drifting in from the terrace. After lunch, he would finally open the battered leather folder that they brought back from Antakya along with the scroll jar.

He hadn't made it that far.

The secure Silentii satellite phone—black, weighty, with its encryption seal worn from years of use—had buzzed on the desk beside him. The caller ID displayed only two words: *Vallente Office.*

Luca had answered, eyes flicking to the others in the room.
"Yes," he said into the receiver.
A pause.
"I understand. I will be there within four hours."

When he looked up, their faces were searching his, reading the tautness in his expression. All he said was " Meeting with Vallenti, today."

 Moments later, he was on the road, heading north toward Rome in his new Audi A4, delivered just this past week. He was too embarrassed to ask Susan and Alister what had happened to his trusty old Pugeot that they had taken last month when they ran from the villa.

The leather folder would have to wait.

The February light was thin, the clouds low, as the kilometers ticked past. He pressed the Audi hard, frustration tightening his jaw. He had been *so close* to learning what else the find in Antakya had contained—and now this summons.

By late afternoon, the walls of Rome rose ahead, ochre and cream under a paling sky. He approached the Vatican perimeter, slowing at the first checkpoint. A Swiss Guard scanned his credentials and waved him toward a gated archway flanked by unmarked sedans. Inside the security compound, a second guard inspected the vehicle before sending him into the subterranean entry tunnel—an unlit, stone-walled drive that angled down beneath the Apostolic Palace.

He parked in the restricted bay, stepped out, and passed through biometric scanners. The air here was cool, silent. His footsteps echoed in the passage that led deeper beneath the Vatican, toward the secured offices of the Ordo Silentii.

The conference room was already full. The senior leadership sat in high-backed chairs around the black-marble table, their expressions drawn tight. Corvus was there, seated near the far end with the other two agents from the Antakya debacle. No one spoke until Luca had taken his place.

Cardinal Vittorio Vallente began without ceremony. "Progress reports."

The answers came one by one, and they were uniformly dismal. No sightings. No confirmed travel records. No intercepted communications. No clues. The fugitives were, once again, ghosts.

Vallente's jaw hardened. His voice, when it came, was sharper than any of them had heard before. Almost a shout. "This is unacceptable. Do you all understand? We cannot sit here and wait for them to reappear on their terms. I want options. Now."

Silence. The kind that prickled at the skin.

Finally, a hand rose—tentative, hesitant—Monsignor Pietro Manzini, Senior Strategist for Field Operations.

"Yes?" Vallente snapped.

Manzini cleared his throat. "There is… something we have never considered before."

Vallente leaned forward. "Well? Speak."

A pause. Then—
"We could use their families as leverage."

Vallente's eyes narrowed. "Like what?"

Manzini swallowed. "I mean… like kidnapping one of their children. Holding them until the scrolls are surrendered."

The words hung in the air like a toxic cloud. For centuries, the Silentii had followed one immutable code, as unspoken as it was absolute: no family, not unlike the old Mafia law.

Luca said nothing, but inside, every instinct went rigid. Susan was the only one among them with a child—Alice—thousands of miles away at a university in California, completely unprotected. And now, seeing the gleam in Vallente's eyes, he knew the idea was being weighed seriously.

He also knew he could not stop it here, not without drawing suspicion.

Luca forced a measured tone. "Perhaps… this could work, but only if the fugitives remain unreachable. The risk is too high otherwise. We would need to know exactly who has children, their current locations, habits, and friends before taking any action. That will take time."

Vallente studied him, then nodded once. "How much time?"

"A week or two, at least. Tracking family members will be delicate work." Luca kept his voice even, pretending ignorance. "I don't even know who among them has children."

The tension eased slightly. Vallente looked around the table. "Very well. Begin immediately. Corvus—coordinate. I want dossiers on all known associates and family members. Locations, schedules, vulnerabilities. Two weeks."

The meeting moved on, but Luca had heard all he needed. Alice was safe—for now. Two weeks to act. Two weeks to build a plan.

By the time he returned to the Amalfi Coast, the sky was deep indigo. It was well after midnight. The villa was quiet. The terrace lights were already out, and the thick stone cliffs muted the sound of the Tyrrhenian Sea. They were all asleep.

Luca quietly walked into the library, glancing toward the unopened leather folder on the desk. He poured a small glass of grappa, stared at the folder for a long time, then left it untouched.

Tomorrow, he would read it. But first, over breakfast, he would tell them what the Silentii were planning.

CHAPTER FIFTY-FOUR

Luca had not slept well. Morning came too soon—only a few hours of sleep. Not enough, but it would have to do.

On the terrace, breakfast was waiting—fresh coffee, melon, and warm cornetti. Susan, Alister, and Thomas were already there—another crystalline day on the Italian Riviera. The sun spilled across the terraces, lighting up the impossible reds and purples on the flowering vines that shaded the trellis. But Luca barely saw it. What was in his head blocked out everything else.

They looked rested. They thought they had time. He knew they didn't.

Luca sat, poured coffee into the small porcelain cup, and finally spoke. "I have disturbing news from my meeting at the Vatican yesterday," he began, voice low. "Our success at hiding your location has created a problem… first for them, yes, but now for us. Something is wrong with Vallente. He used to be calm, methodical—a predator who waited for his prey to make the inevitable mistake. It always worked, eventually. But now… he's lost patience. Almost frantic. He wants you now. What they came up with in that meeting gives us only two weeks to develop a plan and act."

He told them about Rome—how Vallente had summoned him, how the senior Silentii leadership had sat in heavy silence until Monsignor Pietro Manzini raised his hand and said what none had dared before: *Use their families as leverage.*

He described Vallente's reaction, the irrational gleam in his eyes. The talk around the table. How quickly the idea began to take shape. How Luca had pretended to agree, pressing for time under the guise of research. Two weeks to identify who had children, what they did, and where they were. He hadn't said he already knew.

"They'll be looking for family," Luca finished. "Susan, that means Alice. She's thousands of miles away, unprotected. We need to come up with a plan to keep her safe, and we have to move fast."

Susan's face went pale, her hands tightening around her coffee cup. She didn't speak at first, only stared down at the table as if steadying herself.

It was Alister who broke the silence. He reached over, took her hand—it was trembling. His tone was calm, measured, precisely as she remembered from other crises. She turned toward him, and the trembling seemed to stop.

"We already have the plan in place to control this," Alister said, his voice gaining strength. "The blockchain holds the digital twins of the first two scrolls and letters, plus a dead switch that will push the story to the world if triggered. We extend that plan. Right now. Blockchain. Dead switch. Everything we did for the first two scrolls, we do for the third—and whatever's in that leather pouch."

Thomas nodded. "The account's already set up. We just add to it. Once the contents are secured and programmed for immediate release if something happens to us, we control the terms. They can't get their hands on what's already beyond their reach—whether it's the scrolls, us, or any family members."

Susan looked at Alister, surprised by the steadiness she felt just hearing his voice. The calm certainty, the way he took hold of a problem and began shaping a solution—she remembered it from New York, from Paris, from the nights in St Cyr and Antakya. That same quiet reassurance settled deep inside her now, somewhere near her heart.

"But before we can complete the plan," Alister said, "we need to know what's in that last artifact we found. That means reading what's in the leather folder. Today."

"And digitizing it and the scroll immediately," Thomas added. "Same process we used in Ridgewood. High-resolution images, full metadata, multiple backups."

Luca leaned forward. "I can arrange it. There's a studio in Rome I've worked with before—discreet, no questions.

Thomas added, "Susan, you'll play the secretary again, as in New Jersey. Keep an eye on the process. Make sure no other copies are made."

She met his eyes. "Then let's not waste time. Let's find out what's in that folder."

The sound of the sea rose from far below, mingling with the clink of cups and the faint hum of a Vespa somewhere in the hills.

Their plan was in motion.

Luca reached for the weathered leather folder, its edges cracked, the flap secured by an ancient strap close to disintegrating. He placed it on the table between them.

"Then," he said quietly, "let's see what we're dealing with."

From the folder, he removed an ancient leather-bound book about the size of a hardcover novel today. "Until the first century", Luca explained, "ten to twenty-foot-long papyrus scrolls were the traditional way to record information. Then, more modern, innovative people adopted a new approach. They cut papyrus into individual sheets, about nine by twelve inches. These sheets were portable and easier to handle. Many Christians adopted it to demonstrate their break from traditional approaches. Mary would have been one of them. She would have drilled holes along one edge after enough sheets were completed, and then bound the sheets into a book with a leather cover. The Romans called it a Codex, a name derived from the Latin meaning 'wood block'."

Luca took a deep breath and then said, "OK, but this is going to take the rest of today and tonight to translate, so let's get together first thing in the morning."

CHAPTER FIFTY-FIVE

The sun was already warm across the stone terrace when they gathered again. Coffee steamed in white porcelain cups; the scent of citrus blossoms drifted in from the terrace garden. Alister and Thomas looked refreshed, the calm of a full night's sleep still in their faces.

Susan had not slept. Shadows beneath her eyes betrayed the long night spent thinking of Alice, imagining the Silentii's plot against her daughter in a thousand terrible forms. She wrapped her hands around her coffee cup as though it might anchor her.

Luca looked no better. His eyes were rimmed red, his voice roughened by fatigue. He had worked through the night, the Codex open on his desk until the first glimmers of dawn. Still, his expression was almost radiant with discovery.

"I have read many ancient texts," he said slowly, "but nothing like this. It is the most intriguing document from the first century I have ever encountered."

He lifted the ancient leather-bound volume carefully from a side table. Its cracked cover and faint smell of earth gave it a weight beyond its pages. "The scrolls we read told a story—recollections organized and shaped afterward into something coherent. This is not that. This is Mary's diary. Notes taken daily on individual papyrus sheets she carried with her, recording events almost as they happened. It contains one hundred and twenty-five leaves—two hundred and fifty pages of close writing, bound tight, about two inches thick. Her personal diary."

Thomas leaned forward. "When does it begin?"

"It begins on the day she arrived in Ostia, the Roman Empire's great seaport, eighteen miles from Rome, alive with ships and commerce. It was the Second of June in the year 62 CE, and a young and dangerously paranoid Nero was emperor. She could not know that as she entered Ostia, Today this grand old seaport is ruin and dust, but then—then it was the very heartbeat of Rome's power."

He opened the Codex, and the neat, angular script of the first century stared up at them. His finger traced the margin.

"She wrote three, sometimes four times a week. A seamless account in her Galilean dialect—a woman recording what she saw, what she felt, day by day. Let me read you how it begins."

Luca's voice softened as he let Mary's words take over.

Mary's Diary, June 2, 62 CE

From the bow, I saw the city rise in light—the tiled roofs of Ostia shining, sails crowding the harbor, the river carrying the noise of men and beasts. The air was alive with it—salt, tar, garlic, smoke, and laughter. My heart was too full to write what I felt: Rome at last, the center of the world. The place where all roads end and all roads begin again.

And there—on the dock below, among the sailors and merchants, stood the man I missed for so long. Jesus. In the face of success, his dress remains humble. His robe plain, his sandals worn, his shoulders browned by the sun. He waved, and I thought, "This is our beginning."

Luca looked up, his voice steady. "They didn't know then that it was also the beginning of their end. They could not have foreseen that he had only six years left on this earth."

"For the next five years, the diary records their life in detail—happy, prosperous, deeply connected to each other. She paints Rome in living color: the busy streets, the clamor of the port, the confidence she felt walking at his side. She was impressed by how well-known he was. Everyone called him Paulus, the preacher for the shipping fleet of Lucius Aurelius Barrius. Captains, merchants, dockworkers—they all deferred to him. And by extension, to her. She liked it."

He turned another page.

Mary's Diary, June 2, 62 CE

We embraced on the dock. He smelled of sea wind and olive oil. He asked after my voyage, and I told him of the storms near Massalia, and how I prayed each night that God would return me to him. We laughed like children as we walked, and stopped for bread and olives and a cup of Falernian in a tavern overlooking the masts. Men nodded to him, some knelt briefly. He is loved here. I see it in their eyes. I am proud to stand beside him.

"They went first to a mansion near the port," Luca explained. "A property he had acquired through Barrius—a home filled with servants, gardens, marble floors. Later, he also maintained a smaller apartment within the city for business purposes. By Mary's account, it was an idyllic life."

Luca set his hand on the Codex, his voice darkening. "But they had entered one of the most dangerous periods in Rome's history."

"The Rome of 62 CE dazzled with marble and gold, but beneath the surface, shadows stretched longer each year. Nero was still young, not yet thirty, but already feared. He fancied himself an artist, a poet, even a god, but his mind was turning inward, suspicious of every whisper. Within two years, the city would burn—six days and seven nights of flame, devouring ten of Rome's fourteen districts. Whole neighborhoods vanished, temples blackened to ash. And when the embers cooled, the emperor needed someone to blame. He found them in the Christians. The first torches in Nero's gardens were not wood, but living men and women bound to stakes. In the circus, their deaths became sport. This was the atmosphere in which Mary and Jesus—now Paul—were building their life."

Luca's tone dropped lower. "And it did not stop there. In 65 CE, the Piso Conspiracy to assassinate Nero bared its teeth. Senators, equestrians, even poets and philosophers were accused of plotting against the emperor. Nero's paranoia deepened until it touched every corner of the city. Seneca—once his tutor—was ordered to open his own veins. To betray a friend became an act of loyalty. To speak a word could be fatal. Rome itself had become a place where accusation was stronger than truth."

He looked out over the terrace northward onto the blue Tyrrhenian Sea, as though ancient Rome were still visible before him. "And while the capital devoured itself, rebellion ignited abroad. In 66 CE, Judea erupted in open revolt, the zealots driving out Roman garrisons from Jerusalem. Refugees fled west, carrying tales of blood and uprising. To Rome, it seemed part of a pattern—fire in the capital, conspiracies in the Senate, rebellion in the provinces. Order frayed, and in Nero's eyes, every unknown man could be a conspirator. Every whisper could be the spark of another fire."

His hand pressed the Codex as if to steady it. "That was the stage they walked upon. An emperor whose fears burned hotter than the city itself, an empire unraveling, and old acquaintances driven by envy and desperation. Against such forces, even love, even faith, could not protect them. The storm was already gathering—and the traitor was already watching."

Mary's Diary, May 14, 64 CE

I keep the keys to the household. The servants obey; the rooms are full of light and laughter. He preaches on the docks each day, always with the sea behind him. The sailors gather, listening, nodding, eager. When he returns, I wash his feet and we dine together, speaking of the future.

He is happy that the Word is spreading across the sea lanes, his churches reaching to the ends of the Empire. But over dinner, he often shares his concerns. He reminds me that 'Faith' is only the first step in God's plan. Upon it must rise the greater callings of 'Hope' and of 'Love'. He is concerned about how easily men bend faith into rules or wield it for personal power."

"After he visited Corinth, where he once sent his words, he says cracks were beginning to show. The crewman who planted his Church there has told him of quarrels, of voices dividing what should be whole. Of leaders who use the idea of hope to exert control and assert their own power. He plans to visit Corinth again to discover the truth. I think he is losing trust in the crewman who tells him the story.

"Despite these challenges," Luca said, "Mary believed all was going well, and *perhaps they would grow old here. Maybe, at last, they had found peace.*"

"And then, after the Fire in July 64, the tone shifts. She begins to note their unease—the whispering of neighbors, the soldiers in the street."

He read again.

Mary's Diary, August 15, 64 CE

The smoke still clings to the city. Whole districts gone. Rumor swirls like ash. They say the emperor himself played the lyre while it burned. They say he blames us. Paulus tells me not to fear, but I see it in his eyes when the soldiers march past. He knows we are not safe. He writes on his scroll, but no longer carries it with him. It is safer left here at home.

"And then," Luca said, closing his eyes briefly, "a shadow enters the diary. A disheveled man on the docks. Watching. Lurking. Listening."

He opened again to the marked page.

Mary's Diary, October 26, 65 CE

There is a man who comes each day, ragged and smelling of wine. I see him. Try to avoid him. He does not speak. He only watches. His eyes follow Paulus and me...I feel them even when I turn away. Once, when I walked on the dock, the man muttered my name. I do not know how he knew it. But I saw recognition in his eyes, and it chilled me.

Luca looked up. "The diary reveals what Mary learned over the following weeks. This man was Peter—the apostle who denied Jesus in Jerusalem, who fled in fear. He had become a beggar, a drunk, adrift in Rome. Hardly recognizable from the past. One day, in his drunken envy, he stumbled to a Roman sentry and told him a tale—that Paulus was no Roman citizen, but the executed Jesus of Galilee, alive, deceiving all."

Thomas exhaled sharply. "That would have gone straight up the chain."

"Exactly," Luca said. "The guard took it first to the *centurion* on duty at the castra by the Tiber. From there, it reached the *tribunus militum*, then the *praefectus urbi*, the urban prefect himself. Given the climate of paranoia after the Pisonian Conspiracy to assassinate Nero, it would not have stopped there. Word was carried to Tigellinus, Nero's prefect of the Praetorian Guard—and finally, to the emperor."

Luca turned to the next entry.

Mary's Diary, January 15, 66 CE

This morning, he was preaching by the ships when they came. Soldiers, armor glinting, voices hard. They seized him without a word, bound his wrists before the crowd. I ran, but one of the sailors—bless him—followed me. He found me at home, breathless, and told me what I already feared: they had taken him. My Paulus. My Jesus. My love.

Alister took a deep breath, exhaled slowly, and said, "That means the church fathers constructed the story of the Apostle Peter in Rome to cover his real history—abandoning Jesus, and then exposing him to the Romans out of envy. They even built churches over both Peter and Paul to sustain the myth."

Luca closed the Codex. Silence held the terrace. Even the sea seemed quiet, as though it, too, was listening.

"They could not have known," he said at last, "that all those years of happiness were only the calm before the fall."

CHAPTER FIFTY-SIX

Luca leaned forward, his hand still resting on the leather-bound diary. His eyes were hollow with fatigue, but his voice carried a deliberate, reverent weight.

"What happens next," he said quietly, "is something you must hear from Mary herself. But first…a word of context. Nero was not a madman in the simple sense people so often imagine. He was paranoid, yes—but also theatrical, calculating. Everything was about control, about his image. And image was his main concern when he arrested Jesus."

"Rome was still reeling from the Great Fire and the Pisonian conspiracy. The city's trust was brittle, suspicion everywhere. To announce that Paulus—beloved of the seafaring guilds, respected by thousands—was not a citizen at all but in truth the fugitive Jesus who had escaped execution in Jerusalem, would have been reckless. It could have provoked the guilds' anger against Nero himself. But to condemn Paulus as a Roman, guilty of treason—that was different. That turned Paulus into a threat to Rome itself, validated Nero's paranoia, and furnished him with the story of an empire-wide conspiracy. Nero transformed Paulus's death into theater, and the theater into power."

Luca's fingers lingered on the page. Then, with a slow exhale, he began to read.

It was in the last dimming light of day when I came to the Circus of Nero. I had never walked here before. From a distance, it seemed less a place of triumph than a carcass housing death. The air was poisoned: dust and damp earth laced with fresh blood. I knew it too well. The day's violence had left its scent behind.

Beside me walked the Captain who had stood with Jesus that morning when he was arrested. His stride was steady, though the place reeked of sorrow. His face was weathered by salt and storms, his hands made for rope and mast. Barrius had entrusted him with authority to act in his stead, and he knew Paulus's body was more precious than any cargo. He bore a folded writ—an order of transit granting us access to the undertaker's annex, to claim the body. He said nothing, but his presence steadied my panic.

At the gate, two Praetorian guards stopped us. Their bronze helmets caught the last of the sun. The Captain handed them the writ. They glanced at it, more bored than suspicious, and waved us through. They did not look at me. I was only a woman in a cloak—nothing more than a shadow in the dusk.

We did not enter the arena but instead a corridor running beneath the stands. Narrow, unlit, the air pressed close and wet against my skin. Our steps echoed. The sounds of Rome faded; only the hush of my cloak against stone kept me company. The smell grew worse with every step: not just the blood of this day, but the rank of years—sweat, waste, rot clinging to the walls.

At last, we reached a small iron-bound door. An oil lamp sputtered on the wall, its thin flame throwing monstrous shadows. I asked the Captain to wait. He nodded without question. I wanted to go in alone. An old memory fought its way to the surface as I reached for the latch—thirty years past, at Golgotha. That predawn morning when I came to an empty tomb, hoping to anoint the body of the crucified. The same hollow dread filled me now, the same ache of loss.

I opened the door.

Inside was a low, damp chamber. Two rough tables lined the wall. On one, a broken body lay sprawled on a coarse cloth. It was Peter, whom I saw so often on the docks watching Jesus from a distance—the apostle who had abandoned his promise so long ago and still held his anger despite the years that had passed. He smelled of wine. But the table that should have borne Jesus was empty. Empty—except for a shadow at its side. At first, it was only a shape, dark against the wavering lamplight. My breath caught; my heart leapt and sank together. A guard, I thought—someone who had carried him away.

"Sir," I whispered, voice trembling, "if you have taken him, tell me where you have laid him."

The figure turned. The flame flared. Not a soldier's helm—but a face. Familiar, beloved, seared into my soul. I stumbled forward, tears blinding me. "Rabboni," I cried, as I had long ago in another garden, another night.

"Mary," he said.
I reached for him, but my hand closed on nothing. The air was not damp and cold—it was warm. It was him. Jesus.

He spoke again, his words slow and grave:
"Do not cling to me. My work here is finished. Before, it was too soon. But now the Father calls me home. The Church is growing. Built on faith, my ministry will endure."

His voice, tender yet commanding, echoed against the stone:
"Mary, you will follow, but not now. You must live. The Father has a purpose for you here—to record it all, to leave a testimony of how faith survives, and how hope and love take shape—or are betrayed—in the hands of those who claim to follow me. And to tell our story to the world when the time is right."

Then, with sudden urgency:
"You must move quickly. They will come for you and for Barrius, once they learn I am gone. Until then, speak of this to no one. Let the Church grow; let faith take root…and be remembered. But never forget—it is only the beginning."

His outline wavered like heat rising from stone, then began to fade. My eyes strained to hold him, but the more I reached, the more he slipped away. Only his command remained—to live, to record, to guard our story—and it alone carried my feet into motion.

I fled the chamber. The Captain rose at once, reading my face without a word. "We must go," I told him. "Now. To my house. Then to the port. We must reach Antioch. We must warn Barrius. They will come for him soon."

Luca closed the book, his hand still resting on the page. The terrace had fallen silent. Only the faint rush of the Tyrrhenian Sea below reached them.

He paused, then added quietly, "Mary could not have known it, but the very ground where Jesus was executed—the Circus of Nero—would become the heart of Christian history. Built a century earlier, it was first an emperor's playground, a private arena for spectacle. The structure stretched nearly the length of two football fields, a long oval bristling with shrines and statues. At its center loomed a massive Egyptian obelisk—the same that now towers in St. Peter's Square.

"By the time Jesus and Mary arrived in Rome, Nero had thrown open the gates to the people. It was now called Nero's Circus, and he strutted into the chariot stalls, desperate for their cheers. But the horror of its true legacy was yet to come. After the Great Fire, Nero turned his fury upon the Christians. Here they were crucified along the track, their bodies convulsing in agony as the sand drank their blood. Wild beasts tore others to pieces to the shrieks of the crowd. Still more were lashed to poles, their flesh smeared with pitch and set alight—human torches casting a ghastly glow that mingled with smoke and screams, while Nero's guests applauded from the stands. Jesus would likely have been executed here too—though by the sword, not the cross.

"Within a century, the appetite for such horror faded. Attendance dropped, cheers fell silent, and the Circus decayed into ruin. Its arches crumbled; tombs rose where the arena once stood. By Constantine's day, two centuries later, it had become Rome's chief cemetery, a necropolis sprawling across the hillside beyond the city gates. And in time, the Vatican itself would rise upon that layered earth—above the sand of the arena, above the blood of Jesus."

Thomas broke the silence. "That's familiar ground to anyone who has read of ancient Rome."

"You're right," Luca replied, his voice low, "but here is what they don't know. In the fourth century, Constantine ordered the Chamber of the Seven Seals—the Silentii's initiation hall—to be cut into a forgotten Roman tomb within that same necropolis. It remains their sacred chamber even now, hidden under the Vatican and unmarked on any map.

And I don't think it is an accident, or a coincidence, but perhaps God's irony, that the Silentii's chamber lies only feet from the place where Mary saw Jesus rise from death—the very story they are sworn to erase."

He closed his eyes briefly, as though the weight of it pressed down on him. Then, almost in a whisper: "That's Mary's last diary entry. The end of their path together on this earth. And the beginning of hers."

CHAPTER FIFTY-SEVEN

For a long time, no one spoke. The sky above Positano had turned the color of slate, leaving the villa terrace in soft shadow. The only sound was the faint wash of waves below when Luca closed the diary.

Now, it lay on the table between them, its cracked leather cover shut, its voice suddenly silent—unfinished, without closure.

Susan's expression was a mix of awe and unease. Finally, she turned to Luca. "If that was the last entry…what do you think happened next?"

Luca drew a long breath, his tone cautious, as though speaking aloud might fracture something fragile. "I asked myself the same question last night after finishing the diary. And I think we can make a very good guess. You found it hidden in the compartment at the base of the statue in Antakya, alongside the third scroll you brought back two days ago. Mary must have placed the diary there for safekeeping, intending to retrieve it with the scroll before fleeing with Lucius. But the soldiers probably came too quickly, and she and Lucius would have run before she could recover them."

Susan's eyes widened. "Of course—I remember something else now. The compartment was only large enough for one scroll jar and the diary. That means Mary would have kept the fourth scroll with her—the one where Jesus recorded his years in Rome. She must have taken it when they fled…and it was never found."

Alister, silent until now, leaned forward. "But how do we know they weren't caught? That they actually escaped?"

Luca paused, then said quietly, "We know from historical records that Mary lived until an old age in southern Gaul. I believe it was in the stone house where she and Jesus first stayed after leaving Jerusalem so many years earlier. Not in a cave as the Church would have you believe."

Susan whispered almost to herself, "The house in St Cyr."

Thomas, who had been listening intently, finally spoke. "They would have boarded one of Lucius's ships in secret and sailed back to Gaul. He had land in the hills above Fréjus—remote enough to disappear from Nero's view in Rome, and manage his shipping empire from a distance. And Mary would have lived out her days in St Cyr, writing her gospel, preaching at the chapel down the road."

Luca nodded slowly, his thoughts drifting back to his recent visit to the Secret Vatican Library. "When I read the original Gospel of Mary Magdalene, I noticed the last pages were missing—many pages, torn out. Vallente claimed a rogue cardinal destroyed them before he could intervene. But there was something in his eyes, and the way he said it. I don't believe him. I think those pages revealed something the Vatican deliberately silenced—something that, if ever exposed, would be dangerous."

Alister had been silent, listening, until his eyes sharpened as if an old memory had stirred. "The diary recalls their years in Rome and the life they built there, yet her account lingers almost entirely on their household and his preaching at the docks. She mentions his journeys only once—to Corinth, where unrest had already begun and where he was losing faith in the very seamen who had helped found that community. He—and surely Barrius as well—must have returned there many times, and visited other congregations his sailors and traders were planting across the Mediterranean. If that's true—and I am convinced it is— then entire chapters of their lives are missing. And since no pages were torn from Mary's diary, the silence must be intentional."

"I suspect Mary felt these truths too dangerous to preserve, exposing how the church leaders were already bending his teachings. Perhaps she feared that if he ever read her account, he would think she had violated his confidence by laying bare his struggles. Then, years later, when she was living in St Cyr, she may have remembered the last words of Jesus, asking her to live so that she might record "*how faith survives—or is betrayed.*"

He turned toward the setting sun, his voice dropping to a near whisper. "I think those missing pages from Mary's Gospel still exist somewhere—and wherever it is hidden---it records a testimony that Silentii wants silenced."

They could not have known that events were already stirring beyond their sight—currents that would soon pull them far from Luca's villa above the Tyrrhenian Sea, to Corinth and other Mediterranean cities where Jesus and Barrius once walked. It was a past refusing to stay buried, waiting for them like a shadow in the missing pages of Mary's Gospel. Her words, stretching across two millennia, were about to entwine their lives. But for now, they didn't know that…all they had were questions.

CHAPTER FIFTY-EIGHT

Night had fully settled over St Cyr. Cool air drifted down from the mountains. Alice and Sophie had gone inside briefly to fetch sweaters, then returned to the terrace with the last of the rosé. In the distance past the pool deck, the north star already lit the night sky above the town, while thousands of others gathered, competing for room in the darkness.

Alice picked up where the story had left off, her gaze drifting across the old stones beneath their feet. "Mom told me the fourth scroll—Mary must have carried it when she fled with Lucius. And Mary…she would have come back here. To her little stone house in St Cyr. To live out her days and write her gospel…" Her voice softened. "…and preaching at Jesus's chapel down the road."

"And for some reason," Alice went on, "Mom thought Mary buried the fourth scroll beneath that chapel. But, think about it, the only way she could have known that would have been from reading those pages that were torn out of Mary's Gospel. How would she have done that? I think that was part of the story she was going to share with me today…" Alice's voice cracked slightly, "but she passed before she could."

"I mentioned earlier that one of the last things Mom told me was that every Sunday when she went to the chapel, she felt the ground speaking to her—that the scrolls and the diary belonged not to her or the Church, but to the earth itself. To the world we all live in. So she made her choice. She retrieved the first two scrolls from the safe deposit box in New York…and reburied them with the third scroll and the diary right here, beneath this terrace."

Sophie looked down at the stones under her chair, then whispered, almost to herself, "Here. Where we sit now." She swirled her glass slowly, hesitant. "The history that refuses to be erased?"

She drew in a breath, then added more softly, as if repeating a memory not quite her own: "When Mary last saw him, he told her: *Be sure our story survives. Record it for the future…tell it to the world when the time is right. He said…When the time is right.*"

Her head turned sharply. "What did your mother think he meant? *When the time is right?* Do you think the fourth scroll…or those destroyed pages of her gospel…could tell us?"

Alice's gaze shifted to the dark silhouette of the mountains to the west. "That question," she said quietly, "was what the Church feared most. And unless Mom acted, it could have cost me my life. Remember—Silentii planned to kidnap me to ransom the scrolls."

Her voice steadied. "But Mom and Luca realized something. By digitizing the scrolls and Mary's diary into blockchain twins and a dead switch, they had created a trump card. If anything happened to us, the knowledge would be released to the world instantly—and nothing could stop it. Vallente refused reason. He approved the kidnapping. So Luca went higher—straight to the Pope's inner circle."

Sophie leaned forward and, with a quiet gasp, said. "They went to the Pope?"

Alice nodded. "No record survives of how Luca arranged it, or what was said. But Mom told me the outcome. It worked. Luca found out that Vallenti had already been warned about the way Silentii was pursuing its mission. And the information about the kidnapping plot sealed its fate. The Holy Father was furious. Vallente was dismissed. Silentii dismantled. In its place, a new bureau, a new name, still secret—purely technological—charged with protecting the Church's archives through ledgers and AI. For the first time, they could finally breathe."

Sophie exhaled slowly, as if trying to release centuries of tension. "So that was the end."

"An end," Alice corrected softly. "Not *the* end. History doesn't stop. It waits in the shadows."

She leaned closer. "Do you have a SWIL account?"

Sophie gave a faint laugh. "Of course. Everyone does. Mine's with CitiSWIL now. I used to have OmniSWIL, but Citi offered a lower price. Why?"

"Because that's where it all is still securely stored. The scrolls. The Diary. In the 2030s, blockchain was often confusing and mistrusted. So branding experts gave it a friendlier name—SWIL: **S**ecure **W**orldwide **I**nformation **L**edger. People trusted it, and it caught on. That's where our files are sealed, protected by retinal and quantum keys. And by a deadman switch. If no one logs in each year, everything is released. To the world. No power on earth could stop it."

Alice's hand tightened slightly on her glass. "With Mom and Alister gone, only Thomas and I remain. Two keys. Too few. Too easy to accidentally trigger the deadswitch before, as Jesus said, 'the time is right'. We need a third."

She paused, then asked softly, "Would you be willing to hold that key with us?"

Sophie didn't answer right away, her mind seemingly elsewhere. At last, after a long pause, she said, "Of course I will." Then, turning toward the night, her eyes fixed on the North Star shimmering above the dark pool. "But I keep circling back to what we spoke of before... *When will the time be right?*"

She drew a breath. "Alice, I can't shake another feeling—that the question isn't only *when will the time be right*, but also what remained in the story your mother never finished before she passed. What was in those destroyed pages? I think those two are connected."

Alice's breath caught. A chill moved through her, as though her mother's presence stirred in the silence between them. Perhaps Sophie was right—that what her mother left unsaid, the story that ended too soon, was itself part of a larger truth. A truth that would demand to be told—when the time was right.

The cicadas sang louder in the valley. The night seemed to listen.

They finished the last of the rosé in silence. Neither spoke again.

And yet—had they listened closely during the evening on the terrace, past the hum of insects and the rustle of wind—they might have heard the crunch of tires on gravel from the hidden back road above the pool deck. The same road where Susan and Alister had parked Luca's battered Peugeot nearly four decades before, the night Corvus almost caught them.

But this time it was a polished black Mercedes that rolled to a stop beneath the cypress trees.

Inside, a man, now four decades older, with a scarred cheek and close-cropped white hair, watched them talking on the terrace…and listened. At the café in the village that afternoon, he had been seated just out of their view, but near enough to hear them talk. And now again, he waited and listened, patient as the night itself.

From the village below, a faint bell tolled the hour. The sound drifted up into the dark, unanswered.

EPILOGUE

The terrace was dark now, the candles extinguished, Alice and Sophie asleep inside. The night was still, save for cicadas rasping in the valley and the toll of a bell from the village in the hills beyond the pool deck.

On the back road above the pool deck, the black Mercedes remained parked beneath the cypress trees. The smell of its hot engine had drifted quietly into the night air hours earlier, cooling as the day's temperature faded.

The man behind the wheel leaned forward, his scar catching the faint glow from countless stars that lit the night sky. His hair was grey now, cropped close. His body carried the weight of years, but his eyes—cold, unyielding—were the same.

He wasn't supposed to be alive. Whispers of his death had circulated decades ago—burned, broken, lost in the ruins of Antakya. Some claimed he had vanished in a prison transport, others that the Vatican itself had erased him to bury its shame. But like the order that shaped him, he had never truly died.

He had watched from the shadows tonight, the voices from the terrace carrying just enough for him to understand. The scrolls were not out of reach, they had simply gone deep underground.

The Pope might believe that Silentii has been dismantled, its archives surrendered to machines and ledgers. But Silentii had always been more than a bureau or a secret chamber under the Vatican. It was a vow. The silence between words. The shadow between truths. And Corvus—scarred, hardened, half a ghost—was now the leader of something new.

He reached into his coat pocket for a small device. A faint light blinked once, waiting. A message appeared:

Report?

His lips curved into the faintest smile. He had listened well this day. His thumb tapped out ten words:

They don't know. Our grip on Hope is still safe.

The screen went dark. He slipped the device away and settled back into the driver's seat, eyes fixed on the villa below.

A brilliant north star was suspended in blackness above the village as Corvus heard the bell of St Cyr strike midnight, echoing through the hills. It was the star that had guided countless travelers before him. But tonight Corvus needed no guidance. He already knew his path as he whispered the words that had outlived empires, the words that had outlived even the order that bred him.

Hope
is the lie
we rule with.

ABOUT THE AUTHOR

J. Kimball is a scientist, historian, and storyteller whose work blends meticulous research with cinematic suspense. His debut novel, *The Scrolls of Provence*, launches the Silentii Trilogy, a journey across two thousand years of history and faith. He lives in New York City.

What Comes Next

The Silentii Trilogy spans two millennia of leaders twisting the teachings of Faith, Hope, and Love to secure power and wealth. *The Scrolls of Provence* revealed how Faith was rewritten at the very beginning—but that was only the start. For the next seventeen centuries, Hope became their greatest weapon.

In **Book Two**, Susan, Alister, and Thomas travel to ancient biblical sites and uncover the hidden *Book of Hope*—first compiled under Constantine as a manual of "best practices" for bending Hope into obedience. Across the centuries, its lessons were refined by popes, kings, and governments—and in modern times by powerful institutions and NGOs. What began as doctrine became a system, shaping history in ways few could have imagined.

But a newly reborn Silentii is rising—and it will stop at nothing to erase that discovery.

A Note from the Author

If you enjoyed *The Scrolls of Provence*, please consider leaving a short review where you purchased the book, or if you wish, email me directly at JKimballAuthor@gmail.com. Your words help other readers discover the story—and keep interest in history alive by encouraging research and debate.